CW00550993

A. J. Wright has been shortlisted for the CWA Debut Dagger and won the Dundee International Fiction Prize in 2010 for *Act of Murder*. His second novel, *Striking Murder*, was shortlisted for the CWA Historical Crime Novel of the Year. His subsequent novels, *Elementary Murder* and *Sitting Murder*, were published to great acclaim. He has had short stories published in the *Ellery Queen Mystery Magazine* and *Terror at the Crossroads*, an anthology of the best stories from *EQMM*, *Alfred Hitchcock's Mystery Magazine* and others. He lives in the beautiful village of Croston in Lancashire.

PRAISE FOR A. J. WRIGHT:

'This is an absolute gem of a historical crime novel – cleverly and intricately plotted, very well-written and convincingly evoking all the social problems of a late-Victorian industrial town.' – *Crime Review*

'. . . the book vividly depicts the tensions and ramifications of the miners' strike. The mystery is equally strong: the plot is fast-paced and cleverly strewn with red herrings and subtle clues. Highly recommended' – *Historical Novel Society*

'Excellently plotted, with some breathtaking moments, as pieces of the dark past come into the light' – Chris Nickson, bestselling author of the *Richard Nottingham Mysteries*

Hanging
Murder

A. J. WRIGHT

LUME BOOKS

LUME BOOKS

First published in 2019 by Lume Books
85-87 Borough High Street,
London, SE1 1NH

ISBN 978-1-83901-154-2

www.lumebooks.co.uk

Oh, to share a pint or two once more with friends who have gone:

John Edwards; Ray Peycke; Steve Arbury; John Stavers – Leeds University

John Kelly; John and Jimmy Mulligan; Jimmy Ball; Billy Rennox; Terry Critchley – Wigan

John Lewis, my brother-in-law with whom I travelled to Australia (twice!) and New Zealand to watch England Rugby League - Leigh

Jimmy Lewis, my brother-in-law, a proud ex-marine commando, later a coal miner who also worked in Mines Rescue – Leigh

Acknowledgements

Again, a great debt of gratitude to my agent, Sara Keane, of the Keane Kataria Literary Agency, whose advice and support I treasure.

I should also like to express my deepest thanks to Alice Rees and Miranda Summers-Pritchard at Lume Books. Their meticulous editing and sensible suggestions were greatly appreciated!

I never saw a man who looked
With such a wistful eye
Upon that little tent of blue
Which prisoners call the sky,
And at every drifting cloud that went
With sails of silver by.

I walked, with other souls in pain,
Within another ring,
And was wondering if the man had done
A great or little thing,
When a voice behind me whispered low,
'That fellow's got to swing.'

Oscar Wilde – *The Ballad of Reading Gaol*

PROLOGUE

For one person present, it was an object of beauty.

Its circumference was two and a half inches and made of white Italian hemp, four strands thick, and it stretched for twelve and a half feet, with an inlaid brass thimble at its lower end. A leather washer was then slid into place, adjustable, naturally, in order to provide a comfortable and practical fit.

With great care, he moved to the lever on the right of the two trap doors where the condemned man would soon stand. He gripped the ebony handle of the lever and pulled back hard. Immediately, both trap doors dropped open, remaining thus with the aid of the two springs on either side to prevent the doors rattling back. He nodded, satisfied, and ordered the attendant to close the trap doors, whereupon he repeated the routine twice more until he was sure the doors would drop freely.

Then he retired for the night, in the room in the prison grounds traditionally set aside for his use. Sleep would come easily for him, though not for the other one.

The next morning, he stood in the execution shed and looked at his fob watch. Two minutes to eight o'clock. He prided himself on his timing.

A door from the cells swung open, and the condemned man, Benjamin

Goodfellow, was brought in. The prison chaplain, wearing suitably sombre robes, was walking close by his right-hand side, murmuring prayers from the burial service.

A faint smile made an attempt to enliven the hangman's features, but with an admirable sense of place and duty, he quickly suppressed it. *Goodfellow.*

If ever a chap were more wrongly named! There was nothing remotely good about this defiler and murderer of women. Still, he thought, taking some perverse satisfaction, what could be more cruel than what the chaplain was doing – reciting words from the fellow's own funeral service while he still walked the earth? Within his hearing?

No other human being on God's earth would hear the low, melancholy incantations from his own burial service. Only the condemned man is accorded such a grisly privilege.

Managing to combine swiftness with a measured calm, Simeon Crosby pinioned the man's legs firmly, reaching up next to place the white hood over his face. Sometimes, before the hood removed from sight their last vision of life in the physical world, they wished to say something – a name, a prayer for forgiveness, even a last-second denial of guilt – but the practice wasn't now encouraged, and Simeon would much rather they kept their mouths shut. He wouldn't know how to respond other than with a grim silence. It was the reason he had refused to accompany the chaplain to the condemned man's cell. The last time he had met Goodfellow, two weeks earlier, had resulted in the wretch flinging himself at Simeon's feet in the cell and begging him to 'show some fuckin' mercy!' The response the hangman had given – 'Like you showed your poor wife, you mean? She was barely out of childhood!' – had brought a stern note of warning from the governor and an official reprimand from the county sheriff. A condemned cell was no place for gloating, their expressions had said.

'My Ada was a viper!' Goodfellow had yelled, a pathetic attempt to justify, even at so late a stage, the foul crime he had committed. Now, though, he was silent, and Simeon could see the man's legs shaking.

Simeon held his tongue. Any form of converse with the condemned man was to be avoided at all costs.

He stepped back, reached forward and placed the noose over the man's head, hearing the sharp breathing and watching the fabric of the hood sucked in to assume the shape of the man's mouth. Carefully, he placed the rope's knot behind the man's left ear, next to his jawbone. Then he examined for the final time the rope, the man's pinioned legs and the two trap doors before moving quickly towards the lever. There was a dreadful hiatus as he waited for the under-sheriff to give the lethal order.

Once it was given, Simeon Crosby gripped the lever and pulled back with both hands as the man's whole body started to quiver.

Nothing.

He lunged the lever forward, held on tightly and once more tugged hard, forcing the lever backwards.

But the trap doors stubbornly refused to budge.

'Mr Crosby, sir?' said the governor, his voice a blend of anger and horror.

A low keening filled the room. The condemned man was weeping. Crosby saw he had wet himself.

Suddenly, the room felt very hot. He tried for a third time to work the lever and bring about an end to this dreadful, not to say embarrassing, situation, but once more, the doors failed to open.

'That is enough!' The shout came not from the governor but from the under-sheriff who had been standing in the background, anxious that his first official witnessing of such an execution would soon be over. 'Mr Crosby, remove the noose!'

'But it'll take only a minute. Seconds even. Those bolts must be…'

'Now, sir!' bellowed the under-sheriff.

The governor walked over and removed Crosby's hands from the lever. It was coated in sweat.

Five minutes later, Goodfellow was back in his cell, his pallid features rendered spectral by the wide-open eyes and the bared teeth, listening to the ministrations of the chaplain, for whom the situation was both unprecedented and unsupported by anything the Good Book could offer, Lazarus, he felt, being wholly inappropriate.

The news of the failed hanging had spread to the gathered masses outside the prison gates, where two opposed factions had maintained a long vigil: a small group, led by Ada Goodfellow's two brothers, had been there since the early hours to make sure justice was carried out for their sister's murder. The other, much larger group of abolitionists, had sung hymns and prayed. Once the bulletin was posted on the prison gates, trouble flared with the now enraged brothers and their band, having no other recourse than to weigh into the cheering crowd whose prayers had been answered and were now singing hymns of praise and deliverance.

Simeon Crosby left the prison an hour later, under police escort and by a side door, unrecognised. The words of the under-sheriff were still ringing in his ears. Never had he been spoken to in such terms. His reputation was being impugned, despite his protestations of faulty workmanship, warped wood and rusted bolts.

In the following year, he performed twenty-seven more executions, all of which went very smoothly, to the accompaniment of glowing testimonials, before he decided finally, as he put it so jovially, to hang up his noose for the last time.

He had decided to write a book.

CHAPTER ONE

The woman who sat in the railway carriage found it difficult at first. She had smiled, of course, when the three people entered the compartment at Preston – the two men and one woman had acknowledged her presence with courteous smiles and the usual meaningless comments on the weather – but after that initial verbal flourish, the journey settled into silence as the train continued on its way.

Between them, the newcomers had two brown leather suitcases. As the men had placed them on the overhead rack, she noticed that both cases were monogrammed – *SNC* and *GJC* – which might suggest they were related. Two cases rather than three might suggest that one of the suitcases contained clothing for the woman as well. Married to one of them would be the most likely explanation.

It did strike Ellen Brennan as slightly odd that the three of them sat there gazing out of the window, saying nothing to each other. *Perhaps they find it hard to speak to each other because I'm here*, she reflected. So she decided to while away the rest of the journey by contemplating each of them – surreptitiously, of course – and entertaining idle speculations about their backgrounds.

The older man, for instance. He was of a rotund appearance, at least two chins that she could see beneath his greying beard, with heavy eyelids and dark brows that gave the impression of boredom. Her first impression had been that he was a wealthy man, yet here he was sharing a third-class compartment. And the suit he wore was, on closer inspection, rather threadbare and frayed at the cuffs, a curious contradiction to the gold chain looped into his waistcoat pocket. Fifty-five? Fifty-six years old?

The younger man to his left seemed rather anxious, occasionally tugging at his collar as if he felt the carriage was too stuffy. He was watching the passing scene, his eyes flicking from one object of interest to the next. He was broad shouldered, his dark eyes seeming soulful during unguarded moments. His most prominent feature was something she was sure he hadn't been born with: a scar, slightly curved down from his right ear to just below his right cheekbone. He sported a dark moustache, and occasionally, he licked his lips slowly, letting the tip of his tongue brush against the hairs on his upper lip. He too wore a suit, although this seemed a finer specimen than the one worn by his companion. If they were related, they could well be father and son, or perhaps brothers. By the time they reached Euxton Station, she had decided he was rather handsome, despite the scar that she only occasionally caught sight of, as he had his face turned to the right most of the time. Actually, both the scar and his attempts to hide it made him all the more intriguing. An adventurer, then. Or a military man. Survivor of some Indian Mutiny.

Michael would indeed be proud of my observations, she reflected, *though it'd be best to miss out the part about him being handsome. Even detective sergeants get jealous!*

Once the train pulled away from Euxton and continued on its journey to Wigan, she directed her gaze now towards the woman. She seemed of a similar age to the older man, and through the gloved left hand, she could see the raised impression of a wedding ring. His wife then.

Her travelling wear was dark, rather plain, with a small winter bonnet, trimmed with velvet and silk ribbon. There was something about her eyes, though, that suggested both a melancholy and a pride. What had happened to produce such an impression? She had taken out a book entitled *Moths*, according to the gold-embossed spine, by someone Ellen had never heard of – *Ouida*.

Now who in their right mind would wish to read a book about those horrible creatures, she wondered idly. And the book itself was quite thick.

She wished she had the patience and the time to read a book. Any book. But not about moths! Many a time, Michael had urged her to subscribe to the town's lending library, and many a time, she had promised to do so when the cows came home, an expression that had initially disturbed their six-year-old son, Barry, who had wondered how on earth cows would fit into their house.

After a short stop at Standish, during which time no one alighted or boarded, the train chugged its way towards the next stop – Wigan – and for the first time, someone spoke. It rather alarmed her, and she immediately looked down at her clasped hands in an attempt to ignore the fact that she had jumped a little in her seat at the unexpected sound.

It was the younger man who spoke.

'How much longer?' he said to no one in particular.

She noticed he was now sweating quite a lot, minute globules appearing on his forehead like tiny blisters. 'A few minutes,' Ellen said reassuringly.

He gave a curt nod but made no response. Then he turned to the man beside him and said, 'I don't think I shall be there, after all.'

The older man stared at him, his eyes narrowed and a deep frown appeared on his forehead. He seemed to take no notice of the other's discomfort.

'I think you will,' he said in a deep, firm voice, glancing to his right as if seeking the support of the woman beside him.

But she merely kept her gaze firmly on the book in her lap. When silence once more fell, she occasionally glanced through the window at the changing scene beyond, the darkening clouds that gave a sombre background to the number of winding-heads from neighbouring pits and the dim glow of gaslight from the large faded red brick of an imposing building, its several chimneys belching grey smoke into the darkening sky. With a sigh, she would then return her attention to the book, her expression warming as soon as her eyes rested on the page.

The younger man gave a cough, whether through apology or defiance it was hard to tell. Still, the older man's response had seemed to do the trick, for he said nothing more, merely tugged at his collars as if the carriage were uncomfortably hot.

How curious!

A few minutes later, the train pulled slowly into Wigan Station. She watched as her three fellow travellers prepared to disembark, both men reaching up to reclaim their cases while the woman tidied her clothing, smoothing the creases and fixing the bonnet. Ellen, too, stood up as the train came to a halt.

'You live in Wigan, madam?' the older of the men asked her.

'I do,' she said and watched as one of the station assistants swung open the door. She was somewhat annoyed when the man with the scar stepped down from the carriage before she could, without observing the niceties you'd expect.

'Our first visit,' the older one replied, as if that in some way apologised for his companion's lack of courtesy.

She flushed, not really knowing what the proper response would be to that. She said, 'Welcome,' and accepted the assistant's hand as he helped her step down from the carriage. Then, along the platform, she saw her husband making his way towards her, a huge smile on his face.

As he reached her, he gave her a tender peck on the cheek and glanced up at the sky.

'A storm on its way,' he observed. 'How was cousin Bessy?'

'Strong as an ox. And the baby has a fair pair of lungs on him.'

He noticed her fellow travellers, catching sight of the older man's monogrammed suitcase. Immediately, his smile vanished.

'Mick?' said Ellen. 'What is it?'

But Detective Sergeant Michael Brennan merely shook his head and escorted his wife back towards the exit.

'I'll tell you later,' he said.

As they passed through the ticket barrier, Ellen Brennan smiled when she saw a large uniformed figure standing beside a hackney carriage on the station forecourt. 'What's this?' she asked. 'Police escort?'

Brennan gave his constable a wave but guided his wife away onto the main thoroughfare of Wallgate. 'Constable Jaggery is here on official business,' he said.

'Is he waiting to arrest somebody?' she asked.

'No,' came the reply. 'He's been sent by his lordship to escort a passenger down to the station. Matter of professional courtesy.'

'Who's that then?'

Brennan stopped and gave a nod back to the ticket barrier, where his wife's recent companions were emerging.

'So they're important?'

'Not important, no. But necessary.' He smiled at her confusion. 'The one with the beard was at one time, anyway.'

'Go on. Tell me. Who are they?'

'I've no idea who the younger man is, or the woman. But the one with the beard is Simeon Crosby.'

19

'And who's Simeon Crosby? Is he famous?'

'Oh aye,' said Brennan and watched Constable Jaggery approach the three travellers, salute the older man and take their cases, handing them to the cab driver before inviting them to clamber on board. 'Mr Crosby has killed over seventy men. Oh, and two women.'

Ellen Brennan gripped his arm and swallowed hard. 'And Freddie Jaggery's fawning over him?'

'Of course,' Brennan replied with a smile. 'It's not every day we get a visit from one of our official executioners.'

Ellen stood, open-mouthed, as the carriage went past. She could only blink when the hangman gave her a friendly wave of farewell before turning right onto Wallgate. Then she gave a small shiver, imagining someone walking over her grave.

CHAPTER TWO

Captain Alexander Bell, Chief Constable of the Wigan Borough Police, was not in the best of moods. Early that morning, he had attended an inquest at the Silverwell Public House on Darlington Street. The deceased, Jane Waller, had been well known in the Scholes area, that most notorious of hellholes, as an inveterate drunkard who had met her untimely end by being struck by not one, but two snowballs, hurled at her by a couple of local toughs. Both snowballs had contained stones. One struck her in the eye, the other on her ear, and she had returned home complaining of pains at the back of her head. She was soon to become delirious and was dead within twenty-four hours. The post-mortem examination had revealed a small clot on her right eye, and on separating the membrane covering the brain, the pathologist had found a much larger clot. The cause of death was therefore compression of the brain from haemorrhage.

The jury returned a verdict of misadventure.

Because her inebriated state contributed to her demise.

It had meant, of course, that the two miscreants who had brought about her death were guilty of nothing more than a common assault.

Now, as if to compound his misery, he had had to despatch that overgrown ape, Jaggery, to make sure their visitor was brought to the station unmolested. It had been Captain Bell himself who had suggested by telegram that Simeon Crosby arrive a day earlier than planned, thus thwarting the expected hostile reception by those interfering simpletons from the Society for the Abolition of Capital Punishment.

The man was here to deliver a talk on his life's experiences, for pity's sake – not swing some filthy swine from the gallows.

He was musing idly to himself how he could name two who deserved that fitting fate, when there was a knock on his door, and he could hear the hoarse, rasping cough that Constable Jaggery thought was a supplementary indicator of his bovine presence.

'Enter!' he bellowed.

Jaggery swung the door open and stepped inside, followed by Violet Crosby, her husband, Simeon Crosby, and Gilbert Crosby, the hangman's brother.

Captain Bell waved a hand of dismissal to his constable, who closed the door behind him with obvious relief. His three visitors were invited to sit down. After the usual preliminaries, he got down to business.

'You will know, of course, that a small group of people are determined to prevent you from speaking at the Public Hall?'

Simeon Crosby clasped his hands and rested them on his large chest. 'Captain Bell, these people – or their associates – stand for hours outside prison with their candles and their prayers and then hurl the most horrible abuse when I step through the gates. The vast majority are, of course, women.'

Violet Crosby gave a weak smile and said, 'My husband calls them his petticoat gauntlet.'

Captain Bell nodded. As an ex-military man, he recognised at once the reference to an archaic form of punishment where the offender is forced to run between two rows of soldiers and suffer a plethora of blows.

'So you can understand,' the hangman went on, with a sharp glance at his wife, 'that a few females waving placards are hardly the stuff of nightmares.'

'Quite.' The chief constable pursed his lips to prevent an ironic smile from betraying his thoughts. This man has little idea of how ferocious a group of Wigan females can be. 'Nevertheless, it was commendable of you to accept my suggestion.'

'That was my doing, Captain Bell.' It was the younger brother, Gilbert Crosby, who spoke. 'If Simeon had had his way, he would have insisted on a brass band blaring out his arrival and marching us from the station.' The flicker of amusement in his eyes was countered by the frown on his brother's face.

'It's the first time my wife has expressed a desire to accompany me on such a visit,' Simeon said. 'It wouldn't be seemly to subject her to the screeching of protesters.'

'Perhaps I might screech back,' said Violet quietly.

For a moment, there was a flash of anger on her husband's face, but it quickly vanished.

'That, too, would be unseemly, my dear,' was his response.

'You're staying at the Royal Hotel, I see,' said Captain Bell, anxious to move the conversation quickly to its conclusion.

'Gilbert here has taken charge of all arrangements.'

On cue, his brother smiled at their host and said, 'We have reservations at the Royal for two nights. Simeon will present his talk at the Public Hall tomorrow evening – the management informed me the other day that all tickets have been sold – and we will leave on Wednesday morning for Manchester.'

'A city I haven't visited since my retirement two months ago,' said Simeon. 'It must be almost a year since my last, more melancholy visit there. I spent the night as a guest at Strangeways and left quite early the following morning.'

No need to enquire as to what happened in the intervening hours, reflected the Chief Constable. *The Serving of Justice.*

'I have made arrangements for my constables to keep a sharp eye out for the period of your stay here in Wigan.'

'Is that really necessary?' asked Gilbert Crosby. 'The abolitionists are hardly a major force these days, are they?'

'Perhaps not. But over the last few days, posters have appeared urging support for a protest tomorrow night.'

Crosby's eyes widened. 'The abolitionists aren't quite dead yet then?'

The chief constable reached into his desk and brought out a crumpled sheet of paper, which he passed across to Crosby.

If you object to a man guilty of savage murder in your midst, you would do well to visit the Assembly Room at the Legs of Man this Monday at 4 o'clock, where reasons will be given for a strong protest against the hangman Simeon Crosby's presence in this fine Christian town. Thomas Evelyne.

The hangman frowned and passed it back with a shake of the head. 'Never heard of the fellow. We had someone in Carlisle who organised something similar. It's an unfortunate consequence of what my responsibilities involved, I'm afraid.' He gave the chief constable an enigmatic smile and added, 'The protest fizzled out like a damp firework because the police in Carlisle were on their toes.'

Captain Bell gave a defensive cough. 'He sounds like one of these professional agitators, if you ask me. He has also put posters up around the town, urging all Christian-minded folk to attend a gathering in the Market Square tomorrow evening with a view to then marching through the town and disrupting your talk at the Public Hall.'

'I have every confidence in your management of the situation, Chief Constable. This Evelyne won't be the first, and he won't be the last. But as I'm now retired from my melancholy duties he's a little late in his protest, isn't he?'

With a sigh, Captain Bell stood up and walked over to a small safe embedded in the wall. He opened it and took out a small cluster of papers. 'These,' he said with a flourish, 'are letters which have been sent to the local newspapers. All of them complain about your visit. Some of them refer to you as *murderer*, and some refer to you as worse. It is to the great credit of the editors at the *Examiner* and the *Observer* that they refused to publish them and saw fit to bring them to my attention.'

He offered the letters to the hangman, who waved them aside with barely concealed contempt. He turned and replaced them in the safe, closing the door with a heavy thud.

'To these people, Captain Bell, I'm an embarrassment and yes, to some, a murderer in all but name. But what am I to those who have suffered? To the families of those slain by some evil villain? To them, I'm the hand they would love to wield themselves. We can all stand on principles until evil pays us a visit.'

The chief constable blinked. He wasn't used to people delivering speeches in his office. He was normally the one doing that.

'The letters contain what you might expect from those with a warped attitude to the dispensing of justice,' Bell replied obliquely. 'But the good thing is, the letters are written by articulate men and women.'

'And why is that a good thing?' Gilbert Crosby's tone suggested a growing irritation.

'Because articulate people express their outrage by pen and paper.' He let the inference as to how inarticulate people show their outrage hang in the air. 'And, of course, we will have several of our men on duty at the Public Hall tomorrow night,' the chief constable went on, ignoring the concern on Gilbert Crosby's face.

'What is your personal view, sir?' Violet Crosby asked. 'Do your sympathies lie with these abolitionists or with the poor victims and their relatives?'

For a second, Captain Bell's eyes widened. He seemed to consider his response for a while before saying, 'Madam, I served in the army for a number of years. I have nothing but wholehearted respect for the concept of discipline, including the ultimate penalty under law. Take flogging, for instance. It is now, sadly, a thing of the past in the army, with those protesting its use claiming that such a public ritual was degrading. I disagree. For those watching, it was a clear punishment for the crime itself, and it was the *crime* that caused the soldier to lose his integrity, not the ritual of punishment.'

Gilbert Crosby smiled coldly. 'Careful, sir. That might be taken as advocating the return of public executions!'

Simeon Crosby forestalled any response from their host by standing up, a signal for their departure.

Captain Bell gave them directions to the Royal Hotel – some five minutes' walk away – and offered to send one of his constables along with them, but all three of them declined the offer. Once they had left, he stood at his window overlooking King Street and watched them stroll out of the building and turn right into King Street, Mr and Mrs Crosby walking arm in arm, with the younger brother a few feet behind them as if keeping guard. Interesting, he mused as he saw them pass several people on the pavement. What would those people think if they knew the hangman had just passed by?

Suddenly, he became more alert. A man – well-dressed, sporting a bowler hat and a walking cane – had been standing idly against the wall on the opposite side of the street. He caught sight of the Crosbys emerging from Rodney Street and immediately sprang to attention. With a flourish of his cane, he acknowledged the curses of a cab driver and stepped out onto the road, heading, in some haste, directly for the chief constable's recent guests.

'Look out, man!' yelled Captain Bell. But his voice failed to penetrate his office window.

With an urgency he hadn't shown in a while, he wheeled around and made a dash for the door.

CHAPTER THREE

Constable Jaggery later declared that he had never seen the chief constable move so fast. He flung open his door and tore down the corridor and a flight of stairs, yelling all the while something about a murder on *our doorstep*.

Upon hearing such startling news, Jaggery, who had been engaged in conversation with the desk sergeant, turned his gaze to the top step of the station entrance and the literal scene of the reported crime. As Captain Bell hove into view, he was about to point out that he could see no sign of such an outrageous crime when his superior swept past him with the garbled instruction to, '*Follow me.*'

'Tha'd best do as his bloody lordship says, Constable,' was the rather languid comment from the desk sergeant.

With a muttered curse, Jaggery moved to the doorway and caught sight of the chief constable hurtling across the street, narrowly escaping the menace of a passing tram, and launching himself at the throat of a dapper young man whom he flung to the ground, grabbing the poor fellow's walking cane before forcing its tip against his chest.

When Jaggery reached the remarkable scene, he saw the people he had escorted from the station staring down at their would-be assailant with expressions of mirth spread across their faces.

'Constable, arrest this man.' Captain Bell, standing astride his victim, seemed a little breathless, but he maintained the pressure of the cane on the man's chest as if he were wielding his old fullered blade with its point about to plunge into some heathen.

'You're absolutely mad!' said the prone figure, now that the initial shock of assault had subsided.

Jaggery bent down and hauled the miscreant to his feet. With his considerable brute strength, he swung the man round and clamped his hands together, the handcuffs appearing magically and closing around the wrists with a metallic clunk.

'What's the charge, sir?'

His superior frowned. 'We'll begin with assault. Take it from there.'

'Assault!' came the incredulous yelp. 'I never touched anybody. Ask them!'

Simeon Crosby stepped forward, the smile still creasing his features. 'I think perhaps I might speak on this man's behalf, Chief Constable?'

At this point, Captain Bell heard a smattering of sniggers from the crowd that had gathered, intrigued by the commotion. One of the bystanders, a man whose face had seen better days, said, 'Let him go ye bastard. He's done nowt.'

'Aye!' said another, whom Jaggery recognised as a habitué of the Police Court, a rough-looking individual who swayed from side to side in a vain attempt at the perpendicular. 'I seed it all. If that fat bastard's arrestin' any bugger, it should be thee, assaultin' a bloke wi' his own stick.'

There were mutterings of agreement as the crowd swelled.

'Look,' said the hangman quietly. 'I know this man. His name's Ralph Batsford. The only assault he's guilty of has been with a pen.'

'A deadly weapon in the wrong hands,' Captain Bell replied, misunderstanding the comment.

'I'm a newspaper reporter, you cretin!' snapped the handcuffed man.

Jaggery gave him a hefty slap around his right ear. 'Show some bloody respect, pal! That cretin's Captain Bell hisself.'

Simeon Crosby raised his voice so that everyone could hear. 'I'd like to thank the chief constable for his swift action. I must admit, it did indeed look as though my poor wife was about to be embroiled in a daylight assault. From a distance. With the police of Wigan led by such courage in the protection of visitors, it is heartening and reassuring. Now, if your constable will kindly release Mr Batsford, we will allow him to accompany us to the hotel where he can recover his senses – especially his hearing – with a reviving drink.'

'Release the fellow!' barked Captain Bell with as much authority and dignity as he could muster, given the circumstances.

*

'It's all about improvements these days.'

The speaker, Thomas Evelyne, paused and let the irony of his words sink in. There were over twenty people in the assembly room at the Legs of Man Hotel on Standishgate, and in the silence, they could all hear the dulled murmuring from the bar below, punctuated by an occasional raised voice and the slamming of an empty tankard on the counter. It was late afternoon, and there was little light from the small window. The clouds that had brooded malevolently all morning were now shedding their load, and rain smeared the window so that any view through the glass became distorted, fragmented by rivulets that slithered in every direction with no pattern. There was no gas lighting in this upstairs room, and the only illumination came from two oil lamps, one at the front where the speaker stood and another at the rear. Indeed, the lighting seemed most suitable, casting elongated shadows against front and rear walls, creating the macabre impression that the attendance was much larger and they were being observed by a whole phalanx of spirits whose bodies had been excruciatingly stretched by ghostly ropes.

'We surely live in the most enlightened age. For we now have an official guide, from no less an august body than the Capital Sentences Committee itself, a guide that is meticulous in its measurements and providing our careful and considerate executioners with The Table of Drops. How reassuring it is to know that science has removed all doubt, all possibility of a gruesome end such as suffocation or decapitation. Weights and measures, my friends!'

The speaker picked up a sheet of paper from the table before him and held it close to the oil lamp. In the half-light, his face, with its sharp pointed nose, staring eyes and dark beard, glistening with sweat and globules of spittle, seemed more demonic than human. His voice was now low, deceptively so, for as his words gathered momentum, he allowed its volume to rise, reaching its climax with the final simile.

'It's surely comforting to know, for example, that a man such as myself, who weighs twelve stone fully clothed, requires a drop of seven feet six inches producing a force of one thousand two hundred and sixty pounds per foot. It is further comforting to know that the weighing takes place just before the execution and not on entry to the prison, because our judicial system has found that prisoners actually gain weight once they are incarcerated. We feed them, plump and ready, and then we hang them. Like cattle, my friends. Like cattle to the slaughter.'

There were mutterings of both agreement and dissent.

'And how long will it be before our enlightened leaders enact that most sophisticated of instruments introduced by our American cousins – the electric chair? It seems, does it not, that there is no limit to the punitive imagination of the modern world.' He took a deep breath then added, 'And now we have in our midst Mr Simeon Crosby.'

Again, he paused to allow the opprobrium to gain strength. The hiatus was rendered more portentous by the sudden lashing of torrential rain against the window, giving the impression that the Almighty himself had passed judgement.

'A man who, until a few months ago, had been responsible not only for many officially sanctioned deaths, but also, to our certain knowledge, the decapitation of five – *five* – unfortunate souls, simply because he failed to apply the correct procedures. It beggars belief, does it not, that this butcher is now come among us to share his experiences? To *entertain*? Perhaps we should be grateful that this blood-letting accomplice of the state isn't illustrating his talk with magic lantern slides.'

Several members of the audience fidgeted, some turning to their neighbour and expressing their disgust that such a creature should indeed be let loose amongst them.

'Tomorrow night, my friends, Simeon Crosby will stand before the people of this ancient and loyal town and profit from the deeds he has committed. Remember his namesake from Luke Chapter Two. *And behold, there was a man in Jerusalem whose name was Simeon; and the same man was just and devout.* Are these words to describe Mr Crosby?'

After a slight hesitation, during which the audience were unsure as to whether the question were rhetorical or not, many of them responded with a resounding, *No!*

'Is it our duty to sit back and do nothing while he slakes the thirst of a salivating audience?'

No!

'Shall we march to the Public Hall here in Wigan and prevent such vileness from staining the town's good name?'

Yes!

'Then it shall be. We will all meet at the Market Square at six o'clock tomorrow evening and march down to the Public Hall with our determination lighting the way!'

One man, seated in the centre of the room, raised a hand. Once the speaker acknowledged him, he spoke while remaining seated. His voice was low, menacing.

'Is that all you've got in mind then? A march an' a banner? Be more like Walkin' Day than a soddin' protest.'

The room had grown silent, only the rain slashing against the windows could be heard.

Before Evelyne could say anything, the man went on.

'The man's nowt but a murderer hisself, ain't he? Makes a livin' out o' death.' He paused. 'That'd be funny, that. *A livin' out o' death.* So somebody like that won't take a blind bit o' notice of a banner an' a few folk shoutin'. Be like wavin' a snotrag at a wolf.'

Evelyne coughed and flicked a glance at some of the women in the room. 'What exactly are you suggesting, friend?' he asked, wary of the answer.

'I reckon the only thing what'd make that feller sit up an' take notice would be a bit of his own medicine.'

'Surely you don't mean…'

'If there's enough of us, we could drag the bugger from the stage an' wrap a rope around his neck an' scrawp him down Market Street to the Market Square.'

'And then what?' Evelyne asked, an appalled expression on his face now. 'Hang him by the neck until he is dead? A public execution, the like of which we've not seen since '68?'

But the man merely shook his head. 'Just tie the bugger to a railing an' cover the swine wi' tar an' feathers. That'll do wonders for his swagger!'

Evelyne stood there open-mouthed. Another member of his audience piped up, 'Oh aye? We can all bring feathers but who's goin' to cough up for a bucket full o' tar, eh? Ye daft sod.'

There was laughter at that point, more out of relief than humour, and the original proposer stood up, swore at the last speaker and the audience in general, then pushed his way past those seated beside him and cursed his way down to the bar below with a valedictory, 'Lot o' soft shites!' ringing in their ears.

Evelyne made a few final comments and sat down to a great round of applause, and within minutes, the group had left the room. The speaker stayed behind, gathering his notes and reflecting on a job well done. He hadn't noticed the single person left at the back of the room.

'An interesting speech, sir!' came the voice, disembodied by the gloom.

Thomas Evelyne glanced up, peering into the darkness. 'I'm glad you enjoyed it,' he said, with a tinge of curiosity in his voice. 'There's always one, sadly.'

'Of course. Hot air and bluster, men like that. They love the sound of their own righteousness.'

'You aren't from the town?'

'Oh no, Mr Evelyne. I'm a stranger.'

But then, before he could clearly discern the man's features – he was standing behind the oil lamp, and it was all he could do to make out a shape at all – the door swung open and the stranger left the room. The light from the small landing shone briefly on his face.

Evelyne nodded, as if to confirm something.

*

Ellen Brennan felt it quite a luxury to have her husband home during the day. Michael had explained that it was hardly a blessing: Captain

Bell had put him in charge of the following evening's duties involving the visit and talk given by Simeon Crosby, and when Brennan had pointed out that he hadn't had a single day off duty for over two weeks, the chief constable had shown his magnanimity by granting him a full afternoon off.

Their six-year-old son, Barry, was at school, and the two of them sat by the fire and watched the flames dancing in the grate.

'I love this,' Ellen said.

'What?'

'Pouring down outside. And us here. Nice an' warm.'

Brennan smiled. 'I don't even feel guilty.'

'Guilty?'

'Being here when by rights I should be on duty.'

'*Rights?*' Ellen repeated playfully. 'It's our *right* to sit here without worrying about anything else.'

He reached out to hold her hand. The rain was relentless and at times, sounded like a whole hail of pebbles rattling against the window. 'There'll not be much to do today, anyway. Constables have a clever habit of finding the most sheltered place there is on their beat.'

'Need to be a big shelter for poor Freddie,' she said with a comical frown.

'Poor Freddie Jaggery will be as dry as a bone and as warm as that hearthstone. You mark my words.'

They lapsed once more into silence. There was, indeed, something cosy about the warmth and brightness of the fire and the darkening world outside. He looked at the clock – ten past four – and hoped little Barry didn't get too drenched on his walk home. He would come running down the street in his usual race with his best friend, Robert, from two doors along, and doubtless he'd be wet through from the puddles he just couldn't bring himself to avoid.

'This man I shared a carriage with,' said Ellen, breaking into his thoughts. 'Simeon Crosby.'

'It's daft, but I would have said he was well off, what with him being fat and sporting a beard.'

Brennan laughed out loud.

'But then I saw his clothes and, well, he didn't seem so well off after all. His cuffs were frayed, for one thing. Don't they get paid well?'

'Hangmen?' he frowned and thought a little before replying. 'I doubt very much that they do it for the money, Ellen. There's a standard fee of ten pounds for each execution and three guineas for his assistant, if he has one. Nobody'll get rich that way. Besides, the man's retired.'

'But why do it? I mean, surely there're better ways of earning a living?'

Brennan shrugged. 'He'll have had his reasons.'

'Could you do it?'

'What? Hang a man?'

'Or a woman.'

Brennan gave it some thought. 'I think I could hang a man right enough. Someone who's done something awful enough to turn your stomach.'

She watched his eyes and wondered what horrors he'd seen over the years, horrors he never discussed with her once he shut the front door behind him.

'And yet people still murder, don't they? Hanging doesn't put them off,' she said.

He leaned forward, picked up the poker and stirred the coals, sending flashes of sparks flying up the chimney. 'No it doesn't deter, Ellen. Not in the slightest. But it does make sure of one thing.'

'And what's that?'

'Well there's never been one case – not one – of a hanged man coming back and committing another murder. Never.'

She smiled and dug him in the ribs.

Actually, he thought, there had been one such case, although he decided not to mention it to Ellen. A murderer was saved from the gallows because of a botched execution – and the man was taken back to his cell. The experience, however, had disturbed his mind so much that he was admitted to the prison hospital, from where he made a daring escape. Unfortunately, he committed another murder – some poor fellow's wife when he broke into their house looking for food. The man was caught and was eventually hanged – successfully, this time.

No point in relating the sorry tale to Ellen. It would serve only to upset her.

Suddenly, they heard shrill screams from the pavement beyond the front window. The front door burst open, and their son, Barry, stood there, dripping wet, a huge smile on his face.

'I won, Dad!' he said, trying to catch his breath. 'That's t'first time I've ever beat him! An' guess what he wanted me to do?'

'What?' said Brennan with a smile.

'Play knock an' run. But that's not a nice game, is it, Dad?'

'No, lad. It's not.'

Ellen went quickly over to him, wrapped her arms around his wet frame and brought him quickly to the fire.

CHAPTER FOUR

Gilbert Crosby stood at the bar of the Royal Hotel and leaned with his back to the counter. He had an audience of a half-dozen now, and what had begun as a simple and inquisitive customer asking, '*Wheer did tha get that bugger from then?*' soon developed into an entertaining way of passing a rainy afternoon. The old man who had asked the question had pointed directly at the scar on the right side of Gilbert's face, and the subsequent explanation had gradually drawn others in, for Gilbert's was far from a quiet voice.

'Of course,' he went on, 'I was only in Germany a short time. A few days. But I wasn't to know their ridiculous customs, nor their laughable and impossible language.'

'Tha cawn't tell a bloody word Germans say,' said another member of his audience, a small, thin-chested man with a permanent stoop and a face the colour of parchment, a man who had never been further than Blackpool in his life.

'Indeed not.'

'So this German lad offered thee out 'cos tha trod on his bloody dog's tail?'

'That's about the size of it, yes. He was a student at the university, see? They have particular rules about insults and whatnot. So I was forced to meet this student at dawn in some fog-enshrouded clearing in the woods.'

'So wheer did t'get thi sword from, like?'

Gilbert took a long, slow drink and drained his glass, holding it up to the light so that they could all see the frothy dregs clinging to the sides.

'I'll get thee a drink, lad,' the old man offered, and Gilbert clapped him on the shoulder as if they had been drinking partners for years. He passed the glass back to the landlord who gave him a suspicious glance before throwing a towel over his shoulder and pumping the ale.

'Oh they're quite a friendly bunch, the Germans. One of his friends lent me his weapon.'

'Was it thi first time? Wi' a sword?'

'Of course.'

'So tha lost then?' said another of the drinkers.

'Oh no, I won the duel. Slashed the devil's face on both sides.' Here, he stepped forward and swept out his right hand, making swift slicing movements to the right and left of an imaginary foe. 'They judge the duel on who's lost least blood. Then we sat down on a handcart and let the doctors stitch us. Without any anaesthetic, of course.'

'Bloody 'ell!' said one of them.

'Germans!' said another with a sneer. He reached down and aimed a perfect globule of spit into the spittoon at the corner of the bar.

Gilbert raised his eyebrows and shook his head. 'They were amicable after that. And respectful. Took me to a beer hall, and we all got roaring drunk.'

There was a further discussion on the relative merits of fighting a duel with swords or a clog-fight, and after the audience had explained the essential rules of clog-fighting – basically, there were none, and both men stood with arms on each other's shoulders, naked, but for their iron-rimmed clogs and then proceeded to kick each other's shins to a bloody pulp – there was common agreement that the German way of doing things seemed much more civilised.

When his audience had gone, he stood at the bar and looked round. Two men, a young man and an older one, were sitting in a corner, away from the bar. Buoyed by his new-found popularity, he made his way over to them.

'A dreadful day,' he said by way of introduction, nodding to the window where the rain was creating an opaque, distorted view of the street beyond.

The older man followed his gaze. 'Indeed,' he said.

It was a dismissal and a rude one at that.

'Are you staying here at the Royal?' Gilbert asked, still awaiting an invitation to join their company.

He noticed that the younger man seemed rather ill at ease. In circumstances such as this, he immediately raised his hand and touched his scar.

'I hope my duelling scar doesn't upset you!' he said with an attempt both at humour and ingratiation.

'No,' said the younger man.

'We were discussing business,' the older one said.

Gilbert, taking that as the best hope he had of an invitation, pulled up a chair and sat down at their table. 'And what business are you in?'

'Commercial travellers,' the younger one said.

'Very busy ones,' added the older man. By the tone of his voice and the expression on his face, it was clear that there would be little else forthcoming.

Gilbert had the feeling that he had interrupted something – certainly, when the younger one raised his glass to his lips, it was more as a way of avoiding any further engagement than slaking his thirst.

An uncomfortable silence reigned for a few minutes. As a last resort, Gilbert announced that he was visiting the town in the company of his brother, who was *quite a celebrity*.

When neither of them asked the expected next question, he stood up again and glared down at them.

'I hope your sales methods are more communicative than your small talk!' he said and walked away with as much dignity as he could muster.

He walked over to the window and gazed out. Across the street, a row of shops, the interiors illuminated to display their wares through the rainy gloom of a late November afternoon, showed little sign of life. This awful rain!

He turned and gave the lugubrious landlord, who was idly cleaning glasses, a cheery grin. Despite the lack of response from him and the two travellers whose rudeness had irked him, he felt a surge of pride as he reflected on the last half-hour or so. Those fellows earlier had listened to him and been fascinated by his tales of duelling with German students, and not once, in the entire discussion, had he mentioned to them the fact that his brother was Simeon Crosby, the famous hangman.

They had found *him* interesting.

Him and his scar.

Putting the rest of it to the back of his mind, he decided that the afternoon had been a delight. For the first time in a while, he felt lucky.

Once Gilbert had left the bar, the older man drained his glass and said curtly to his young companion, 'I need a cigar.'

*

While his brother was thus engaged in the public bar downstairs, Simeon Crosby sat at the small table beneath the window of his room and made one or two alterations to the presentation he would

41

be delivering to the good people of Wigan the following night. He would begin, as he always began, with his favourite, audience-catching anecdotes, relating some of the more unfortunate consequences of not having a widely experienced hangman in charge of the rope. Slipshod botched executions by those who had long since passed into executioner folklore. Such as the time one of his predecessors, the notorious Bartholomew Binns, who was a known drunkard, completely misjudged both the thickness of the rope required to hang a diminutive prisoner and the length of the drop, with the result that the poor wretch, fully expecting a swift passage to the Lower Regions, was seen to swing round and round once the lever had been pulled, and instead of dying from a fractured spinal cord, was seen to writhe in agony as death made its slow advance through strangulation.

Or the time back in the good old days of public executions, almost thirty years ago, when George Smith made the unfortunate mistake of failing to attach the rope firmly enough to the beam above the trap door. Once Smith pulled the lever, the prisoner, pinioned and blindfolded and helpless, plunged through the opening and fell unhanged to the ground below. As the public – most of them drunk and raucous – witnessed this abominable display of ineptitude, they jeered and hurled insults aimed not at the condemned man this time (whose crime was now seen as secondary to this most public of humiliations) but at the hapless hangman, who was forced to climb down and give orders for the injured prisoner to be hauled back up and for the rope, still in place around his neck, to be reattached to the beam – this time more securely.

That was the last time there was a public execution in Staffordshire, he would add, *and poor George Smith got the blame!*

The biggest laugh, however, was always reserved for the tale of the four men in Derbyshire, almost eighty years ago, who had been condemned to death for setting fire to a field of corn and hay (*pause for gasps of shock at the brutality of the Bloody Code of former times!*) On the day of their execution, they stood ready to be despatched by the hangman when it came on to rain most heavily (*surely a meaningful comment from the Almighty on the fire and devastation they had caused!*) To the shock and amusement of the thousands watching the executions, the men begged for umbrellas to shield them from the rain.

Perhaps, my friends, they hadn't realised that if they got to hell sufficiently drenched, it might help dull the fierce flames the devil had waiting for them!

Levity, he knew, was the perfect seasoning if applied at the right moment.

There was one mishap, however, that he would refrain from mentioning, while in the spirit of honesty, he would share with them a further mishap from a few years later. It was to be the central focus of his talk.

The first, unmentionable, incident concerned a condemned man who was due to meet his maker at Norwich Castle back in '85. He had caved his wife's head in and hurled her down a well. He was arrested and put on trial for murder, found guilty and sentenced to be hanged. On the day of his execution, the rope was placed around his neck and all due ceremonies observed. The trapdoors swung open, but to the surprise and subsequent horror of all those watching – the sheriff, the prison governor, chaplain and several members of the press, including, of course, the executioner – the rope unexpectedly jerked upwards before dangling like a lifeless snake. This was followed rapidly by a dull thud and the uneven rolling of a decapitated head in the pit below.

The hangman had miscalculated the length of rope.

Simeon Crosby shook his head at the unforgivable error. The fact that he himself had been the guilty hangman would naturally preclude him from mentioning that particular incident in his list of anecdotes.

Besides, since he had perfected his *Table of Drops*, and every one of his subsequent customers had gone to meet his maker *corpus et caput intactus*, so to speak, it irked him that some of his detractors were spreading the lie that more than one of his subjects had been decapitated. Lies beget lies, and people prefer to believe varnished calumnies than the unvarnished truth, for no matter how many times he denied such rumours, they continued to follow him like horse muck.

He had severed one head. No more.

The second incident concerned the ironically named Benjamin Goodfellow. Simeon maintained that the lever and the trapdoors were in perfect working order when he had rehearsed the execution only the day before. Why the mechanism should refuse to operate a matter of hours later had been a positive conundrum at the time. It was only much later that some idiot in the prison admitted he'd fooled around with the contraption on the eve of execution. Still, he had been exonerated, and that was all that mattered.

But the unfortunate event had its uses. In the book, a whole chapter would be devoted to it, on the advice of Ralph Batsford, who said it provided rich material. It was, he'd argued, an excellent example of the Inevitability of Justice, and tomorrow night, he would share the anecdote in a section of his speech he would call *Justice Always Prevails*. For hadn't he had the rare privilege of ensuring justice was finally done when, after Goodfellow had escaped from prison and killed once more, he had been caught and finally renewed his acquaintance with the hangman?

I am the only executioner to hang a man twice for two separate crimes!

As at his last talk in Carlisle, it was his climactic boast. It had brought forth a thunderous applause from the audience.

He sighed, read through his notes and gave a satisfied nod before turning to the bed behind him, where his wife, Violet, lay sleeping.

The train journeys – from their home in Lancaster to Preston, then Preston to Wigan – had been tiring, he had to admit. It had come as a surprise when she had asked to come with him this time: since he had retired from his post a few months earlier, he had travelled to various towns and cities to deliver his talk, but she had never shown any desire to accompany him until now. He should regard it as a compliment, he knew, that his wife should show her support for him in such a way. But he had a vague feeling that marital loyalty had little to do with her presence.

Over the last few weeks, he'd had an idea that she wasn't being completely truthful with him. Small things, surreptitious movements, unexpected flushes of embarrassment which he put down to the sensational nature of the novel she was reading.

But he wondered, nevertheless.

Batsford, he suspected, had talked her into coming, more than likely to add the personal touch to his memoirs. To be fair, the journalist had proved most helpful in his suggestions for the whole concept.

Still, he was probably concerned over nothing. She would see for herself the way people regarded him, especially women: that expression of fascination and disgust whenever he was introduced to them. The disgust, of course, was natural, he'd told Violet before they travelled. It was the fascination that was more surprising and (although he didn't admit it to his wife) more enjoyable. He supposed it was the proximity to a dispenser of death, one who did so with the full blessing of Her Majesty.

Only soldiers on a battlefield shared such a privilege.

There was a knock on the door.

Crosby glanced across at his wife, whose sleep remained undisturbed by the knocking. He left the table and his notes and moved quickly to the door in case whoever it was knocked again.

When he opened the door, he found Ralph Batsford standing there.

Crosby looked back to his wife and stepped out into the corridor, pulling the door closed behind him.

'Batsford,' he said with more than a hint of pique in his voice. 'I thought I said I wasn't to be disturbed? My notes aren't quite…'

Batsford frowned and placed an arm on the hangman's shoulder. 'There's disturbed, and then there's disturbed,' came the cryptic reply.

'What the blazes does that mean?'

'It's what you will be when I tell you.'

'Tell me what?'

'Disturbing news, Simeon. Disturbing news.'

CHAPTER FIVE

Haydock Lodge, Private Asylum for the Restoration and Care of the Insane, lay two miles from Newton-le-Willows Station on the LNWR line, just under eight miles from Wigan. It had formerly been owned by a prosperous country gentleman, and its advertisement in the *London and Provincial Medical Directory* proclaimed proudly that:

The accommodation is of a superior character, the apartments being spacious, cheerful, and admirably arranged for the purposes of classification, without entailing any objectionable features, such, for instance, as one suggestive of restraint.

Of its numerous patients in residence, nineteen were listed as having no occupation, thirty-six were designated as living on their own means, while others had formerly held occupations in areas as diverse as governess (two, female), sempstress (one, female), solicitor (one, male), salesman (cutlery), and chartered accountant (one, male).

It was one of the more unsavoury aspects of an attendant's duties to escort the patient to the water closet, with a view to observing the necessary natural function of bladder and/or bowel. Particular care had to be taken with one such patient, Oscar Pardew, who, in his more lucid days, had worked in the Indian Civil Service. Oscar had two unfortunate habits: the first was more than likely a consequence of his days in the Raj, for he insisted on shaking hands with all and sundry with a handshake so firm, the recipient often yelped in pain. His other, more revolting habit, involved the swallowing of buttons and coins, much to the annoyance of the other patients and on several occasions prompting hysteria from the sempstress, whose collection of clothing fragments would never get finished for the ball if that man continued to eat her finest black glass buttons with their delightful reliefs of animals and plants. An assurance from the attendants that she might well see them returned to her in due course brought forth a barrage of the foulest language.

During one such visit to the water closet, the attendant, whose name was Simpson, stood as far from the open door as he could while maintaining sight of Oscar. Closet duty was, by its very nature, unpleasant, but having to scrutinise the consequences for extraneous matter and then removing it was beyond the call. Sometimes, they simply ignored it and allowed Pardew to do the business and manage his own cleaning. And the time he took to do it!

While Simpson stood in the doorway connecting the closet room with the narrow corridor that led back to the main lounge area, he was joined by Potter, another attendant. The two of them smoked a cigarette, and after sharing a quite salacious reference to the visibly and audibly straining Oscar Pardew, allowed their conversation to drift to other topics.

'I wouldn't miss it. Not for anythin',' said Potter, inhaling deeply before blowing forth a perfect set of smoke rings.

'An' I'm bloody well stuck 'ere. Don't fancy swappin'?'

'I most certainly don't. Not every day you get to meet a bloke what kills for a livin'.'

They both laughed.

'My uncle heard Simeon Crosby speak, you know,' Potter said. 'Over in Liverpool a month ago.'

'I know. You said.'

'He reckoned some of those tales'd make your hair stand on end.'

'You told me.'

'Even got to shake his hand after. Said it felt strange, shakin' the hand that pulled the lever.'

'Why?'

'Because of what that hand had done.'

Simpson shrugged. 'Anyroad, I can always catch him again. The bugger's retired, ain't he? He'll be makin' more money by talkin' about hangin' folk than actually hangin' 'em!'

'Rumour has it he's writin' a book about his experiences.'

Simpson straightened his back in a show of righteous indignation. 'Now that's crossin' the line, I reckon.'

'Why? It'd be a seller, right enough.'

'An' what about the families, eh? All them as is left behind when he watches 'em drop?'

'What about 'em?'

'They'll not be best pleased readin' about their loved ones an' their last minutes in this world, will they?'

'Well they won't be readin' about it if they don't bloody well buy the thing. Nobody's forcin' 'em. Besides, if they're related to a bad un there's no tellin' they're not as bad. Just luckier.'

Potter inhaled once more, swirled the smoke around his mouth before exhaling. This time, Simpson noted with satisfaction, the smoke rings were misshapen, fragmenting weakly within seconds.

There was a loud, painful grunt from the closet.

A few moments later, Oscar Pardew was standing in the doorway and holding up, with some pride, what looked like two ha'pennies soaked in filth that dripped thickly to the ground.

'A penny for your thoughts, my dear *badmash*,' he said with a grin.

*

Barry Brennan frowned and twitched his nose. While his mother was in the kitchen getting their tea ready, he was standing at the front window watching the rain bounce on the pavement beyond.

'Dad?'

'What?'

'Do you remember when we went to the park? For the gala?'

Michael Brennan smiled at the memory. Back in May, on Whit Monday, the Grand Gala at Mesnes Park had been expected to raise a large sum for the Infirmary in Wigan, but the rain had kept many away, with the result that, after the expenses of the many acts booked to perform were taken into account, the gala made precious little for the fund. But, despite the foul weather, he recalled how excited his young son had been to see the feats of the Brothers Anistine on the Flying Rings, the child bicyclist, Young Adonis, who did impossible things on a drawing-room table, and more than anything else, the Grand Display of Fireworks at the end of the day (although the much anticipated Mammoth Whirlwinds, Roman Candles and Whistling Rockets had proved to be vulnerable to raindrops).

'I do, lad. It was a good day.'

'It rained.'

'It did.'

'Why did it rain then?'

His son had recently taken to asking questions of superficial simplicity, requiring him to respond with frankness.

'Because the sun had gone away.'

'Why? If God knew there was a gala in the park why did he make the sun go away?'

'Well, sometimes we don't know why God does things. If we did, we'd be like God ourselves, wouldn't we? We don't always have sunshine, and we don't always have rain.'

'We have snow, too!'

'That's right.'

'It snowed last week.'

'It did.'

'So why is it raining today? Did God get fed up of the snow? Happen he sent the rain to get rid of the snow, melt it, eh, Dad?'

'Happen.'

'But it were good, all that snow. We had snowball fights at school.'

Brennan ruffled his son's hair.

'So why did God make it rain on Gala Day then?'

'Ask your mother,' Brennan said, just as Ellen came back into the living room.

*

'Well?'

Simeon Crosby sat across from the journalist in the lounge area of the Royal Hotel. There was only one other person in the room, and he was reading a newspaper with his back to them.

Ralph Batsford leaned forward and spoke softly. 'You know there'll be some protest tomorrow night?'

Crosby sighed. 'There's always protests. Protesters are like bloody ants. Can't get rid.'

'Agreed. But I have a bad feeling about this one.'

'Why?'

Batsford shrugged. 'I went to a meeting across the street. Public house called the Legs of Man. They were organising the protest for tomorrow.'

'Like I said. Ants.'

Batsford shook his head. 'One man suggested they drag you from the Public Hall and – what was the colourful word he used? Ah, I remember: *scrawp* you down the street to the Market Square where, he suggested, they cover you in tar and feathers.'

Crosby blinked. 'They wouldn't bloody dare!'

'Oh, I think the man who made the suggestion would dare. He seemed angry enough.'

'There'll be police there. The chief constable said so.'

'Depends on how many.' He sat there silent for a few moments to let the implications sink in. 'I need hardly remind you of the consequences of such an attack.'

'Consequences?' Crosby's voice rose, causing the man reading his newspaper to turn round and glare at him. 'I'd be covered in tar and bloody feathers. That'd be the bloody consequence!'

Batsford shook his head. 'What I mean is, it wouldn't look good.'

'Course it wouldn't bloody well look good! I'd be tied to a post like a black chicken!'

'Not what I meant. I was talking about the publicity. For the book.'

Crosby blinked and gave it some thought. He had high hopes that the book he was writing – or rather, the book that Batsford was writing, with information and anecdotes provided by himself – would make his fortune. How many people over the years had urged him to write a record of his experiences for the edification of the country at large? But it was only when Batsford had approached him after the

Goodfellow affair with the notion of a memoir, secretly penned by Batsford, containing everything the general public would be clamouring to read, that he grew warm to the idea. It took him a length of time to agree, but once he had, his imagination grew. He even pictured himself signing copies of his book, not only in this country but further afield – America, say?

'An old editor of mine,' Batsford went on, breaking into his vision of a drinks party in some Manhattan Club, 'was in Dublin in '83 when the students of Trinity College threatened to tar and feather the Lord Mayor himself after he was invited to attend the University's Philosophical Society. They were planning to tar and feather him and drag him into the examination hall where the meeting was to take place. Imagine the outrage. The humiliation.'

'What happened?'

'Why, the Lord Mayor decided against turning up.'

Crosby's face grew an alarming shade of red. 'You're suggesting I do the same? Skulk in my room like some coward?'

'Think of it, man. The disgrace of being hauled through the streets by a jeering mob and then given what is commonly regarded as the ultimate humiliating punishment... It isn't the sort of publicity we need, is it?'

At that point, the hangman stood up and thrust out his chest with some pride.

'I've never skulked in my life. And I can stand up to any man. If you think for one second, Batsford, that I would stand there and allow myself to be – what was it – *scrawped* down the street of this godforsaken shithole in the armpit of the north then you don't bloody well know me!'

Batsford, recognising the man's mood, forebore from pointing out that armpits don't have shitholes.

With that, Crosby turned on his heel and left the lounge.

Batsford waited a few moments and then headed to the staircase to return to his own room. He knew that the Crosbys were planning to dine in the hotel tonight and not venture forth. He had been invited to join them but had politely declined. Crosby and his wife were dining alone together, for the odious Gilbert had declared a wish to *sample the evening delights* of the town. *Alone*, he had pointedly stated, the single, loaded word aimed directly at Batsford, who had no intention of being in the fellow's company any longer than was professionally necessary.

No, Batsford had much to occupy his mind and needed the privacy of a quiet supper in his room to decide how to proceed.

Tomorrow, he would deal with the troublesome matter.

*

When Simeon Crosby returned to his room, he saw his wife sitting up in bed, reading the novel she was currently devouring: *Moths* by Ouida.

'Feeling refreshed, dear?' he asked with an ironic glance at the novel she was holding.

Violet Crosby raised her eyes and then turned her head to look at the rain-spattered window. 'Do you know where I am at this moment?' she asked.

'Wigan in the rain!' he declared somewhat dramatically.

'Well, no. As a matter of fact – or should I say as a matter of *fiction* – I've just been walking through the myrtle wood near the Villa Nelaguine on the Gulf of Villafranca.'

'And no doubt the sun was beating down, and all was right with the bloody world.' He spoke without rancour. It was a common theme between them – her yearning for the romantic refuge of her novels while he had his feet firmly planted in the grimness of the here and now.

'Well not really,' she said, holding the volume up as if for proof. 'A seventeen-year-old girl from Northumberland is now the Princess Zouroff in a loveless marriage and—'

He held up his hand. 'For God's sake don't spoil the ending for me!'

She smiled, knowing full well that he would rather have his eyeballs skewered than read the sort of novel she enjoyed. 'What did Mr Batsford want?'

He gave her a stern look. 'How did you know? You were asleep.'

'I was resting my eyes. Well?'

Simeon Crosby gave a little cough. 'Just wanted to clear up a few things about the book.'

'Ah,' she said, recognising the telltale sign that he was lying.

'I've reserved a table for eight o'clock,' he said as he moved to the window. Once there, he gazed down at the scene below. Several people were taking shelter beneath the canopies of the shops opposite. Large puddles had formed in the road. He watched as two rough-looking boys came running along the pavement and stopped suddenly, waiting for a man who was walking towards them. He wore a dark brown ulster, a bowler hat and was pulling his muffler close to his chin. The boys watched him stop at the kerbstone for a tram to pass by; then they chose the exact moment when he stepped into the road to launch themselves at the largest and nearest of the puddles, sending what seemed like waves surging towards their unfortunate victim, soaking his coat and the lower sections of his trousers before rushing down the street, giving him a flick of their hands in the air and what must have been a string of obscenities, to which the poor chap responded in kind.

Simeon smiled. Those two miscreants might one day make that fateful walk to the gallows. They wouldn't be rushing then, he reflected.

'Just the two of us?' she asked.

He turned to face her.

'Just the two of us,' he replied.

She sighed and returned forthwith to Villafranca.

*

The generally agreed diagnosis of Oscar Pardew's mental condition was Insanity by Virtue of Delusion. This manifested itself through what was termed a Monomania of Suspicion, whereby the patient has created a delusion of persecution which originated, he claimed, during his time on the sub-continent. It was his contention that a curse had been placed upon him by some holy man as a result of some slight. The incident was doubly unfortunate for Pardew, as he was accompanied by the district officer – his immediate superior in the Indian Civil Service – and the disturbance in the village that ensued gave him a quarrelsome reputation a mere month into his posting in Calcutta. The curse, and the D.O.'s obvious disapproval, had played on his mind, and once he contracted a fever, he felt that the whole world was conspiring against him, urged on by the holy man. His mind, therefore, created a whole litany of disasters that would subsequently befall him.

During his period of convalescence, the sense of persecution waned, and he grew in strength as the fever abated. Even the D.O. visited him and wished him a speedy recovery. He returned to his work in the ICS, feeling much refreshed, spending a great deal of his time studying for his departmental examinations and longing for the expiry of his first year in his new life, when he would no longer be referred to as a *griffin* and would be regarded as a valued member of the service.

But in his second week back at work, he received an urgent and distressing letter.

His father had been brutally killed in a card game gone wrong.

The curse, he realised, was alive and well.

In profound distress, he was shipped back to England where, after hearing the gruesome details of the murder and discovering that his father had been buried two months earlier (*What in God's name did you expect, Oscar? That we keep our dear father on ice while you sail the seven seas?*), Pardew finally succumbed to the horrors of his life, and his mind let go of reality. Finally, his unstable condition was too much for them to cope with and so they had him committed to the asylum.

He had been placed in a private room, paid for by his family, where he spent every night singing some baleful ditty to a small framed photograph of his elder sister sitting in a chair, her hand stretched out to hold the hand of the older man seated beside her: his father. It had been a specially commissioned photograph, which his sister had claimed would give him comfort. Indeed, he showed the photograph of *Dead Father* to others in the asylum, a bizarre reversion of the normal practice of proud parents showing off their children.

He told others, in his more lucid moments, that the song he sang over and over was a remnant of a folk tale he had learned in India when he was a mere griffin. It told of a prince wandering the land and coming across a graveyard, where a headless corpse sat lamenting its fate by a freshly dug grave:

On earth I was even as thou,
My turban awry like a king,
My head with the highest, I trow,
Having my fun and my fling,
Fighting my foes like a brave,
Living my life with a swing.
And, now I am dead,

Sins, heavy as lead,
Will give me no rest in my grave!

One day, one of the other patients had asked him a question about the song.

'How can the corpse talk if it's headless?'

Another asked, 'How can it talk if it's dead?'

Yet another said, 'And what happened to his turban?'

'How can you be a griffin?' asked one. 'That's a lion's body and an eagle's head. I drew one at school.'

'I *was* a griffin!' Pardew had ranted. 'Everyone's a griffin when they first go out there. Everyone. You calling me a liar?'

Then, confused and angered by the interrogation, he had begun to hum the tune and rock to and fro until the attendants had come to his rescue. But always, he held the small framed photograph close to his chest, and he looked for all the world to be singing *Dead Father* to sleep.

It was part of his nightly routine, too, once his door was locked from the outside, to delve into an old copy of *The Graphic*, where he relished the writings of Mary Frances Billington, whose reports from India under the heading *Woman in India* transported him back to the subcontinent, a place he still harboured hopes of returning to once the fog and the fever in his head had dissipated. Tonight, for instance, he read avidly about the most common crimes of Indian women, foremost of which was infanticide as a way of gaining revenge on violent husbands.

'That's not right,' he whispered, directing his comments to the small photograph that now rested on his bedside table. 'Poor innocents, Father. A good sessions judge would make 'em swing for it and no mistake about that. No, sir.'

He also read an article about the executioner in this country, Simeon Crosby. Or rather, an article devoted to those who had been affected in some way by the hangman's actions. Relatives of those whom the condemned person had murdered.

Like Oscar himself. A bereft son.

Hadn't that same executioner been the topic of conversation between the two attendants?

He turned to look at the photograph of Dead Father.

'It's like you're telling me something,' he said softly. 'It's like I can hear you, Father. Simeon Crosby! He's the one who...' But he stopped, looked round, wondering if, even now, someone was standing outside his room, listening, sniggering.

Later, as he lay in his bed, all the lights extinguished and the darkness giving shape to all kinds of distortions peopling his room, he closed his eyes, as always facing the photograph of his sister and his dear father, and listened to the nightly sounds from the dormitory beyond his door, the coughing, the mumblings, the rhythmic thump-thump of a fist against the dormitory wall. Behind his eyelids, he saw fantastic outlines silhouetted in reds and dull greens and tried to follow their fluid movements with his eyeballs, only to find the shapes vanishing at the outer edges of his shuttered vision then returning from the right-hand side and begining again their slow movement across his mind. He could never quite get them to stop, never quite focus on what the images were. He imagined them to be sandgrouse, and from somewhere, he remembered a shooting expedition and suffering a reprimand when he asked why, if sandgrouse were so vile to eat, were they even shooting them from the skies?

Tonight, though, he saw a new shape suddenly appear, one that assumed the definite features of firm lines that became a rectangle, then a rectangle within a rectangle, then a man's upper torso in profile staring to his left.

It was a playing card.

A knave.

A knave whose head suddenly vanished.

And, as the vision remained still, not sliding off to the left as all the other images did, he could hear a faint whisper, and the whisper was coming not from the dormitory beyond his door but from inside his head.

It was the headless knave.

Oscar Pardew then watched the outline of the card fizzle, the way a real one would if you set a corner alight. He could almost smell the burning!

Though he kept his eyes shut in case the vision vanished, he strained to listen and nodded several times and said, *Yes I will*, even though his lips stayed perfectly still. His father, his dear father, was calling to him, cursing the one who stabbed him through the heart. *I know!* Oscar assured him silently. *He was cheating and you exposed him, and he waited for you, and he stabbed you... Yes. I promise. I will, Father.*

Once the vision had faded into windblown ashes, he felt a warmth inside him as if the card were still burning. Everything was clear now.

It was as if you made those two talk about him, Father, while I was doing my business. You were directing me.

His plan was formed. He smiled to himself, almost sniggering beneath the bed sheets, where he clutched a small purse, filled with coins, to his chest.

'My treasure chest!' he whispered to himself and giggled at his own joke.

He pulled back the sheets, reached to his right and gently took hold of the photograph, which he placed inside his nightdress for safekeeping.

Then he let forth a scream of anguish.

CHAPTER SIX

The billiard room of the Ship Hotel on Millgate, not twenty yards from the Royal Hotel, still retained that slightly sickening smell of freshly painted wood, having been reopened only a few months earlier. There were over fifty people in the room, and the odour had grown thicker as the evening progressed, what with the cigar fumes hovering like some miniature storm cloud over the green, mingling with the reek of damp clothing from the incessant rain they had all eagerly rushed through to get there.

Diggle, a Liverpudlian and the billiards champion of the north, was facing a challenge from a local amateur, Eddie Gorton, with the game a target of a thousand points, the challenger, Gorton, being credited with a start of four hundred. Diggle had already made an impressive thirty-four when, to the delight of the local crowd, he failed a simple cannon. Gorton responded with a delightful slow screw off the red, earning an even louder roar of approval from the locals.

'I thought this Diggle chap was a champion?' Gilbert Crosby said to the man next to him, one of the faces he recognised from his earlier audience in the bar of the Royal and who had asserted that it would be a privilege if Mr Crosby would allow him to buy him a drink.

The man leaned closer, anxious lest their conversation was overheard.

'Playin' to the crowd, Mr Crosby. Wouldn't do if he cleaned up early, would it?'

'I dunno,' Crosby replied. 'I'm sure I would. Pride, y'see.'

'Aye,' said his companion, who didn't see at all.

'Who do I speak to?'

'About what?'

Crosby smiled. 'A wager.'

'Tha means a bet?'

Crosby nodded.

The man pointed to a small weasel of a man standing in the far corner of the room, next to the door leading downstairs to the main bar. 'Benny Liptrot,' he said. 'He'll take thi money right enough. Who art backin'?'

'Why, Diggle, of course.'

The man laughed. 'Benny's not daft. Tha cawn't back Diggle. Tha can only back Eddie. But he'll give thee a better start than four hundred.'

Crosby shrugged. As he moved through the crowd to Liptrot, there was another roar – Gorton had just made a respectable break of twenty-five, making the score 493–442 in Diggle's favour.

Within less than a minute, Crosby had handed over five pounds in return for a start for Gorton of six hundred points, which meant Gorton's score was now 642. If Diggle had it in mind to produce a crowd-pleasing display of thrilling, nail-biting billiards, he might well allow the challenger to encroach close enough to produce, for Gilbert Crosby at any rate, a most rewarding outcome. Benny Liptrot, holding the note up against the table light, had made some humorous reference to his scar:

We don't go in for that sort o' stuff round 'ere, pal – if tha doesn't pay up, all tha gets is a thick lip. But tha's already paid so tha're awreet.

His two larger companions laughed at that, one even going so far as to shake Crosby's hand with the grip of a bear.

Once he'd made his way back to his new-found friend, Crosby was feeling quite pleased with himself, especially after he saw Diggle once more make a hash of what seemed to be a simple cannon. But as the game progressed, it became patently obvious that Diggle was not only playing deliberately badly on occasion but also that he was playing to instructions. He saw the weaselly Benny Liptrot – who had been taking bets more frequently as Diggle's game periodically faded – give a series of curious signals involving his forefingers pressing against his temples that could well have been mistaken for an incipient headache. Except that, upon seeing the signs, Diggle became elegantly potent, notching up a break at one stage of 178 including some masterful nursery cannons, resulting in a win for Diggle by one thousand to 726. Even with the extra two hundred Gilbert had negotiated, Gorton's final score was 926. Seventy-four points adrift. Gilbert was five pounds down.

'Hard luck,' said his drinking companion.

'Luck has nothing to do with it,' he replied through gritted teeth. He saw Liptrot leaning over a table where he was making a great show of counting his money – piles of coins, a smaller pile of banknotes, along with two pocket watches, a woman's dress ring and, unbelievably, a silk umbrella.

'Told you. Benny's not daft.'

'No, he certainly isn't.' Gilbert drained his glass and moved through the smoke and guffaws of laughter and past the small group commiserating with the loser Gorton. When he reached the bar, he ordered a whiskey then turned to observe Benny Liptrot, who was now beaming with satisfaction and nodding at something one of his larger associates had said. At that point, Diggle extricated himself from a large gathering of men, who were all eager to pass on their congratulations and bask in some reflected glory, and began to head for the door that obviously led to a smaller, more private room. One of Liptrot's men opened the door, patted the victor on the back as he moved into the room. The man kept the door held open, for within seconds, Liptrot, who by now had pocketed all the winnings, apart from the umbrella which he began swinging in imitation of a toff, followed Diggle inside. The door was firmly closed behind him.

'You little bastard,' said Gilbert softly.

*

From the short time he had spent in the sick room at Haydock Lodge when he was first admitted, Oscar Pardew knew that it was the only place in the entire asylum where the windows were left partially open. Every other room had doors and windows securely locked. But in the sick room, the rules demanded a full supply of fresh air to counteract the noxious fumes from patients with lung diseases, weeping and festering sores, unhealthy perspiration and *those of wet and dirty habits.*

It was the reason he was there now, feigning a set of painful stomach cramps, the general view being that, if his condition were to deteriorate with foul consequences, at least in the sick room the impact would be tempered by the circulating air. One of the attendants had taken the unusual step of opening the damper on the grate in the fireplace. Although no fire burned there this night, the open flue would provide extra ventilation. The resultant fall of dislodged soot could easily be cleaned away in the morning.

Now, as the attendant dozed at his desk at the far end of the room and as the other patients – some five in total – snored and groaned and uttered nonsensical words into the darkness, Oscar slowly, silently, threw back the bed covers and stepped out of bed, making sure that the photograph was secure against his heart. The attendant grunted, arms folded and feet resting on a chair, and settled back with his head drooped low on his chest.

Conscious that this was the most hazardous phase of his escape, Oscar crept towards the window halfway along the room, keeping a wary eye on the patient who rested beside it, an elderly chap whose lungs were fading fast and whose condition rendered it vital that he be placed as close to the open window as possible. Oscar smelt the soiled linen when he stopped beside the man's bed. The attendants were under the strictest of instructions to remove such noisome items as soon as they were discovered, but he knew that the night-time, and the lack of official supervision, meant that such orders were often ignored. Who wants the trouble of waking, cleaning, changing and settling at such a late hour?

A laxity for which Oscar, tonight, was truly grateful.

As he reached up and gripped the lower sash to force it upwards, he heard a sound.

A sharp stab of breath.

He turned to his right and gazed down. The elderly man was wide awake, his eyes flaring open and a look of sheer terror on his face. Oscar held his breath and waited for the scream that would stir the attendant and force him either to abandon or continue his flight.

But there was no scream.

Instead, the old man swallowed hard, his eyes still intensely staring at the figure standing by the window. Then he whispered something Oscar couldn't quite catch.

'What?' he mouthed before bending down, both to hear better what he said and to forestall anything louder.

'Not ready!' he rasped. He was beginning to show signs of agitation.

Oscar glanced up, saw the attendant rub away an imaginary fly.

'Not ready for what?' The last thing he wanted to do was engage this old fool in conversation.

'I'm not coming,' said the man, shaking his head.

'No. No, you stay here.'

'Not my time yet. You hear?'

'I hear.'

He patted the old man's hand gently. The skin was clammy but cool to the touch. He'd seen enough of death in India to recognise the signs.

'I've not finished with things yet. Not… finished.'

'No. I won't come back. Not for a long time.'

The elderly patient raised his head from the pillow, and when he spoke next, globs of spittle slithered from the corners of his mouth.

'I'm never going. Hear? Tell Him that. And…'

Oscar bent low, one eye on the sleeping form at the end of the room. 'And what?'

'Tell Him to fuck off.'

Once more he patted the cool, clammy hand. It seemed to give the old man some reassurance, for he let his head rest on the pillow and within seconds, had closed his eyes in all the semblance of a sleep that was closer to death.

Five minutes later, Oscar had traversed the extensive park that surrounded Haydock Lodge, having broken the flimsy lock of the greenhouse where he knew the gardener kept several items of clothing for the patients, including boots of various sizes, for when they made themselves useful in helping with the plants and shrubs. Dressed now as a common labourer, he flitted across the grass, watching the moon slide its way behind a bank of thick clouds, before entering the nearby wood. From there, it would be a short stretch to the railway station at Newton-le-Willows, where, if his luck held, he would be able to catch a train on the LNWR line.

To Wigan.

*

'There's a bloody stink round 'ere, sergeant!'

Constable Freddie Jaggery took out a rather grubby-looking hand-kerchief and held it against his nose, much to the amusement of the desk sergeant.

'It's out the back, constable. Came in last night.'

'What did?'

The sergeant, who had by now become accustomed to the foul stench drifting in from the parade yard at the back of the police station in Rodney Street, consulted his notes before replying.

'A cartload of filth. Namely two boxes of dabs, two boxes of gurnets and a box of conger eels. Sanitary Inspector's been earlier. Said the bloody fish were turnin' green. Dabs curled up double when he held 'em.'

'Don't tell me,' said Jaggery. 'Zach bloody Ellison.'

'The very same.'

Jaggery shook his head and blew his nose. He had arrested the fish seller on more than one occasion, and to Jaggery's certain knowledge, he had twenty-eight convictions to his name.

'Go and have a look. Inspect the evidence.'

'No thank you, Sergeant. I've seen me breakfast once this mornin'. Buggered if I want to see it again.'

'You'd have thought last night's rain would have deadened the smell.' The desk sergeant shook his head. 'Just shows, eh?'

'Aye,' returned Jaggery, unsure what it showed.

'You seen the roster board, Constable?'

Jaggery frowned. The fact that the desk sergeant had made a point of asking if he had seen it meant that whatever was on the board would mean extra work for the constables. Or the bloody infantry, as he and his fellows often remarked under their breaths. 'No, Sergeant.'

'Well let me just say it's gonna be a bloody long day,' came the reply, coated with a bitterness that suggested the new orders didn't just apply to the infantry.

Before Jaggery could mutter a response, he felt the slap of a hand on his shoulder, followed by a breezy, 'Good morning, Constable.'

He turned and felt his heart lurch. Whenever Detective Sergeant Brennan spoke in such a hearty manner, it was the prelude to something singularly unpleasant. He wasn't wrong.

'We have a walk ahead of us,' said Brennan. 'And the sun is shining. I can tell you all about the notice placed on the board by the chief constable himself on our way.'

'Where to, Sergeant?' Jaggery gave the desk sergeant a lugubrious stare.

Brennan smiled. 'Where better on such a cold, fresh morning as this, away from this foul stink?'

Jaggery shrugged. 'Mesnes Park?'

'No, Constable. Even better. The Dog.'

Jaggery tried hard to suppress the smile that was breaking out.

The Old Dog Inn, known also as a music hall, held a prominent position on the corner of Old Market Place and Cooper's Row. The proprietor, Horace Seddon, had sent a pot boy down to the station to ask particularly for Detective Sergeant Brennan as he had *summat to tell*. On occasion, Seddon had been very useful in providing information that later turned out to be of interest, and so, with little to occupy him until the evening when the order from the chief constable took effect, Brennan made the short walk with at least the prospect of a frothing glass of ale in front of him, a thought gleefully shared by his constable.

But when Brennan explained exactly what the chief constable's notice said, it darkened Jaggery's mood considerably.

*

That morning, Ralph Batsford ate a solitary breakfast. The dining room of the Royal Hotel was a compact place, with space only for ten tables. Simeon and Violet had ordered breakfast in their room, and Gilbert had simply failed to respond when Batsford had knocked on his door. He had done this more out of politeness than any real desire to dine with the fellow: he found him at times lofty, disdainful, even envious of the closeness that had developed between the journalist and his hangman brother. Still, it had been a relief when there came not even the grunt of a dismissal from the man's room and so he sat at the table furthest from the door and enjoyed what he had to admit was a rather delicious breakfast of bacon, eggs, sausage and kidneys. There was only one other table occupied – two men, one of them older than the other, deep in conversation and unaware of his presence – and he appreciated the companionable silence, a contrast to the rattle of carriages, the hiss of a tram and the clanging of clogged feet from the street beyond the window.

Last night, he had come to a firm decision on what he should do. All he needed now was the opportunity.

*

When they reached the narrow entrance to Cooper's Row, Constable Jaggery had had time to absorb what he had just been told. He stopped and turned to his sergeant.

'You mean, every single one of us?'

'That's what the notice said.'

'But the wife'll have me tea ready.'

'So will mine.'

'How can his bloody lordship expect us to work all day and straight on till God knows when? Who does he think we are?'

Brennan shrugged. He had to admit, the unusual notice, ordering all uniformed men and detective officers to remain on duty until otherwise commanded, was out of the ordinary. He knew the chief constable was anxious to see the talk by Simeon Crosby pass off without any interruption, but it was scheduled to end sometime around nine o'clock. Twenty minutes to see the last of the straggling audience off the premises and into the numerous pubs in town and that should effectively be an end to their duties. Yet Captain Bell had told him of the threatening letters sent to the *Wigan Observer* and, more importantly, reminded him of the protest that would begin in the Market Square and continue towards the Public Hall in King Street.

Captain Bell's real worry was that if Simeon Crosby were to be attacked in some way, the adverse publicity that would inevitably follow would reflect very badly on him. The chief constable was most protective where his personal reputation was concerned. Brennan knew, for instance, that the man had only been in office for two years when, in 1892, he applied for the post of Chief Constable of Warwickshire. When he failed to be appointed, he had let it be known that the main reason was the wave upon wave of violence, of drunkenness, of criminality in general that raged throughout the borough of Wigan and that he had fought for two years to hold back like some latter-day Canute.

A gross exaggeration, Brennan felt at the time, motivated not simply through a sense of loyalty to his hometown but through a straightforward view of the facts: Wigan was no better or no worse than any of the towns in the county. Captain Bell hadn't been appointed to the Warwickshire post for the simple reason that a better applicant was chosen.

No need to blame the town for that.

Still, he'd have an eye on any future prospect, and an assault on the most famous executioner in the country, albeit retired, wouldn't reflect well on his control of the borough's more volatile elements.

And so, Brennan reflected with a consoling smile in Jaggery's direction, every man must do his duty.

The door to the Old Dog was open. A young woman on her hands and knees, with a piece of matting to cushion her knees, was scrubbing furiously at the steps. She slid herself to one side as the two of them entered the pub but kept her concentration on the partially scrubbed steps, as if her previous good work might be sullied if she took her gaze away for an instant.

Once inside, Brennan was greeted by the dubious odour of stale beer and the clinging remnants of cigarette and cigar smoke. The proprietor, Horace Seddon, was busy wiping down the long, curved bar counter that swept from the public house side of the building to where the music hall took over. Brennan had brought Ellen here once, to see a Mr Arthur Anderson, who was billed as a *female impersonator*. Ellen had spent his entire performance criticising the outfits and the make-up that he wore, and talking over his several monologues which Brennan might well have found funny if he'd been given the chance to hear them.

'Ah, the great detective hisself.'

Seddon leaned over the counter and shook Brennan's hand, giving Jaggery a cursory and not very friendly nod, recalling, no doubt, an occasion only last year when the overly large constable had entered his premises while a ventriloquist was performing and brought with him Seddon's wife. Jaggery had met her weaving from side to side in Market Place, one bloodied hand clapped to her mouth, while in the other hand she held up what looked like a jagged tooth, which she claimed had been forcibly dislodged by her *swinin' pig of an 'usband*.

The ventriloquist, unable to compete with the way Mrs Seddon threw her voice at all and sundry, had stormed offstage, dragging his dummy along the floor behind him to a chorus of boos and shouts of *watch the poor sod's head!* Eventually, the victim had calmed down sufficiently, aided by a large glass of gin and a promise of new shoes and a new tooth, and she withdrew her claim of assault, leaving Jaggery with nothing but a pint of frothing beer to show for carrying out his duty.

'Now, Horace,' said Brennan. 'What's this all about then?'

The proprietor gave the bar counter a final flourish with his cloth and nodded to a small table beneath the alley window. 'Get yourselves settled,' he said, 'an' I'll bring you a livener.'

Jaggery held his breath. The tantalising prospect of a morning pint depended on what sort of mood Sergeant Brennan was in – easy-going or temperance – so he tried to maintain a blank expression until he heard the answer.

'Might as well,' said Brennan as the two of them sat down. 'It's going to be a long day for Constable Jaggery and myself.'

Once the tankards were brought over and Seddon had joined them at the table, Brennan took a long sip of the establishment's justifiably celebrated ale and waited for his host to explain why he had sent for him.

'You know it's not like me to complain, Sergeant,' Seddon began. 'Live an' let bloody live's what I say. But there're some things you can't turn a blind eye to.'

'Such as?'

'Now I've got all the time in the world for Royal Murray. What he's done to the Alex is nowt short o' stupendous. Though why he couldn't keep the name 'stead o' changin' it is beyond me.'

Brennan suppressed a smile. It was common knowledge that there was no love lost between Seddon and Royal Murray, the owner of the Empire Palace, formerly known as the Alexandra. Both establishments competed for business, a fact made more urgent by their close proximity to each other: the Empire and the Dog shared the narrow alley, known rather grandly as Cooper's Row, and those queuing to enter both places were often amused by the ribald and derogatory comments each owner hurled at the other, a form of free entertainment that often surpassed what went on inside.

'Anyroad, last night, after chuckin' out time – allus before twelve, you know me, Sergeant Brennan – after chuckin' out time, I were just lockin' up when I heard a noise from out yonder.'

He nodded behind the two policemen, in the direction of the alleyway. 'What sort of noise?'

Seddon leaned forward in an attitude of confidentiality. 'I heard their side door open. Still a helluva lot of noise comin' from that place, even at that time. That's against the law, that is.'

Brennan sighed. 'You've brought me here to report a breach of Royal Murray's licence?'

He knew full well that the town had more than its share of music halls. It had long been a bone of contention with Captain Bell, who objected to any new applications to the Borough Licensing Sessions, his view being that with twenty-six establishments already being licensed for music there was, as he put it at the latest hearing, *absolutely no need to place this extra straw on the poor camel's back*. As a consequence of such a proliferation, the rivalry that existed between the respective licence-holders was excitable, to say the least.

But Seddon shook his head and laughed. 'God no! No landlord would do that to another. It's unchristian is that.' He paused to allow his religious rectitude to sink in. 'No, it's what I heard after the door slammed shut again.'

'Go on.'

'Two of 'em. Talkin'.'

'Who?'

Seddon shrugged. 'Two blokes. One of 'em says, *What's in it for me?* T'other says, *Ten pounds.*'

Now, as Jaggery gave an appreciative whistle, Brennan's curiosity was aroused. 'What exactly were they talking about?'

'I'm not sure an' that's the truth. But I did hear that first chap say, *Best spend thi money on summat else. I like breathin', me.*'

Brennan thought for a while. Constable Jaggery took another drink, frowning at what he'd just heard.

'Did you see them?'

Seddon pursed his lips. 'It were dark. An' there's sod all lightin' once I puts my light out. I were tryin' though. I peeped through that door yonder.' He indicated the frosted glass of the side entrance door and the trim of clear glass that ran around it. 'But like I say, it were dark.'

Brennan rested his chin on one hand. What could possibly be worth ten pounds?

'They stood there sayin' nowt for a while then they started whisperin' low-like so I couldn't hear what they were sayin'. Then they seemed to agree on summat 'cos some money exchanged hands an' the two of 'em shook hands an' both left.' He paused before adding, 'There were one thing I did catch sight of though. I only caught a glimpse, mind, so I wouldn't swear to it.'

'Well?'

'One of 'em – the one offerin' the money – turned for a second so I could see him side on, like. I reckon the moonlight caught him or summat. Anyroad, it looked to me he had summat wrong with his face.'

'What do you mean?'

'Well, like he had a scar runnin' down it.'

CHAPTER SEVEN

Once they had left the Old Dog, Brennan paused at the end of Cooper's Row and placed a hand on Jaggery's arm. 'Now you can speak,' he said.

He had noticed the way his constable's head lifted mid-slurp at the mention of the scar, followed by a slow wiping of the mouth and, as was common whenever he wished to convey something of a secretive nature, a heavy cough.

'I reckon I know who that bloke is. The one with the scar.'

'Well?'

'That hangman I escorted from the station. He had a brother.'

'A lot of people do.'

'Aye, but how many have a brother wi' a scar, eh?' Jaggery's voice contained a triumphant note, as if he'd just laid down three aces.

Brennan, who hadn't really taken notice of the hangman's brother at the station, frowned. What would Simeon Crosby's brother be doing outside the Empire Palace after midnight with someone and offering him ten pounds? What did the fellow have to do to earn such a handsome sum?

They turned right as Cooper's Row met Market Place.

'The Crosbys are staying at the Royal, is that so, Constable?'

Jaggery nodded. The Royal Hotel was a matter of yards away, at the top of Standishgate. He smiled to himself. Perhaps they might be offered a butty. He'd heard they do a bloody good ham butty at the Royal. Bound to have a plate of mustard to hand, an' all.

*

To anyone who bothered to give him a second glance, Oscar Pardew gave every appearance of someone down on his luck. The collarless shirt had seen better days, its faded white stained by smears of varying shades of green. The jacket he wore was snagged at the sleeves – a result of numerous encounters with thorns and bushes of varying prickliness – and where the buttons had once been, now thin strands of cotton hung limply down. His trousers seemed at least a size too big, and the waistband was secured with what looked like twine. Yet he passed from the station unnoticed, for his outward condition, at any rate, was nothing remarkable – there were others similarly attired scattered throughout the town, unfortunates, who for some reason or other had been unable or unwilling to secure any sort of meaningful employment and who were tolerated rather than accepted by those who passed them by.

Oscar had never been to the town before. He hadn't walked a hundred yards before a cold clamminess began to make him shiver. It wasn't the unfamiliar accent, the strange words, or even the hard features of many of those he walked past. It was rather the noise of it all – trams rattling past, horses clopping and neighing, pulling wagons whose wheels creaked and groaned as they crossed the tramlines and the cobbled surface of the street. Sometimes people stared, and he imagined them sneering at him.

That fellow's a certified lunatic. No cause or no right to be here.

For a while, he sought refuge in the doorway of a shop and closed his eyes, fearing that the noise would soon overwhelm him and cause his skull to crack.

'Hey!'

Oscar opened his eyes to see a man wearing a dark suit and straw hat standing before him, arms resting on his hips and scrutinising him with more than a passing interest.

'Yes?' said Oscar, taking a deep breath.

'Are you badly?'

'Certainly not.'

'Well then. Are you comin' in?'

'What?'

The man pointed to the shop door, which was propped open by a wicker basket containing all manner of footwear from slippers to shiny leather boots.

'By the look of them buggers,' said the man indicating Oscar's laceless shoes, 'tha could do wi' a pair of my sturdiest. I've some tough buff calf inside if tha fancies?'

'I haven't the foggiest what you're talking about,' said Oscar.

The man grabbed Oscar by the shoulder and brought him close to his chest before pointing to the sign above the shop entrance. 'What does that say, pal?'

Oscar, who could feel the man's strength draining his own, said feebly, 'Craddock's Boot Bazaar.'

'Bloody 'ell, it can read!'

There were titters of amusement, and Oscar realised, with some humiliation, that a small crowd had gathered.

'Now,' said the man, who Oscar presumed was Craddock, 'if tha not comin' in, tha gooin' out!' and with a hefty push, he propelled him into the street.

As the shop owner turned to go back inside, accompanied by several of his customers, Oscar walked back to the entrance and stood in the open doorway. 'You do realise,' he said in a voice loud enough to make the gathering inside turn and face him, 'that your sign is nothing short of a lie?'

Mr Craddock frowned. His customers watched him closely. This was an unexpected bonus, their faces acknowledged.

'What did t'say?'

'A bazaar is made up of a warren of streets and alleys. It is also littered with garbage of an unspeakable stench. I know, because I've seen more than one bazaar – more than one *actual* bazaar, that is – in Delhi.'

'Why you cheeky little bastard!' yelled Craddock, who picked up the nearest object he could find – a shiny ooze calf boot in the latest West End shape – and hurled it across the shop, missing Oscar's right ear by inches.

Before the shop owner could develop a more physical attack, Oscar decided to withdraw hastily, running across the road and causing a hackney carriage to swerve violently to avoid a collision. With the curses of Craddock and the cab driver ringing in his ears, he ran down a narrow alleyway between a bank and a public house. It wouldn't do, he realised somewhat belatedly, to be a focus of attention now. Why, they'd have him escorted back to Haydock in a heartbeat, which would mean he'd be unable to do what he came to do.

He pressed his hands against his chest, where the framed photograph was lodged. His father – his dead father – nay, his *murdered* father – would never forgive him if he failed now.

*

Constable Jaggery was disappointed. Not only did the manager of the Royal fail to offer them any sort of complimentary sandwich, he seemed

78

more than a little put out, his attitude towards himself and Sergeant Brennan almost hostile.

'I would never have allowed the booking if I had known!' James Eastoe snapped as he escorted the two policemen into his office. He was a small man, smartly dressed, his hair kept in place by a judicious application of macassar oil.

On the previous occasions Brennan had met the man, he had seemed quite affable, though staunchly defensive when it came to the affairs of the Royal Hotel.

'Known what?' Brennan asked. He had only mentioned the name of Gilbert Crosby and asked for his room number, nothing else.

'A hotel is the recipient of a motley cross section of the populace,' Eastoe began, standing at the window and gazing out onto Standishgate. 'It's a great pity we cannot demand a fuller profile of our guests than name and address.' He turned round to face his visitors. 'If I had known that the Crosbys – or shall we be more exact and say the name Mr Simeon Crosby? – if I had known his *identity* rather than simply his name, well then, I would have refused the booking.'

'You had no idea he had been the country's executioner?'

'Crosby is not an unusual name, Sergeant Brennan. Besides, I do not have oversight on every booking made. Although,' he added with a self-deprecating smirk, 'I think there has indeed been an oversight of another colour here.'

Brennan shrugged. 'That's as may be, Mr Eastoe, but I'm not here about the hangman.'

At the last word, Eastoe visibly flinched. 'I have very decided views about capital punishment, Sergeant. Very decided.'

'You'd let the buggers go free?' Jaggery said.

'Certainly not! Miscreants should be punished. And punished severely.

But to take a life… it's barbaric. It renders the state no better than the wretch who committed the crime.'

'You wouldn't say that if it were your missus or littlun what got done in,' Jaggery responded. 'You'd want to see the bugger swing to high heaven.'

'I don't think he'd swing in that direction, Constable.' Brennan's voice carried a sharp undertone that Jaggery recognised: he should make no further contribution to the debate. 'Besides, as I said, we're after a word with his brother, Gilbert Crosby. So if you'd let me know his room number? Unless he's already breakfasted and left?'

The manager gave a dissatisfied grunt and bade them follow him to the front desk. A few minutes later, they were standing outside Room Seven, with Eastoe tapping on the door. There was no response, so Brennan gave a nod towards the set of keys the manager held dangling from his right hand. With a sigh, he complied and swung the door open.

It was a small room, a double bed resting against the wall shared by the neighbouring room. A small wash basin stood on a set of drawers beneath the window overlooking the main thoroughfare beyond, and a tall wardrobe stood at the diagonal between two walls. A carpet of indeterminate colour covered part of the wooden floor.

The bed was empty, the sheets and blanket undisturbed.

'This bed hasn't been slept in,' said Brennan, turning to the manager. 'Unless the maid has already been in?'

But Eastoe shook his head. 'It's too early. She only starts on the rooms at eleven.' He glanced down at his pocket watch. 'Half an hour to go.'

'Had Gilbert Crosby left word that he wouldn't be sleeping here last night?'

'Not that I'm aware of. I can ask downstairs at the desk.'

'Do so. Meanwhile, perhaps you could take us to Simeon Crosby's room? He is his brother, after all.'

'I am indeed, sir!' came a voice from the open doorway. 'What's all this about?'

With unseemly haste, the hotel manager mumbled something about having other duties to attend to. He offered Simeon Crosby a curt nod and breezed past him, leaving the latter with a puzzled look on his face.

Brennan introduced himself and the three of them moved along the corridor to the next room.

'My wife has taken the opportunity to go for a walk,' he explained as they entered. 'My colleague, Mr Batsford, has been told of your wonderful park and kindly offered to escort her. I have my speech for tonight, you see?' He indicated a table by the window, strewn with papers. 'Best if I'm left alone, iron out a few wrinkles.'

Brennan saw Jaggery looking round, nonplussed. 'And who exactly is Mr Batsford?'

Crosby smiled. 'A journalist of high renown. He's providing, shall we say, technical help. I'm writing my memoirs, don't you know? He's making sure it's presented tastefully.'

Making sure you don't overstep the boundaries, Brennan thought. *A hangman's seen much more than he can write about.*

'Only yesterday,' Crosby went on, 'your esteemed chief constable tried to have him arrested by this grand specimen. Thought he was an assassin, for goodness' sake!'

Jaggery coughed modestly, unaware that Brennan had taken the depiction *grand specimen* with an ironic pinch of salt.

'I'm sure your good wife will find Mesnes Park delightful,' Brennan said, 'but we'd rather hoped we could speak with your brother. He appears not to have slept in his room.'

Was there a flicker of discomfort in the hangman's eye? It was quickly replaced by what Brennan considered to be a forced chuckle.

'I'm not my brother's keeper, Sergeant Brennan. He's a grown man. And grown men find unfamiliar towns have familiar attractions.'

'When did you last see him?'

'Last evening. Before he decided to pay a visit to the public house along the way. He'd heard there was a billiards match being played there.'

'The Ship,' Jaggery explained in a low voice.

'What is this all about, Sergeant? Is it a crime not to sleep in your hotel bed?'

'Not at all, sir.' Brennan eyed the man carefully.

There was an edge to his voice. Defensive? Of his brother or himself?

'Is it usual for him to do something like this? I mean, Wigan is hardly Manchester. Or London. Public houses and music halls close at a civilised hour. Strictly overseen, I might add, by the Watch Committee.'

And enforced with vigour by the chief constable, he failed to add.

'As a matter of fact it isn't out of the ordinary. Gilbert comes and goes as he pleases. He may have met someone, for instance.'

He let the idea float in the air for a few seconds. Both policemen knew what he was referring to, and both realised it was indeed a possibility. The Ship, they knew full well, was a place renowned throughout the town for its prostitutes, who advertised their going rates by crudely chalked prices on the soles of their shoes. Brennan had often wondered what they did when it was raining.

'But you haven't explained why you wish to speak with my brother.'

It was a sensible question, Brennan acknowledged. But one which should have been asked as soon as they met.

'Oh, just something that came up,' Brennan replied with annoying evasion. 'Perhaps you might send word down to the station when your brother does turn up?'

Crosby seemed on the point of saying something but thought better of it. Instead, he held up his hands and accepted the commission. 'And now, I really must get back to my speech. I gather all the tickets have been sold, and I don't wish to disappoint.'

'I understand, sir. I myself will be there tonight to supervise those on duty.'

'Good. I can rest easy, then.'

He ushered them out, with Brennan sensing some irony in the man's parting words. He shut his door with some force.

He's either annoyed with me for making the query or angry with his brother for being the cause of it, Brennan thought.

As they walked back along the corridor to the stairs, he heard the soft click of another door closing behind him, but when he turned round, he saw nothing. Every door was shut, and the corridor silent.

Had someone been listening to their conversation?

He kept the suspicion to himself. Yet when they got downstairs, he asked Mr Eastoe, who was hovering by the main doors waiting to see them out, if he could take a look at the hotel register.

'Why?' said the manager. It seemed to be one further irritation for him to bear.

'Out of interest,' said Brennan with a smile.

Sighing, Eastoe went behind the front desk and opened the hotel register with an angry flourish.

Brennan gazed down at the list of names against rooms.

'Might I ask what you are looking for?' Eastoe said crisply.

'The rooms on the second floor,' Brennan began. 'There are four of them?'

'Yes.'

'Mr Crosby and his wife in Room Eight; Gilbert Crosby in Room Seven; Mr Ralph Batsford in Room Six. The only other room is Room Five.'

'Amazing deduction, Sergeant.'

Brennan ignored the insult and read out the name of the occupant of Room Five. 'Mr David Morgan. Address in Chester. Who is he?'

Eastoe frowned. 'A delightful young man, Sergeant. A commercial traveller, in fact.'

Brennan tapped his finger against the name and gave a nod, closing the register and sliding it across the desk. 'Is he a regular guest?'

'No, Sergeant. His first stay. He's been here since Saturday. Lovely manners.'

'I see.'

He bade farewell and left the hotel. As they stepped outside, the sun was pale and held little warmth, the cold seeming to grow in strength as the morning progressed.

'Strikes me, Sergeant, that bloke Crosby knows more than he lets on. *Am I my brother's keeper*, my fat arse.'

'You know who first said that, Constable? About his brother's keeper?'

'Who?'

'It was Cain, when God asked him where his brother Abel was.'

'And where was he?' Jaggery asked, wondering if Mickey Brennan was actually comparing himself to God.

'He was dead, Constable. Cain had killed him and left him in a field.'

'Bit of a bugger, eh, Sergeant?'

'Indeed.'

But as they made their way back to the station, Brennan's thoughts weren't on the brothers Crosby, nor on Cain and Abel. He was wondering why the occupant of the only other room on that corridor, presumably Mr David Morgan, should have been eavesdropping on his conversation with the hangman.

CHAPTER EIGHT

Thomas Evelyne sat in the small private room he'd requested at Ringham's Oyster Bar in Market Place and mopped up the juices of his beef and oyster pie with a wedge of crusty bread. He ate alone, preferring his own company in the hours before the storm he hoped he would unleash later in the day.

He was surprised that so many people had turned up at the Legs of Man the previous night to hear him speak. Some might argue that the twenty or so sitting there in the upstairs room of a Wigan public house could hardly be described as the vanguard of a great movement and that the days of real protest, back before public hanging was abolished and the authorities took their justice indoors, were now over. But he really didn't care if his audience consisted of one or a hundred and one: he felt an almost messianic desire consume him, and to have the most famous hangman in the country travelling round, promoting not only what he had been doing for the last twenty years but also garnering publicity for the book he was purportedly writing… it was an abomination.

The man had death on his conscience – or if not his conscience, then on his hands.

Evelyne would make the man suffer for what he had done, the taking of life, while he gloried in the title of official executioner. He had sat in the audience up in Carlisle and listened with growing fury as Simeon Crosby had positively gloried in what he'd done.

Tonight, Evelyne mused as he dabbed at his beard with a napkin, would be different. Tonight the whole world would see. If those twenty from last night could encourage twenty more, why then it would be quite a march through the town to the Public Hall.

He smiled to himself. He wondered if some of the more impressionable marchers might be encouraged to do more than shout and hurl abuse? A few stones, maybe, a few smashed windows. Any damage would be all to the good.

There was a knock on the door, and the waiter, a spotty-faced youth, entered.

'Anything else, sir?'

'No, thank you. The pie was excellent.'

The waiter began clearing the table when he said, 'Oh, I varneer forgot.'

Evelyne had spent only a day in the town, and the language of the locals occasionally flummoxed him. '*Varneer?*'

The waiter, misunderstanding the purpose of the repetition, nodded. 'Aye. But then I remembered. There's a woman askin' for thee.'

'A woman? Where is she?'

'In t'main room. Said it were urgent, like. Should I get her?'

Evelyne frowned but nodded. 'Very well. *Get her.*'

The youth turned round, almost dropping the pie dish in the process and moved quickly, leaving the door open. Within a few seconds he returned, ushering a young woman into the room.

'I'll gi' thee some privacy,' said the waiter with a knowing wink before closing the door behind him.

Evelyne stood and looked at the woman. She was around twenty-three or twenty-four, not a beauty in the conventional sense, by any means, although there was something about her bright green eyes and the way her nose seemed to turn up at its tip that gave her a sort of pert attractiveness. She stood before him in a trim grey jacket, ankle-length pleated skirt and a white blouse. The hat she wore slightly off-centre, lending a slight air of mischievousness to the otherwise staid outfit. Her hair was jet black and tied in a severe bun.

He wasn't used to female company, not for a while at any rate, and so he hid his nervousness behind a façade of confidence.

'Thomas Evelyne,' he said, extending his right hand.

She gave an equally confident smile, returned his handshake and said, 'Maria Woodruff.'

He drew up a chair and placed it opposite his, inviting her to join him, which she did with a graceful, 'Thank you.'

'And what can I do for you, Miss Woodruff?' he asked.

For an uncomfortable few seconds she said nothing, merely stared at him, a hesitant expression on her face. Her confident mood seemed to have faded as she searched for the right words.

'I'm sorry,' she said suddenly and took a deep breath, the sort you take when about to jump in at the deep end of a very cold pool. 'You see, I'm a newspaper reporter.' She spoke more firmly now, with a tone almost of defiance, as if daring him either to scoff or contradict.

He did neither. 'A growing band,' he said. 'Female ones, I mean.'

Miss Woodruff, who seemed on the verge of launching into a spirited defence of the New Woman, was taken aback.

Evelyne smiled. 'I have seen several of Mr Ibsen's plays. My wife insisted. And very worthy they are, too.'

'You don't agree with the view that a woman's duty is to purify the home by her lifelong devotion to husband and children, to virtue and to self-sacrifice?'

He gave an elaborate shrug. 'A friend of mine – an unbeliever in your eyes – visited America last year. He told me they have female doctors and female preachers and yes, even female journalists, but what he saw little sign of was female women.'

Before she could respond, he raised a hand and added, 'I think he was in jest. The world is fast changing, Miss Woodruff. In my view, women have as much right as men to follow whatever they wish to. If you wish to become a journalist, then...'

'I don't wish to *become* one. I *am* one.'

'Then I apologise.'

She nodded, an acceptance of his apology. 'And I'm writing a series of articles about capital punishment in general and Simeon Crosby in particular.'

Evelyne bristled at the name.

She went on. 'My articles are published in *The Graphic*, as a matter of fact.' She raised her chin proudly.

He looked impressed. *The Graphic* was a highly respected magazine. 'In that case, why do you wish to speak with me? I detest the fellow Crosby and everything that he stands for. If I had my way...' Here he stopped himself, the expression on his face one of restrained anger. 'I apologise. There are times when I forget I'm not standing on a platform.'

She clasped her hands in a demure show of understanding. 'I fully accept your principled stand, Mr Evelyne. Our purposes are not at odds. I have no intention of writing a eulogy. For my earlier articles, I have spoken with families of those who have been victims of crime, seeking their views of capital punishment.'

Evelyne frowned. 'I would have thought their views were unanimously in favour?'

'For the most part, yes. Although some of them expressed the wish to see those who took their loved ones from them suffer the much longer punishment of life imprisonment. Some feel that hanging is a merciful end.'

He raised his eyebrows. 'I never thought I'd hear *hanging* and *merciful* in the same sentence.'

'*Sentence* indeed,' she said with a smile that rendered her features more alluring. 'My new article will concern in part the impact of Mr Crosby's visit on the ordinary people of the town. What is now known as the human interest dimension.'

'I am not an ordinary person of the town,' he said politely. 'I've never been to Wigan. I don't see how I...'

She raised a gloved hand. 'You're leading a protest at tonight's meeting. Last night, I gather you addressed people from the town to gain support for your abolitionist cause. I should like your perspective on how your cause was greeted. Unanimous agreement? Any dissent? How many women attended? That sort of thing.'

With a slow shake of the head, he said, 'You know, of course, that there are fewer advocates of the abolitionist cause than twenty years ago?'

'Yes. It is a great pity. I tend to the opinion that most murderers are insane. To commit that most heinous of crimes must require some loosening of rationality. Is it, therefore, right to hang an insane person?'

A strange expression appeared on Evelyne's face. It seemed to his visitor that he actually seemed irritated by her observation.

'Surely that is an argument worth pursuing?' she asked.

Evelyne cleared his throat. 'The taking of any life is an abomination, Miss Woodruff. Wouldn't you agree?'

'Of course.'

'And if the government pursue the taking of a life as a policy of law then surely they are guilty of an abomination, whether the condemned unfortunate is sane or insane?'

'I agree. But—'

'—And the laughable claim that it is a deterrent!' Here his voice began to rise, causing Miss Woodruff to shift in her seat.

He saw her discomfiture at once. 'I'm sorry, I tend to get carried away.' He took a deep breath. 'You wished to know how my meeting was received last night?'

'Yes.'

'With a lukewarm enthusiasm. Some professed anger at the visit of an official murderer. Some merely wished to cause trouble for the fun of it. We even had a suggestion that Crosby be tarred and feathered.'

'Goodness.' She placed a hand to her neck, as if she herself were in imminent danger of such a threat. 'I see.' She paused, appeared to be considering something. Then she spoke, in a lower voice this time. 'Do you mind if I make some mention of your movement in my article?'

He frowned. 'Movement is far too grand a word.'

'But you are an abolitionist?'

'I am.'

'Then what is your opinion of the fact that the Society for the Abolition of Capital Punishment is fast losing its influence? That the Howard Association has taken up the mantle? What is your vision of the future? Do you think—

Evelyne held up his hand. 'Please, Miss Woodruff. I have no wish to be a part of your article. Worthy though it will undoubtedly be.'

'But if it furthers your cause?'

'I'm not a member of any society. I have no link with the Howard Association or the Quakers or any official body. I'm just someone who believes in direct action.' He sat back, his face now breaking into something approaching a smile. 'Might I suggest that you come to the Market Square this evening – it's just down the road, about a hundred or so yards away from where we are sitting – and seek the views of those attending? Mind you, they're quite a rough lot, here in Wigan.'

'Where are you staying, Mr Evelyne?'

He gave her a long, hard look. 'The Queen's Hotel. Hardly a grand affair. Why?'

'I should like to speak further. There are… other questions I should like to ask.'

He slowly shook his head. 'There won't be time, I'm afraid. I shall be leaving this place first thing tomorrow morning.'

She bowed her head gracefully. 'Very well. But I shall certainly take the opportunity to hear you speak to the masses.'

'You have a ticket for tonight's entertainment?'

She shook her head. 'Mr Crosby's talk? *Entertainment* is hardly the word I'd use. But no. I have no desire to hear what he has to say. I am much more interested in what his wife has to say.'

'His wife?' He raised his eyebrows. 'She's here with him? In Wigan?'

She gave a rather mischievous smile, leaning forward to adopt a more confidential air. The action somehow made her appear more human. 'I have taken the liberty of communicating with her. And she has finally agreed to speak with me. Hers is the voice I wish to hear above all others. *Living with the hangman. A wifely perspective.*'

'The man has no sense of propriety. To bring his wife with him when there may well be noisy protestations…'

She shrugged. 'She insisted. After I'd made the suggestion, of course.' She gave another smile, this time conspiratorial.

'So he knows nothing of the interview? Surely he would never allow that? Not when he's hoping to make his fortune writing his memoirs with Mr Batsford. It would somehow steal his thunder.'

Her voice now adopted an almost secretive tone, yet as she spoke, he couldn't help thinking that there was something of the child in her, confessing to something very naughty.

'He indeed knows nothing about our little arrangement. While he is addressing his salivating audience in the Public Hall, I shall be conducting my interview with his beloved wife in their hotel room. She has agreed to feign a headache. It's rather exciting, don't you think?'

Evelyne held up his hands in appreciation of her initiative.

'Then I wish you good luck,' he said. 'And I look forward to reading your article, especially Mrs Crosby's views!'

She stood up and again shook his hand. 'Thank you for speaking with me. I hope your protest is heard loud and clear by Mr Crosby. A pity I won't be able to speak with him. Not tonight, at any rate. I've heard that he speaks with no journalists except one.'

'Yes. The redoubtable Mr Batsford. He had the audacity to attend my little gathering last night. He thought I didn't recognise him.' He stood and opened the door for her.

'Mr Batsford is a disgrace to the noble calling of journalism, Mr Evelyne. He should spend his time reporting the news plainly and without prejudice, not acting as diarist to the hangman.' She spoke with feeling, and a little colour began to suffuse her cheeks. She frowned and appeared to be on the verge of saying something but then she shook her head and dismissed the unspoken comment. Instead, she added, 'I shall be at the Market Square this evening and speak with as many of your followers as I can.'

With that, she swept from the room, leaving Evelyne with a rather confused expression on his face.

*

The Pavilion Café in Mesnes Park was half empty, despite the throng of chattering mill-girls seated on the benches surrounding its outside perimeter, taking in the fresh breeze that made such a pleasant contrast with the dust-heavy atmosphere of the nearby Rylands Mill. Many of them had brought their own food in snap tins, very few of them using the facilities inside the café.

Ralph Batsford and Violet Crosby sat inside. The noise from the girls thronging the park at midday had encouraged them to seek comparative silence; away from the chatter, the two of them could hear themselves talk, and that, after all, had been the prime purpose Batsford had had in inviting Violet Crosby to join him in the town's foremost park. Both of them took a sip of tea, Violet giving a little smile as she replaced her cup.

'Something amuses you?' Batsford said.

She indicated the girls who sat outside, their backs towards them and their heads moving in animated conversation. 'I remember when I was their age. Worked in a shop in Morecambe. We'd often spend our free time in Summer Gardens. Lovely place. And they had a pavilion there that *was* a pavilion.' She waved her hand around the café. 'How many folk do you think this *pavilion* holds?'

Batsford shrugged. 'Hundred or so. At a squeeze.'

'The pavilion in Summer Gardens held over ten thousand. Imagine that, eh?'

'Amazing.'

She took another sip of tea and looked directly at him, the glow of nostalgia that had flittered across her face now replaced by something much more serious.

'Now, Mr Ralph Batsford. There's no one can hear us. We're just two people having a midday cup of tea. So, why don't you tell me what's on your mind, eh? You didn't invite me to this park, lovely though it is, to admire the gardens.'

Batsford clasped his hands together and leaned forward. 'There's something we need to discuss,' he said, quietly but firmly.

'Go on,' she said with a sparkle of amusement in her eye.

With his eyes cast down as if he were examining the wood grain of the table, he said, 'It has to stop before it begins. If Simeon were to find out...'

Playfully, she cupped her mouth with her left hand to simulate shock.

'Why, Mr Batsford, sir, I really have no idea what you're referring to. Upon my soul, sir!' She spoke in a high-pitched, sing-song voice, the way a coquettish heroine might speak in one of her beloved novels.

'It isn't just Simeon who would be hurt, is it? There'd be yourself, whether you see that now or not. No one can foresee the consequences of such a course of action.'

'And you, of course, Ralph. There'd be you and your... feelings to consider, wouldn't there?'

He sighed heavily. A group of mill-girls seated on a bench beyond the window burst into raucous laughter. The timing gave him the strangest sensation that they were actually laughing at him and his predicament. Violet Crosby gave him her sweetest smile.

This was not going to be easy.

*

Oscar Pardew read the poster with interest.

He'd almost missed it as he shuffled along the row of terraced houses. He had no idea where he was headed, but the long street swept away from the centre of town where the loudest noises were, and he needed to find some sort of quiet place, a place that was free from crowds and all the hubbub of a bustling town. Halfway along the street, he passed what had once been a shop, but now thick wooden slats were nailed to its window frame and a letting sign pasted across at an angle. The space had afforded room for numerous posters advertising services such as *Stammering Cured! Fig and Lemon Jam – The Most Delicious & Healthy Jam Ever Made! Dutch Bulbs At Low Prices!* And in the centre of such temptations was a dark-edged poster proclaiming the *Blood-Curdling Tales From England's Pre-eminent Executioner: Once Heard – Never Forgotten! Mr Simeon Crosby In Person.*

Oscar smiled when he saw the details of time and venue. *Wigan Public Hall. King Street. 7.30. Tuesday 13th November.* That was today. He'd heard right, then, back at Haydock. His mind had worked wonders, and he hadn't been confused, no cloud blocking things out. He peered closer, saw the price of a ticket, saw also, a handwritten addendum which declared that the event was now sold out.

Then, as he progressed further down the street, something else caught his eye. A narrow poster that appeared to have been hastily stuck to the wall beside another derelict shop. It was Crosby's name, printed in thick bold letters, that made him stop and take notice.

Whereas Mr Simeon Crosby should consider – does his murderous noose reform or deter? Mass Meeting Tuesday 13th Market Square Wigan. 6.30.

A March of Mercy.

He screwed his face in an effort to ponder the question, but no answer came soaring through the clouds taking shape in his head. Instead, he shrugged and carried on walking, letting his mind reflect on the fact that today was Tuesday, and tonight, he would do what he had come to do. It didn't matter about not having a ticket. He didn't have any wish to hear Mr Crosby speak about his experiences and what he could tell from how the condemned faced him and what they did and what they said. But the other meeting – the Market Square, wherever that was. He could go there, couldn't he? They were going to have a meeting about Mr Simeon Crosby and then there'd be a march of mercy. He liked the sound of that.

But he wouldn't let it distract him.

There was only one thing he *needed* to do. He would do it for his beloved father. He reached into his shirt and took out the small framed photograph, gazing at it for a while. Remarkable, he thought, how a photograph can almost bring someone back to life.

'If only I could,' he said, reaching down and kissing Dead Father.

*

When Brennan and Jaggery got back to the station, Brennan immediately reported to Captain Bell's office and explained what little he knew about the mysterious conversation involving Gilbert Crosby the previous night, as well as the fact that he never returned to the hotel.

'Simeon Crosby says it isn't at all out of character?' the chief constable asked.

'It's what he says.'

'You have doubts, Sergeant?'

'I don't like things half-heard, sir. This business about ten pounds and Gilbert Crosby insisting that the thing had to be done last night. I'd like to know what *thing* is so urgent.'

Captain Bell walked over to the window and gazed out. It was a habit of his, and sometimes, Brennan resented the fact that he spent half his time addressing the man's back.

Finally, he said, 'In India, not all that long ago, they used a particular kind of executioner. You've heard of the caste system, Sergeant?'

'I have, sir.'

'Well, over there, they employed men of a low caste to act as executioners. Imagine the ignominy of being hanged by someone of a lower caste. But these hangmen were grossly unpopular. So hated, in fact, that they were forced to seek shelter in the very prisons that housed the ones they were hired to execute.'

Brennan watched his superior's shoulders rise and fall as he sighed heavily.

'They were also former criminals themselves. Marked in some way around their eyes to show their lowly and shameful status. It was ironic that they were scorned and insulted by the people, while the condemned man was regarded as almost holy. Men, women and even children would reach out and touch him.'

'Yes, sir,' said Brennan, unsure how to respond.

Captain Bell whirled round. 'The point is, they got it wrong, didn't they? In hiring low caste criminals, they turned the people against capital punishment at a stroke. Very short-sighted, Sergeant.'

'Yes, sir.' *Remarkable how a conversation that began with Gilbert Crosby had now changed course – and continent.*

'And I wonder if Mr Crosby writing about his experiences and touring the country like some nonsensical magic lanternist isn't having the same effect as the low castes. Giving the ultimate punishment a bad name.'

'He would argue the opposite, sir. Sharing his experiences, as it were.'

'And causing possible mayhem, Sergeant Brennan, as it were.'

'Quite, sir.'

The chief constable clapped his thin hands together, a sign that the time for philosophy had passed. 'I'm sure you'll get to the bottom of Gilbert Crosby, Sergeant.'

Brennan forebore from making some ribald joke at the chief constable's expense. Ribaldry had no place in this man's office.

'Now to more practical matters. This rabble-rouser, Evelyne – is he garnering any sort of support?'

Brennan shook his head. 'I don't think so, sir. From what I can gather, there were around twenty people at the meeting last night at the Legs of Man. If that's any indication of what to expect tonight, I don't think we'll find things too difficult. It's hardly in the same league as the problems we faced this time last year.'

'Indeed, Sergeant.' Captain Bell's voice adopted a sombre tone. The miners' strike of a year ago had brought the town great hardship, when feelings were hot among the miners, who saw the police as the supporting arm of the coal owners. It hadn't helped that the army had been called in as a precaution and installed in the Drill Hall. Fortunately, there had been no large-scale riot, as there had been over the Pennines in Featherstone, where two miners had been shot dead by the military, but it had been a close run thing nevertheless. And the murder of a prominent colliery owner hadn't helped matters.

'The men are all prepared, Sergeant. You are in charge, of course. Just make sure no one does anything silly. Remember, we are the arm of the law. The strong arm of the law.'

Brennan knew exactly what his superior was saying.

If in doubt, strike out.

*

The temperature had dropped considerably as the day wore on. The gas lamps that stretched the length of Market Street seemed to lose their glow against the bitter chill of the approaching night.

It was that time of evening when the mill-girls and the pitmen and the foundry workers had already made their way home from work and were either eating their tea or having what they commonly referred to as *a nod* before turning out for the night. For most of them, the local pubs would provide a warm and convivial refuge for a few hours, where gossip could be exchanged or grievances aired to the background rattle of dominoes or the dull thud of darts. As a consequence, there were few people on the street itself, other than the two police constables who stood across from the Market Square and observed the proceedings with barely concealed annoyance at the boredom and the cold. They muttered curses under their visible breaths.

For some thirty or so, whose social conscience proved stronger than the cold or the desire for smoke-filled bars, the Market Square was tonight's draw. Thomas Evelyne stood in the covered entrance to the Market Hall, wrapped his muffler close around his neck and watched the numbers grow – slowly, it had to be said. Still, it was rather pleasing to see that so many people from the town had heeded his call. If he hadn't decided to come here and organise the march and the protest outside the Public Hall, why, they'd be with the rest of their friends, doing what they did every night of the week. Hadn't he woken something inside them – some spirit of righteous protest? Yet even these people were blind to the abomination of what people like Simeon Crosby were doing in the name of justice.

Simeon Crosby.

How he hated that man!

A smile creased his face when he spotted three clergymen walking towards the assembling group, and he wondered idly what the collective noun for clergymen could be. A *trinity*, perhaps? Whatever the term was, he felt a glow of satisfaction: having members of the church march alongside him would do his cause no harm whatsoever. Further, he reasoned, it would lend a certain sanctified gravitas to what he was hoping to achieve tonight. Then he noticed, with a smile, that Miss Woodruff, the woman journalist he had spoken to earlier that day, had suddenly made an appearance and was making a beeline for the three clergymen, notepad in hand.

He looked at his watch: time to address the gathering, give them some final words to fire their anger and urge them to be vociferous in their condemnation of such an unwelcome visitor.

He found a sturdy wooden box, the sort of container used to transport vegetables from farm to market, turned it over and planted both feet on it, testing his weight. Satisfied it wouldn't split mid-speech, he raised his arms high above his head. Gradually the message got through to those gathered there, and the excited chatter slowly subsided. He cleared his throat and began to speak.

'Friends. We have in this town a representative of justice. Or so he would like us to think. He has, on a regular basis, fastened a rope around the neck of someone found guilty in a court of law. He has, on a regular basis, gripped the lever that, with one forceful pull, sends the condemned man to his eternal judgement. And now, on a regular basis, he flitters from town to town, like some vampire bat sated with blood, to describe his experiences in gruesome detail. I mentioned eternal judgement just then. For who is the only one who can deliver such a judgement? Who is the only one who should hold sway over the life of every man, woman and child on this earth?'

He paused and directed his gaze to the trinity of vicars standing to his left. The oldest of them, a grey-haired gentleman with watery eyes and cheeks of a mottled pink, folded his hands across his chest and shouted, 'Only the Lord our God, sir. Only the Lord our God.'

The two alongside him both added loudly, 'Amen!' and the word rippled along the crowd like an echo in a long tunnel.

Evelyne raised both hands. The crowd fell silent. 'It is now being suggested that, in order to show how merciful and considerate we have become, the authorities should make arrangements for the condemned man to be visited by a mesmerist to prepare him for the gallows. Or better still, inject him with an anaesthetic to replace the glasses of gin or brandy with which he is traditionally dosed. What kind of people are we, when those who suggest those things claim they are examples of a humanitarian approach to judicial death? It is far, far better to remove, not a man's life, but a man's freedom. Life imprisonment, not legal strangulation!'

The crowd cheered and the trinity applauded politely.

'But surely, my friends, even though the capital penalty is still woefully upon us, surely it is an abomination for someone like Mr Simeon Crosby to glory in its squalor, make a profit, not only from the grubbiness of his employment but also the lurid accounts of the things he has seen and done? One march like ours will never bring about the abolition of hanging, but this single march of ours can and will bring about the strangulation of a wicked man's voice. He must be stopped, my friends. Simeon Crosby must be prevented from speaking tonight! Let us, therefore, march with Right and the Almighty on our side and make every effort to keep this monster from corrupting the good people of this town!'

He jumped down from the wooden crate and strode purposefully to his left, towards where the trinity were standing.

'Gentlemen,' he declared. 'I would consider it a great honour if you would lead the march to the Public Hall. Your presence would lend our purpose a certain gravitas.'

The three vicars murmured to each other before nodding their assent. They took up their position at the head of the group, and Evelyne fell in behind them as they began the march along Market Street towards the Public Hall, some three hundred yards away. He glanced quickly behind him. The rest of the crowd were following, as were the two constables, who seemed more cheerful than earlier.

He caught sight of a dishevelled-looking individual who shuffled along at the rear of the group, to whom Miss Woodruff had now attached herself. She seemed to be engaged in conversation, and at one point, the man reached beneath his coat and took out a small object. He spoke to her with great animation for several seconds and seemed to be urging her to look at the object more closely. Then, she seemed to step back with an expression of disgust and horror on her face and moved quickly away from him. The man merely shook his head, as if he were disturbed by a swarm of bees.

Oscar Pardew had a confused expression on his face. Why did the woman leave him? After all, he'd merely introduced her to Dead Father. He looked up, to the head of the crowd, to the man who had been speaking to them. That man had called Simeon Crosby a monster. Despite the wisps of cloud that were slowly beginning to take shape behind his eyes, he made every effort to keep focused on what he had come to do.

He glanced down at the photograph, could almost feel his father's stern gaze, watching what he would do next.

*

At that moment, Ralph Batsford locked his room in the Royal Hotel then walked along the corridor towards Simeon Crosby's room. The door opened and Simeon stepped out, his face registering surprise at seeing the journalist.

'Ralph? I thought we were to meet in the bar?'

Batsford shrugged. 'Just thought I'd give you a knock. Make sure you were ready.'

Crosby gave a quick glance back into the room.

'Is Violet ready?' Batsford nodded towards the open door.

For an instant, there was a flash of annoyance on Crosby's face. Instead of answering, he stepped back towards the room and said loudly, 'I hope you feel better soon, dear. Perhaps your headache might go away if you put that silly romantic volume down and got some sleep.'

With that, he closed the door.

Batsford sighed. 'Still no sign of Gilbert?'

Crosby shook his head curtly, giving the impression that any mention of his brother was unwelcome. Then his mood seemed to lighten, and he held up a small leather case which he patted gently. 'The best speech I've ever given,' he said with some pride.

'Violet is unwell?' He stepped towards Crosby's room. 'Perhaps we should send for—'

Crosby slapped him on the shoulder and said, 'All that reading, my dear chap. All that reading! Best to leave her to her rest, eh?' With that, he led Batsford along the corridor to the stairs. 'And I have an audience waiting,' he added.

'You also have three very large constables waiting in the hotel foyer, Simeon, all ready to escort you to your awaiting carriage. It seems the chief constable is taking no chances with your well-being.'

At the top of the stairs, Batsford glanced back down the corridor, a deep frown creasing his forehead.

CHAPTER NINE

Detective Sergeant Brennan had deployed his men wisely.

Four constables were standing at the top of King Street, where the marchers would have to pass in order to make their way down towards the Public Hall. No carriages had been allowed to enter, and the chief constable, at Brennan's bidding, had asked for the tram service to be suspended for a half-hour while the expected protest took place.

He had given orders for the men to give a stern and no-nonsense response to the group as they passed by, a timely reminder that the forces of law and order were in no mood to tolerate anything other than an orderly demonstration from those wishing to register their protest at Crosby's presence. Halfway along King Street, another four men, two on either side of the street, stood with heads held erect as if on inspection, and outside the Public Hall, four constables stood on the steps, two on each side, to provide a barrier that would keep the marchers out. On the lowest step, in the middle of the two lines, stood Constable Jaggery, his large presence and scowling features enough to discourage even the most dedicated of protesters.

Already a queue of ticket-holders was waiting patiently against the wall of the building, and judging from the expressions on their faces,

Brennan could see they were both unnerved by the sight of so many policemen and excited at the prospect of hearing what the cause of their presence had to say. He noticed there was roughly an equal mix of men and women waiting to enter. He felt slightly taken aback by the sight of so many women, wondering why they would choose to listen to the morbid and probably gruesome reminiscences of an executioner. He couldn't imagine Ellen sitting there and taking in such horrors.

Suddenly he heard the sound of distant voices. He looked up the street and saw one of his constables raise an arm. It was a signal that the marchers were almost at the top of the street.

'Look at 'em,' said one man in the queue. 'Holy bloody joes.'

'Aye,' said another. 'They'd be singin' a different tune if it were theirs what got done in. They'd be skrikin' for blood then, the soft bastards.'

Brennan turned and gave the attendant on the door a curt nod. 'Right, son,' he said. 'Let 'em in.'

Quickly, the attendant opened the hall door and ushered in those waiting.

''Ave your tickets ready, if you please!' he announced.

The audience filed in, some of them exchanging pleasantries with the policemen as they passed through, as though, for the moment, they shared the same firm belief in the forces of law and order.

Then Brennan raised his arm once more and the constables halfway along the street immediately took up fresh positions across the street itself to form a human barrier.

He saw the marchers now at the top of the street, where King Street and Wallgate formed a junction. They were singing the hymn *Nearer My God To Thee.* The constables stepped forward and had a word with the three vicars at the head of the march. They all gave a sharp nod, and the four officers led the way down King Street. The marchers appeared to be following the commands of the police – Brennan could see there were no arguments or raised voices, nor was there any arm-waving, and he wondered if tonight's display would, after all, proceed along orderly and civilised lines.

He was ready if it didn't.

*

Under normal circumstances, it would take all of two minutes to make the journey by carriage from the Royal Hotel on Standishgate to the Public Hall in King Street. But these were far from normal circumstances, and Captain Bell had insisted that the carriage, containing Simeon Crosby and two police constables take a circuitous route that would take them down Millgate and at the bottom of that steep incline, via a sharp right into Rodney Street, past the police station and then finally right into King Street, thereby avoiding the route taken by the marchers from Market Square.

Batsford, meanwhile, stood shivering in the icy cold on the steps of the Royal and was informed that the chief constable's orders extended only to Mr Crosby and his wife and that the journalist was to be accompanied by the remaining constable on foot.

As Crosby was clambering into the carriage, one of the constables asked, '*Where's the missus, like?*' He was clearly discomfited by the unexpected absence of Mrs Crosby. It was also clear that this deviation from the chief constable's orders was something he didn't really know how to respond to.

'Mrs Crosby is indisposed,' her husband replied. 'She won't be accompanying us.'

'I see,' said the constable, looking at his two colleagues for support.

Both of them shrugged, and one of them, an older, more world-weary chap, added, 'Nowt we can do. Unless we go an' skulldrag her out of her room, like.'

Simeon Crosby leaned out from the carriage's interior. 'I beg your pardon?'

The constable gave an apologetic cough. 'Sorry, sir. It were a joke.'

But Crosby's face showed what he thought of the man's humour. 'There'll be no skulldragging. Do you hear?'

'Yes, sir. It were only—'

'—My wife is not to be disturbed.'

'No, sir.'

As one of the constables climbed in beside him with the other already ensconced beside the driver, Crosby leaned from the carriage and addressed Batsford, who had been watching the exchange with interest.

'You might as well get in here with me. Plenty room now.'

But Batsford shook his head. 'I need the exercise,' he said. 'I'll see you there.'

Crosby grunted and rapped on the carriage roof. With a snort, the horse pulled away.

Batsford turned to the constable who was standing beside him. 'I really don't think I need an escort, Constable.'

The policeman was young, and Batsford noticed the beginnings of a moustache. He wondered how long it had taken those flimsy hairs to sprout.

'Chief constable's orders, sir.'

The journalist gave a quick glance back towards the hotel steps. 'Well, if you don't mind waiting…?'

'Waitin'? What for?'

'I've left my notebook in my room. A reporter without his notebook is like, well, like a constable without his truncheon.'

The young policeman smiled. 'I'd be buggered baht it.'

'And so would I, Constable.' He started to move back towards the steps of the hotel.

''Ere, how long will you be, only—'

Batsford held up his hand. 'As long as it takes, Constable. No more and no less.'

The policeman sighed and walked to the bottom of the steps, watching the reporter take them two at a time.

*

The trouble, when it came, took everyone by surprise.

The marchers, with the three vicars at their head, closely followed by Thomas Evelyne, had halted a few yards from the steps of the Public Hall. The glow from the gas lamps dotted along King Street highlighted the size of the group, and Brennan estimated there were no more than thirty present. The bitter cold of the evening made their combined breaths form small clouds. When he issued his order for the constables to stop the marchers, they had all complied, following the example of the trinity leading them. Many of them stamped their feet, not out of annoyance or impatience, but merely to generate enough energy to create some suspicion of warmth.

The singing had faded away, and it seemed to Brennan that now they had reached their destination, they were at a loss as to how to proceed.

At that moment, further down the street, he heard the rattle of carriage wheels and the clip-clop of the horse's hooves on the cobblestones. The sight of a policeman seated beside the driver brought a ripple of murmur as people understood the carriage's import, but even then, they remained more like placid observers than enraged protesters.

Once the carriage reached the Public Hall, Brennan stepped forward and waited for the door to swing open. He was somewhat surprised to see Simeon Crosby clamber out unaccompanied by his wife, but the important thing now was to get the man safely inside so he could deliver his eagerly awaited talk.

It was as the hangman placed his foot on the first step that a loud yell pierced the air.

'Murderer!'

He saw the one who had been at the head of the march along with the vicars – Evelyne, presumably – turn to the others in an attempt to generate a loud vocal protest. Several of them complied, but then a man, a dishevelled-looking individual who had been standing at the back of the protesters, surged through the crowd shouting, 'Crosby! Simeon Crosby!' and pushing all and sundry out of his way in his eagerness to reach his quarry.

Someone yelled out, 'Look out – he's got something in his hand!'

Within seconds, pandemonium broke out as the police constables flanking the marchers plunged into the mass of bodies in a desperate attempt to grab the man, those hurled aside expressing their outrage in the vilest terms. As the man continued to force his way to the front, two more constables leapt into the midst with truncheons raised, but this occasioned more anger, more shoving, more expressions of resentment and indignation directed towards this uniformed intrusion into their ranks, and soon, the hitherto disciplined but hesitant band of protesters had transformed into a chaotic melee of swinging fists and cursing tongues.

Brennan grabbed hold of Crosby and almost lifted him off his feet in his haste to usher him into the relative safety of the auditorium. Once he'd gained the topmost step he wheeled round and called out to Constable Jaggery, 'Nobody gets past, Constable! Nobody!'

Jaggery nodded, turned his attention to the mass brawl developing before his eyes and lunged forward, grabbing the first figure he could see and dragging him forcibly from the scrimmage by the neck.

'Now meladdo!' he yelled in the man's ear. 'How about some fist?'

'You brute!' came the unexpected reply from, as Jaggery could now see, a quite elderly man. 'You have torn my collar! My clerical! You fat oaf!'

'Jesus!' said Jaggery, realising his error at once. He let the man go and waded further into the brawling mob. Several of the women protesters had rushed to the pavement, partly to get out of harm's way but also out of a desire to observe the proceedings from a better vantage point. As if by some miracle of prestidigitation, dozens of men appeared from nowhere – or rather from the vaults of the nearby public houses, having watched the scene unfold – and joined in the general disturbance, swinging fists in pleasurable abandon and taking particular delight in taking aim at the unfortunate constables, who suddenly saw themselves as objects of violent attention. Jaggery fought like a man possessed, grabbing two at a time (taking a second to check their neckwear) and cracking skulls together before moving through the mob, tossing man after man from the mass of bodies to land with an unceremonious crunch against the nearest wall.

Of the man rushing through the crowd, there was now no sign.

Inside, the scene could hardly be more of a contrast. Brennan escorted Simeon Crosby to the front of the auditorium where the curtains on the small stage were draped in sombre colours, befitting the nature of the talk the man was about to give. By now, every seat was taken, with some at the back of the hall standing. There was the muted sound of chatter from the audience, a sense of anticipation at what promised to be a gruesome insight into the dark world of prisons, last-minute confessions and the ultimate price paid by those who rob some poor soul of his or her life.

'I think I can manage from here, Sergeant Brennan.' Crosby's eyes glimmered in the gas lighting as he gave various members of his audience a cheery wave. He leaned closer to Brennan and whispered, 'They're always amazed to see me smile, you know. It's as if they think I go round with a permanent scowl on my face!'

'They only think of you in a certain situation, Mr Crosby.'

'The imagination's a powerful thing, is it not?'

'Indeed it is.' Brennan thought for a moment then asked, 'I was expecting your wife to accompany you.'

Crosby gave a slight cough. 'Under the circumstances don't you think it was for the best? Her not witnessing that rabble outside?'

'Of course.'

'Besides, she was complaining of a very painful headache. She reads to excess, Sergeant. Many's the time I've threatened to apply leeches to her temples!'

With that, the hangman shook Brennan's hand and made his way to the wings, where the manager of the Public Hall was waiting for him and pulling at his shirt collar, indicating both anxiety and relief.

Brennan checked that two of his constables were standing by the exit doors. He gave them a curt nod and made his way back to the foyer of the hall, where the sound of scuffling and intermittent grunts, punctuated by the occasional obscenity, told him the affray beyond the closed doors was far from over. Time to join in, he told himself and barked the order to the constable standing on the inside to, 'Open 'em, lad. Quick as you can!'

The doors swung open, and Brennan launched himself forward, adding to the forces of law and order.

CHAPTER TEN

By the time Simeon Crosby's talk had come to its conclusion (to a standing ovation), the disturbance outside the Public Hall had ended. Several arrests had been made, either for assaulting a police officer or disturbing the peace or, in some of the more violent cases, under both charges. Detective Sergeant Brennan stood in the foyer, nursing a set of bruised knuckles, having watched the animated audience make their way out into the cold night air. Their eyes were sparkling, and he heard snatches of their conversations:

Can tell a tale all right.

Just think on what he's not told us!

I never knew they give 'em a drink afore they drop.

Bloody scandalous!

Aye, an' a bloody waste an' all!

That were t'best, yon mon singin' wi' t'rope round his neck!

Aye. Happen he liked a drop!

General laughter.

He was waiting for Crosby and the journalist, Batsford, who had arrived half an hour late and who was recognised at once by Constable Jaggery. With commendable devotion to duty, Jaggery had relaxed his stranglehold on one unfortunate marcher and made it his business to ensure a safe passage for the reporter.

Now the two men appeared through the door that led into the auditorium, Crosby's face flushed with the success of the evening. Batsford seemed preoccupied, merely nodding when the hangman spoke.

'I hope the show went well, Mr Crosby?' Brennan asked.

'Indeed it did, Sergeant. I gather it was quite a show outside as well, eh?' He gave a little chortle.

Brennan nodded. 'Perhaps as well your wife didn't come. Mob anger like that isn't very pleasant.'

Crosby shrugged. 'Her loss,' he said.

It took Brennan a second to realise the man was referring to his talk and not the violence outside.

As they left the building, Brennan had the same carriage waiting to take Crosby and Batsford back to the hotel. He opened the carriage door and waited for them to enter.

'Is this necessary?' Crosby said with a wave of the hand to show that King Street was now devoid of protesters.

'It's a necessary precaution, Mr Crosby. I'll accompany you to the Royal. The chief constable would expect it. Besides, I can't see all of them going straight off home. Not when they've had a taste of the rough stuff.'

With a resigned shrug, Crosby clambered inside, Batsford following, while Brennan climbed up and sat beside the driver.

Within minutes, they were pulling up before the steps of the Royal Hotel, where Brennan was surprised to see a small group of people standing outside the building. At first he thought it was the protesters waiting to give the hangman another indication of their abolitionist views until he saw one of the constables also standing there, speaking calmly and nodding in response to what someone was saying. Nevertheless, Brennan took no chances and climbed down, ordering the occupants of the carriage to remain inside until he found out what was going on.

When the constable saw Brennan, he gave a wave and beckoned him over.

'Constable?'

'It is nowt, Sergeant. Bit o' bother, that's all.'

'*Bit of bother?*' someone said. '*Bit of bother?* You call a smashed window a *bit of bother?* I call it rampant hooliganism!'

Brennan now recognised the speaker. It was the hotel manager, James Eastoe, whose hair, which earlier had been elegantly combed and kept in place by macassar oil, was now elevated in several unkempt directions at once.

'What's happened?' Brennan asked.

'Look!' said Eastoe, pointing at a large window that belonged to the Eagle and Child, the public bar side of the hotel. 'Even a detective from Wigan can work that one out!'

Ignoring the insult, Brennan examined the damage. Shards of glass stuck out around a large hole, with shining slivers of glass spread across the wooden floor inside. A large brick lay on the table nearest the window. A workman was carefully removing the fragments of glass, placing them in a metal container. Propped against the wall lay a large square of wood and a toolbox containing a hammer and nails of varying sizes.

'Did you see who did it?'

'I don't spend my time standing on the steps of the hotel, watching the world and his uncle go by. I have a hundred things to attend to inside the hotel. More than a hundred, truth be known.'

At this point, Crosby called out from the carriage window, 'Can we get out now, Sergeant?'

Brennan turned to the constable and told him to escort the two gentlemen inside.

Once he saw Crosby emerge from the carriage, the manager raised an accusatory finger. 'There! He's the one!'

Brennan turned. 'You're saying Mr Simeon Crosby smashed your window?'

'As good as! If he weren't staying here, we wouldn't have become a target.'

Crosby seemed about to respond as he stepped from the carriage, but Batsford placed a restraining hand on his shoulder and, accompanied by the constable, walked the hangman inside the hotel.

'The protesters, you mean?' Brennan asked. 'I thought we'd dispersed them. Those we hadn't arrested anyway.'

Mr Eastoe tried to smooth his hair into position. 'It's stretching the imagination to suggest anyone else but a protester, Sergeant. I have been manager here for years and never, in all that time, have I had a brick come sailing through the window. And the talk in the hotel bar has been of the disturbance in King Street. Two and two make four, Sergeant. Or they did when I was at school.'

With a sigh, Brennan began speaking to others standing outside the bar, in case any of them had seen anything. Several of them had been drinking inside when the brick came through the window around an hour earlier. None of them had noticed anyone loitering outside, and he was about to give up and leave the manager to his cleaning-up operation when the doors at the top of the steps swung open, and the young constable came rushing out.

'Sergeant!'

'Yes, Constable. What's the matter?'

'You'd best come up.'

Brennan's heart skipped a beat. 'What's happened? Where's Mr Crosby?'

'In his room, beatin' his chest an' cursin' fit to burst. It's his wife, Sergeant. She's lied there on the bed wi' her eyes wide open. Looks like she's dead.'

CHAPTER ELEVEN

When Brennan reached Crosby's room, he found Simeon Crosby kneeling beside the bed, clasping his wife's hand. Ralph Batsford stood beside him with a consoling hand on his shoulder. In the bed, Violet Crosby lay face upwards, the deep red mark around her neck indicative of some kind of ligature having been applied. Her eyes were wide open, and as Brennan moved closer to inspect the body, he saw spots of red on the poor woman's eyeballs. The bed cover was thrown back, and she appeared to be fully dressed, her cream-laced blouse crumpled and partly torn to expose the neck. A length of thin rope lay on the pillow to the right of her head.

As Brennan reached for it, Batsford said, 'It was wound tightly around her neck, Sergeant. Simeon did what he could but by that time…'

As if registering the policeman's presence for the first time, Crosby glanced up. His eyes were brimming with tears.

'My Violet,' he said, almost in a whisper. 'Who did this vile thing to my dear Violet?'

Brennan held the piece of rope, noted its criss-cross pattern and looked more closely at the victim's neck, where the pattern seemed faintly impressed into the wound around her neck.

'I think we should go to my room, Simeon,' said Batsford, directing his gaze not at the hangman but at Brennan, who gave an appreciative nod.

But Crosby shook his head. 'I'm not leaving her!' He clasped her hand tightly, bringing it close to his lips.

Brennan leaned towards him. 'Mr Crosby. You need to allow me to do my job. There are certain things I need to…'

'I've seen death before, Sergeant. I'm not a bloody fool!'

Before he could launch into a tirade, Batsford placed an arm beneath Crosby's and made an effort to raise him to his feet. Brennan did the same, and Crosby finally stood. It was as if the act of standing had deflated whatever anger he felt towards the world, for he gave a slow nod and said heavily, 'Come on then. Let's leave the detective sergeant to do his job.'

Batsford gave Brennan a weak smile of apology – the ironic, accusatory implications of Crosby's words accepted as unfair – and they both left the room. Brennan saw the young constable standing in the doorway.

'Get the manager, Mr Eastoe, Constable. I need this room locked and guarded. Go on. Hurry up!'

As the constable rushed away, plainly relieved at being given something to do that would remove him from this dreadful scene, Brennan stood by the door and examined the lock.

'Was this door locked when you got back?' he asked Batsford, who was in the process of escorting Crosby to his room.

The journalist thought for a second then shook his head. 'Simeon just walked in. I was about to unlock my own door when I heard him yell…'

Brennan saw there were no marks to indicate a forced entry, nothing untoward around the lock or the door handle. The door key was in the keyhole on the inside. Quietly he closed the door and turned to the body on the bed. He noticed a leather-bound book on the bedside table, went over and picked it up. He'd never heard of the author – Ouida – nor the novel – *Moths* – but it somehow angered him that the poor woman had, sometime earlier, been reading and escaping from the real world, a world where her husband hung those who were guilty of the most appalling crimes... and now someone had entered her room and strangled her.

But the lock hadn't been forced.

'Bloody hell*fire*!' he muttered to himself.

*

Mr James Eastoe looked like a man enduring all the weight of the world on his small shoulders. Worry lines were etched along his forehead, and as he sat behind his office desk and attempted to answer the detective's questions, he continually licked his lips and clasped and unclasped his hands.

'I must say, Sergeant, it's unfair to expect me to know that.'

'But Mr Crosby says he left his wife in their room feeling distinctly unwell. He said nothing to you when he left?'

'Nothing. Nothing at all. If I'd known, of course I would have sent someone up to see if she needed anything. But as I was unaware of her illness... We do allow our guests their privacy, you know.'

'Of course. Did anyone see or hear anything on that floor? A shout? Sounds of a struggle?'

'Not that I'm aware of. I've spoken to Gray, who mans our reception desk, and he tells me there was nothing untoward. Nothing to cause undue concern.'

'I shall wish to speak with Mr Gray.'

Eastoe took out his watch and checked the time. 'He is due to finish at ten thirty, Sergeant. At which time our night receptionist takes over. It's barely ten o'clock now. I shall make sure he's available when he comes off duty.'

Brennan shook his head. 'I'll speak to him now, Mr Eastoe if you don't mind.'

'But he's still on duty.'

'And so am I. And I won't be off duty for several hours yet. So if you please…' Brennan gave a curt nod to the door behind him.

'I cannot leave the desk unmanned. It's a dereliction of duty, both his and mine.'

'Then if you ask him to step in here and take over his duties yourself for a short time, that would provide us all with a solution to your problem.' He smiled at the now crestfallen manager, whose sunken shoulders and tightened lips indicated his grudging acceptance of defeat. 'And while you're there, perhaps you can prepare a list of all your other guests staying tonight.'

Eastoe snorted. 'I can tell you now, Sergeant. There are only two other guests, apart from the Crosby party. Both of them commercial travellers.'

'Then I need their names and room numbers.'

The manager turned away, unaccustomed to being on the receiving end of orders.

Within a minute, the receptionist, Mr Gray, was standing in the doorway, regarding the detective with curiosity and suspicion. He was in his fifties, Brennan guessed, with hair the colour of his name, and his dour countenance, exaggerated by his pinched features, gave him an appearance more suited to a disillusioned parson than someone whose job it was to meet and greet guests of the hotel.

'Mr Gray, please sit down,' said Brennan with a wave of his hand towards the chair Eastoe had just vacated.

Gray shook his head. 'I'll stand if it's all the same. I spend most of my time sitting down.' He suddenly thrust a hand forward. It contained a torn-off piece of paper. 'Courtesy of Mr Eastoe,' he said.

Brennan took the paper and looked at it quickly. Two names, along with room numbers, hastily scribbled. He could imagine the manager's mood when he wrote them down. He placed the paper in his notebook.

'Thank you. I just want to ask a few questions about tonight. Mr Eastoe tells me you have no knowledge of any disturbance from the second floor, where Mrs Crosby was found.'

'I heard nothing. It's two flights of stairs.'

'No reports of anything from residents or employees of the hotel?'

'Nothing came to my attention.'

Brennan sighed.

'Apart from the woman, that is.'

Brennan frowned. 'What woman?'

Gray shifted his stance, less formal now, more confidential. 'Pretty young thing, Sergeant. I'd been outside after some young ruffian had hurled a brick through the bar window. When I came back in, I saw her standing by the front desk. I hadn't seen her come in, but in all the commotion…'

'What did she want?'

'Asked to see Mrs Crosby.'

'What time was this?'

'Five past eight. Ten past. Something that way.'

'Did she give her name?'

Gray nodded and a ghost of a smile crept onto his lips, a sign that he was privy to something the policeman would wish to know. 'She called herself Miss Woodruff.'

'Woodruff?' Brennan took out his small notebook and wrote down the name. 'What did you do?'

'I asked her if Mrs Crosby was expecting her, and she said she was. I was a bit flustered, I admit, after all the shenanigans outside. So I told her to sit in the reception area then sent our bellboy to Mrs Crosby's room.'

'Did she get to see Mrs Crosby?'

Gray shook his head. 'Indeed not. When the boy came back and said there was no answer, that was that.'

'The woman left?'

Gray gave a sharp cough. 'Only after demanding to go up to the room and try for herself. I refused, of course. She took umbrage at that, called me officious, would you believe? Told me she had an appointment with Mrs Crosby, and perhaps she'd simply fallen asleep. I insisted she leave at that point. And she did. With most unfeminine grace, I might add.'

'The boy heard nothing from the room? Any sounds at all?'

'He would have mentioned something like that, wouldn't he?'

Brennan agreed, making a mental note to speak with the boy later. And, of course, he needed to find this Miss Woodruff. He wondered what business she had with Mrs Crosby, especially when no one expected the poor woman to be in her room in the first place. Until tonight, she had been fully expected to travel to the Public Hall with her husband to listen to his speech. Mr Crosby had told him his wife had a headache. Yet this Woodruff woman told Gray she had an appointment to see her. Was the woman lying? Or did she really have an appointment? In which case the *headache* could well have been a fabrication. And that would mean that Violet Crosby had deliberately misled her husband and lied about her headache.

A lot of supposing there, Mickey lad.

He thanked the receptionist and asked him to send the bellboy in.

The boy, whose name was George, came in sheepishly and stood by the door, giving Brennan the impression that if he were to raise his voice just a fraction, the boy would be off like a frightened hare. His eyes were watery, not so much indicating the imminence of tears but more a sign of his youth. He seemed to be barely old enough to have left school, despite the fact that the leaving age had recently been raised to twelve. His dark blue uniform, trimmed with yellow piping, looked at least one size too big for him.

'How old are you, George?'

'Thirteen and a bit, sir,' came the high-pitched response.

'How long have you worked here at the Royal?'

'When I turned thirteen, sir.'

'So you've been here a bit then?'

Brennan had meant it as a joke to settle the boy's nerves, but from the expression on his face, he realised it had sounded more like an insult.

'It were me dad got me the *position*.' He pronounced the word with a hint of pride. 'Said as I weren't to go anywhere near the pit.'

Brennan nodded, understanding the father's concerns. It seemed the entire population of Wigan was split down the middle: parents – fathers mainly – who insisted their sons would follow literally in their footsteps and gain employment down the mines, and others who were adamantly opposed to the idea, insisting that no son of theirs would ever set foot *down yonder*. Both Brennan and his wife were firmly in the latter camp where their son Barry was concerned.

He went on quickly. 'Tell me about when you went up to Mrs Crosby's room. After the woman asked to speak with her.'

The boy shrugged. 'I did as I were told.'

'You knocked on the door?'

'I did.'

'And did Mrs Crosby answer?'

'No, sir. I heard nowt. I mean, nothing.'

'Did you try opening the door?'

George looked shocked. 'I'd get sacked if I did that. They don't answer, you walk away. Them's the rules.'

'Was there anyone up there on the second floor?'

George frowned in concentration then said, 'Didn't see nobody, sir.'

'You came straight back down?'

'Yes, sir.'

'And you saw no one on the way down?'

'Yes, sir.'

'Yes? You saw someone?'

'Well, didn't 'zackly see him.'

'What then?'

'More like bumped into him. On the stairs.'

'A man? Who was he?'

Again the concentrated frown. 'Like I said, I didn't 'zackly see him. Just ran into him. Kept me head down an' mumbled how sorry I were then kept on runnin' downstairs. I were in a bit of a hurry, like.'

'You say you bumped into this man on the stairs. Was he going up or on his way down?'

'Goin' down, I think.'

'Did you see him on your way up the stairs to Mrs Crosby's room?'

The boy thought for a minute then said, 'No, sir.'

'Mrs Crosby was in Room Eight,' said Brennan. 'Is there anywhere someone could hide? I mean between the top of the stairs on the second floor and Room Eight?'

When he spoke next, George's voice had dropped lower. 'Room Eight's round the corner on its own. Then there's Rooms Five, Six and Seven. And there's a store cupboard next to Room Five, near the top of the stairs!' His voice was now raised excitedly. 'I reckon he were a guest.'

Brennan said, 'A guest here in the hotel?'

George nodded. 'I reckon so.'

'What makes you so sure?'

'How would he know me name if he weren't stayin' here, eh?' There was a small look of triumph on his face, as if he'd given a demonstration of his deductive powers. 'He said, *Now, now, what's the panic, George?*'

'But you don't know who he was?'

'They all know *my* name, sir,' he said with a touch of pride. 'But as to *his* name...'

Could be important, thought Brennan, but then again it might be nothing at all. Hotels have guests and guests use the stairs. According to Eastoe, there were only two other guests staying at the hotel. Wouldn't be too difficult to discover the man's name.

'You don't know the woman who made the request? Miss Woodruff?'

'Never seed her before, sir.'

'What did she say when you got back?'

'Seemed annoyed, as though it were my fault! Told me to go back an' knock 'arder. Mr Gray told me that wouldn't be necessary an' I were to run along an' get on wi' me duties like.'

Brennan thanked the boy, who left the room with far greater confidence than he'd shown on entering. He'd given the detective some information, his attitude said. He could imagine the boy getting home and proclaiming to his proud parents how he'd actually been helping the police with their enquiries.

*

The Queen's Hotel in Lower Wallgate had none of the select features of the Royal. It boasted neither manager nor bellboy, for in truth it was little more than a public house with rooms to let. Its situation, past the railway station on the road leading out of Wigan town centre and heading out towards Pemberton, had proved an ideal spot for Thomas Evelyne to stay. He could, of course, afford a much grander place than the Queen's, but once he discovered where Simeon Crosby was staying for his temporary sojourn in Wigan, Evelyne had decided the further away from that man the better. He sat now, in the vault of the Queen's, nursing a pint and contemplating the events of the night.

The march hadn't stopped Crosby's speech, but then that wasn't really the object of it anyway. No. He'd been careful to explain to Miss Woodruff only that afternoon that his purpose was to expose the man and the vile things he had done, and although the march had come to a violent end, as far as Evelyne was concerned, his purpose had been achieved.

At some cost, though. He reached up and touched the throbbing and growing lump on the top of his head. *Bloody police!*

Still, he took a long sip of his ale and wondered, for the umpteenth time, how it was that he himself had escaped with mere bruises when some of the others had been beaten senseless by the police. He could still feel the rush of wind when the largest of the constables had taken a swing at his head with his truncheon. And later, the kindly priest who'd ministered to him and his throbbing head!

But the one who'd stormed to the front of the march, yelling out the hangman's name! The same dishevelled character he'd seen talking with such animation with Miss Woodruff as they left the Market Square.

Evelyne shook his head at the naivety, or to be more blunt, the sheer unadulterated stupidity of the man, thinking he could get close to Crosby. Strange, though, how the man simply disappeared after the charge. Once he'd reached the steps of the Public Hall, all hell had broken loose and punches were being traded as if Armageddon were close at hand.

But the man had served a purpose all right. Now the papers would be filled, not with reports of Crosby's speech but with all that occurred as a consequence of his presence in the town. And that could only be a good thing for his cause.

At that point, as he drained his glass and stood to head for the bar, he happened to glance outside. Across the street, passing a row of shops, he spotted the very man he'd just been thinking of. He was hurrying along, staring down at his hands, shaking his head and casting furtive glances behind him, looking for all the world like a man worried that he might have someone chasing him. He was the actual instigator of the melee that had followed, and one would have expected him to be spending the night nursing both grievances and bruises, yet here he was at liberty.

Evelyne thought about stepping outside and calling out to the poor fellow, to buy him a drink for rendering the evening such a success, but then he saw him slip into a narrow alleyway that ran between the shops.

'Like a rat,' he thought. 'Like a cornered rat.'

He had better things to do than go after him, so he caught the landlord's attention and ordered another pint. It was an occasion to celebrate, after all.

*

The man Thomas Evelyne had just been watching – Oscar Pardew – was in no mood for celebrating. Not at all. He couldn't take his eyes from his hands, which were streaked with blood. He stifled a sob and wiped his hands against his trousers. Then he felt inside his pocket and pulled out a bloodstained photograph, the small glass frame now gone. There was a smear of red on his father's chest, and if he hadn't been so angry with what had happened, he would find that almost funny. The stain was where Dead Father had been stabbed.

'I'm sorry, Father,' he said softly. 'But I'll clean you up.'

He'd tried so hard to get to the hangman and carry out his promise to Dead Father, but those people, especially those policemen, had prevented him. Even threatened to put him in a police cell, and he'd had enough of being locked up, thank you very much, even though the family told him Haydock Lodge was more of a hospital than anything else, and where better to heal the wounds that couldn't be seen?

He was puzzled, however. He'd thought (or had he been told? He wasn't quite sure about that now, not when the clouds started to swirl around inside his head and make the events of the day vague, unclear), but he'd thought if he were to run through the crowd and shout out Mr Crosby's name, then the people would make a gap, like the parting of the Red Sea, so he could reach the hangman, and even the police would stand to one side once they saw how eager he was. It had been so clear, that vision. And it was so annoying when visions didn't come true.

The big policeman had called him some terrible names and – what had the brute shouted?

I'll swing for you, you little bastard! Come here!

That was it, Oscar recalled with pride: that's exactly what the lumbering slow-footed moron had yelled at him. And it had been funny at the time, what with him within touching distance of the country's most famous hangman:

I'll swing for you!

He'd struck Oscar on the chest. That's when he'd heard and felt the glass smash. He had screamed loudly, pulled free of the fat policeman's clutches and run back the way he'd come, turning once to see the policeman chasing him with all the elegance of an overfed elephant.

And then…

He reached out and pressed his hands against the cold, rough surface of a wall. Tiny pieces of grit stuck to his bloodstained palms.

Where was he?

It was dark and cold, and all around him were high walls and an enclosed path that led to a road where he could just make out the lights from a public house.

He shook his head. Perhaps the clouds would break up, give him a clearer glimpse of where he'd been and what he'd done.

*

Brennan made his way up to the room occupied by Ralph Batsford. He nodded at the young constable now standing on duty outside Batsford's room, and he pointed to the door along the corridor, to Crosby's room. The body had been removed and was even now on its way to the mortuary, where it would await the tender solicitations of the House Surgeon at Wigan Infirmary, Dr Monroe, who would be examining the poor woman's remains.

'Make sure no one goes in, Constable,' he ordered before opening the door to Batsford's room.

There he found Simeon Crosby slumped in a chair by the window. He was leaning forward, his hands clasped together and his head bowed, but his was no prayerful attitude: he stared at the threadbare carpet, his eyes red and raw from the tears that still brimmed on the surface. Batsford was standing beside him, his hand placed gently on the hangman's shoulder. It was a silent tableau of grief, Brennan felt, but he had things to do, and the mood of mournful stillness would, of necessity, be broken.

Batsford cleared his throat. 'Mr Eastoe has arranged for another room to be made ready. Simeon can hardly spend the night—'

Brennan held up a hand to show he understood. 'Mr Crosby,' he began in his most respectful tone, 'I'm afraid there are some questions...'

That was as far as he got. From the corridor beyond the closed door came the sound of raised voices, angry voices and what sounded like someone being slammed hard against the corridor wall.

CHAPTER TWELVE

When Brennan stepped into the corridor, he saw the young constable pinned against the wall by a powerful-looking individual whom he recognised at once by the scar on his right cheek.

Gilbert Crosby, who had been missing all day.

'Let him go!' Brennan ordered.

'Is it a crime to knock on a brother's door?' Gilbert's voice was hard, unyielding.

'No,' Brennan replied reasonably. 'But it is a crime to assault a policeman. And if you don't let him go this second, I'll break your arm.'

There was something in the sergeant's tone – controlled anger, resolve and more than a hint of relish at the prospect, that caused Gilbert to loosen his grip on the constable's throat.

The young policeman straightened his uniform and looked at his sergeant with an expression that was a blend of apology and shame. 'I'm sorry, Sergeant, only he took no notice when I told him...'

'That's all right, lad,' said Brennan reassuringly. 'You did well.'

'What's all this? Where's my brother? Where's Violet?'

Brennan pushed open the door to Batsford's room. 'You'd best go in. Your brother's had some bad news.'

A few minutes later, after he'd found out what happened to his sister-in-law, Gilbert Crosby stood beside his brother and patted his shoulder gingerly in what seemed to Brennan to be a less than effusive show of shared grief. Were these two brothers incapable of showing emotion to each other?

'I was about to ask your brother some questions, Mr Crosby, but seeing that you've suddenly reappeared and seeing that you didn't occupy your room here last night, I'd like to know where you've been.'

Gilbert Crosby cast a quick glance in Batsford's direction, but the journalist had removed himself to stand by the window and was gazing out at the gas-lit scene below.

'Out and about, Sergeant.'

'Where exactly?'

'Here and there.'

Brennan frowned then nodded. 'Very well. Once I've finished speaking with your brother, we can continue this fruitful little chat in more suitable surroundings. The station's only a short walk away.'

Gilbert's face flushed. 'It's rather private,' he said with a nod in Batsford's direction. He evidently wished to keep his wanderings away from journalistic interest.

'Very well. We'll speak in a few minutes. For now, I'd like you to remain where you are and say nothing. Is that clear?'

Gilbert gave a sharp nod. He appeared to dislike being given orders.

Brennan approached Simeon Crosby, who raised his head in acknowledgement of the imminent questioning. 'Mr Crosby, this is a very difficult question, but can you think of anyone who might have wished harm to your wife?'

Crosby shook his head. When he spoke, his voice was low, flat, much of his self-confidence now absent. 'Violet was a good woman, Sergeant. A good woman.'

'But did anyone hold a grudge against her?'

'No one. Why should they? She had the sweetest nature…' He gave a short, bitter laugh. 'All she did was support me. And read.' He sobbed. 'If it hadn't been for that damned novel she was reading, she'd have suffered no headache, would have been with me…' His voice broke, the futility of hindsight seeming to stifle his words.

Brennan recalled the novel he had seen on her bedside table.

Crosby took a deep breath and regained his composure. He slowly shook his head. 'You know, I think she met far more people in her novels than ever she did in the real world. Novels *were* her real world.' He cast a quick glance at Batsford, who remained steadfastly looking through the window, his dim reflection on the glass showing a fixed stare, his eyes seemingly unfocused and unmoving.

'You say she had complained of a headache tonight. That she felt too unwell to accompany you.'

'Yes.' Crosby's tone was curious, cautious now.

'Was that unusual?'

Crosby looked up at him. 'What do you mean? The headache or the fact she didn't come with me?'

Brennan shrugged. 'Both.'

In a sudden movement that surprised the detective, Crosby stood up and faced him squarely.

'My wife frequently had headaches, Sergeant. As I told you, she read voraciously. It tends to bring on eye strain and headaches. Tonight was to be the first time she accompanied me to the talk. Batsford here will agree with me that she often suffered from such headaches.' He turned towards the journalist, whose sudden stiffening of pose indicated an awareness of what had just been said.

Batsford turned round. 'That's quite right, Sergeant.'

'I see.' Brennan paused before continuing. 'When you left your wife, was she in bed?'

'Yes. With that infernal book in her hands, despite the pain it must surely have brought her.'

'Forgive the next question, Mr Crosby. You might find it a bit indelicate, but, well, was she wearing her night dress?'

Crosby's eyes widened. 'What sort of question...'

Brennan held up his hands. 'I apologise, but I do need to know.'

'Why?'

'Because she was fully dressed when you found her.'

Crosby frowned then seemed at a loss. Finally he said, 'I didn't notice... in all the... I didn't notice.'

Brennan went on. 'Did she give any indication that she might be expecting someone?'

Now, Crosby's eyes flared in anger. 'What the blazes do you mean by that?'

Batsford stared at the detective, his expression one of distaste.

'It appears that a young woman called earlier tonight.' He placed undue emphasis on the words *young woman* in order to remove the sting of any suggestion of impropriety in his question.

Batsford stepped forward. 'What young woman?'

'She said her name was Woodruff. She told the attendant downstairs that she had an appointment to see Mrs Crosby.'

'Nonsense!' Crosby snapped. 'My wife had no *appointment*. She had a headache!'

Brennan gave Batsford an enquiring look, but the journalist signalled his perplexity.

He now turned to the journalist. 'Did you speak with Mrs Crosby earlier tonight, Mr Batsford?'

'The last time we spoke was earlier in the day.'

'Ah, I remember. You took Mrs Crosby to Mesnes Park.'

For a moment, Batsford's eyes widened in surprise. 'She needed some fresh air. Simeon here needed some time on his own. To prepare his talk.'

Crosby looked at the journalist then at Brennan. He gave a short nod to confirm what he had just been told.

'You didn't see her at all tonight?'

Batsford glanced at Crosby. 'I was about to knock on their door to walk down with them, but when I got there, Simeon here was already leaving.'

'You didn't see or hear his wife?'

The journalist appeared to give this some thought. 'No. I heard Simeon bid farewell to Violet. He said something about putting down the volume she was reading and to try to get some sleep. He seemed most concerned for her welfare.'

'I see.' Brennan waited a few moments before asking his next question. 'The trouble we witnessed tonight. At the Public Hall. It seems tempers were quite high. Has anyone made threats against you, Mr Crosby? Personal threats, I mean.'

Crosby gave a close-lipped smile. 'You think the riot tonight was an expression of support? Your chief constable himself told me about letters that had been sent to your local newspaper. But for every vociferous objector, there are hundreds of silent supporters. The death penalty can be the final arbiter of justice.'

He fell quiet, and Brennan wondered if he were even now thinking about the punishment that would be meted out to the one who murdered his wife, perhaps regretting the fact that it wouldn't be his hand that pulled the lever.

'It was hardly a riot, Mr Crosby,' Brennan replied. He'd seen riots during the miners' strike last year. The skirmish outside the Public

Hall was a mere picnic by comparison. 'But I meant something more individual, threats directed at you face to face perhaps, that we haven't been made aware of.'

Batsford cleared his throat. 'You could do worse than speak to the fellow who organised tonight's march and its consequences, Sergeant. I happened to attend a meeting he conducted last night at that pub across the way.' He gave a nod in the direction of the Legs of Man Public House in Market Place. 'He was most anxious that Simeon here be silenced. One bright spark even suggested tarring and feathering him.'

Brennan took out his notebook and pencil. 'I've seen the posters. Evelyne, isn't it?'

'That's the one. Unpleasant chap. Righteousness oozing out of every pore.'

'Right then.' Brennan closed his notebook, a signal that the interview was at an end. 'That should be all for now.' He turned to Gilbert Crosby, who had been sitting in a small upright chair all the while, head down and hands clasped, uttering not one word. 'And now, Mr Gilbert, perhaps we could have a little chat in your room. Just to change the scenery, eh?'

*

It won't do, Maria Woodruff told herself. *It simply won't do.*

She had to be sure!

She looked down at her hands – delicate, slender, milk white – and they were trembling.

And yet, what damage they could do!

The room she had taken at the Victoria Hotel was spacious enough, although it was situated at the side of the building that overlooked the ramshackle Wigan Railway Station, and there were times when the noise of trains arriving and departing, the hiss and belch of steam, the clank of the locomotives coupled with the slamming of doors and the shouts of platform guards, made her close her eyes and think longingly of the forest near her childhood home, the gentle susurration of the brook, the shrill whistlesong of invisible birds high in the branches, the soothing breeze and the fluttering leaves and the cool, welcoming soil as she lay hypnotised by the occasional flashes of sunlight…

She had been so happy as a child!

Strange, she thought, gazing down at the notebook that lay on the small table before her. Things never turn out the way you wish them to.

In a perfect world, where everything happens that you want to happen, tonight would have gone so differently. But as she had walked along with the others from the Market Square, as she had spoken to that strange creature with his abominable photograph and tried to make enquiries about his purpose for being in the march, she had realised that, despite the deep desire she had to make a success of what she was undertaking, why, things occurred that forced you into another pathway altogether.

Like the time she had ventured into the forest with her closest friend back then, Beatie. And the mist, that had been clinging to the fields, had slowly grown in strength to fill the entire forest with a thick, impenetrable fog, and familiar paths, that they had always rushed along with giggles and a dizzying sense of abandon, suddenly became mysterious and stealthy and treacherous. Trees, whose shapes were ordinarily so familiar, assumed the twisted features of ghoulish ogres, slowly swaying and spreading their skeletal arms towards them in a hellish embrace…

The man who had chased them was nothing more than a vagrant, but his sudden appearance behind a fog-shrouded bush had terrified them.

Since that day and those terrors, she had always regarded the forest as a place of deception, a place of secrets, and there were times when it was best left alone.

Left alone.

The phrase had an unwanted resonance and she shivered.

I shouldn't have come to this place.

But even as the thought took shape in her head she discounted it. For that would be the same view *he* would express. And she would never give him the satisfaction of proving him right. She hated him.

She gave a long sigh and picked up her pen. She opened the notebook, flicked through several pages until she came to the one she wanted to examine – for the umpteenth time.

There was no mistake. Either it was a coincidence of epic proportions or...

She began to underline what she had written some time ago. She would need to delve further into this. It wouldn't do at all to regard the day as any sort of failure. She had plenty to write about. Of course she did.

But she had to be sure of her facts. A good reporter must rely on her facts. And a likeness behind a glass frame was hardly proof.

Five minutes later, she stared in frustration at the number of underlined words in her notebook and placed her pen, very carefully, on the table. She looked around the room and was suddenly filled with an enormous sense of worthlessness. She remembered the painting in her father's study – a vivid copy of Titian's *Sisyphus* – where the Corinthian king, who had tricked the gods on several occasions, was condemned to forever carry a rock to the top of a mountain, only to see it roll back down, and he was forced to start all over again.

Life is hard, my dear, if you thwart the gods, her father had warned her in that stern way of his.

She'd had no idea what *thwarting the gods* meant, and she had no intention of doing anything to upset any god, mythical or Christian. Not back then, at any rate. No, she would have to seek another opportunity to speak with the man, ask him about the face that lay behind the glass frame.

Suddenly, she heard a commotion below her window. Raised voices, a gaggle of women, by the sound of it. At first, she thought they were arguing, but as she raised the window slightly, to allow the sounds to become clearer, she heard one woman say, 'Well don't just take my word for it…'

One of her companions said, 'Aye. I heerd it an' all. Nelly Clegg got told off her old man. He were in t'bar.'

'Bloody place is goin' to the dogs.'

'Aye. An' all Ding Dong Bell can do is prosecute hard-workin' land-lords for afters.'

'You *sure* that woman were murdered? I mean, in t'Royal, of all places?'

'Aye. Throat cut from ear to ear. Blood all over t'place. Swimmin' in it, she were.'

'Couldn't be bloody swimmin' in it if she were dead, you daft sod.'

'You know what I mean. Anyroad, I got told 'er 'ead were just hangin' on wi' a bit o' skin.'

'Bugger off!'

Laughter then, and the sound of clogs fading away.

Maria quietly closed the window and moved to the door, where her coat was hanging from a peg. She could feel her heart beating faster as she opened the door and stepped onto the small landing, wondering if she should really be doing what she was about to do.

Thwarting the gods, Maria?

*

Throughout the interview, Gilbert Crosby stood with his back to the window, hands clasped firmly behind his back and his chest thrust so far out that he appeared to be peering over it whenever he responded to Brennan's questions. Brennan had seen the attitude before – the stance was a physical attempt to dominate proceedings, along with a supposedly hidden intention to avoid any awkward questions by bluster and, if need be, outright lies.

'I don't see that it's of any concern of yours, Sergeant. What I choose to do with my own time is my own business.'

'I agree,' Brennan replied. He'd sat in the upright chair by the door, one arm across its back, a leisurely pose, deliberately at odds with his companion's. 'And under normal circumstances I would accept your refusal to answer.' He paused. 'But, of course, you'll agree these are not normal circumstances. Your sister-in-law has been found murdered.'

'And I'm devastated. As is my brother. But I don't see how my whereabouts have any bearing on what took place. You should be out there—' Here, he swept his arm dramatically backwards to indicate the Sodom and Gomorrah beyond the window, 'hunting the beast down.'

'And I will. But I wouldn't be doing my job if I didn't make full enquiries of everyone close to the victim. You're her brother-in-law. You travelled here with her. And yet you absent yourself from the hotel for an entire day, not sleeping in the room you've paid for. At the same time, you fail to support your brother at his public meeting when I presume he would have appreciated your presence. It's curious behaviour at the best of times. And this is the worst of times, is it not? So. I'll ask you once more. Where have you been for the last twenty-four hours?'

Gilbert seemed about to give an angry retort, but by some supreme effort of will, he controlled himself. 'I was occupied. With a woman.'

'A prostitute?'

Gilbert blinked. 'You're very direct.'

'I don't have time for subtlety, Mr Crosby. You were with the woman all last night? All today?'

'Yes.'

'What's her name?'

Gilbert snorted.

'I need her name.'

'Why?'

'She's your alibi.'

The man's eyes widened. 'You're suggesting... what? That I killed my own sister-in-law?'

Brennan shook his head. 'I'm suggesting you tell me the name of the woman you slept with.'

Crosby took a deep breath and gripped his hands tighter behind his back. Brennan noticed the scar that ran along the right side of his face seemed to throb and become inflamed, a sign, perhaps, of the immense effort of will to control his anger? He saw how this man could become very violent very quickly.

'We didn't get as far as names,' he replied, imbuing his words with a lewdness he appeared to be relishing.

Brennan sighed. 'Address then.'

Gilbert smirked. 'It was dark. Both when I arrived at the doxy's house and when I left. Haven't got round to installing gas lighting where she lives.'

'Where did you meet her?'

'At choir practice.' When he saw the policeman bristle he added, 'Where do you think? I met her on the street.'

'You offered someone ten pounds last night.'

This seemed to throw Gilbert, for he blinked rapidly and set his lips firmly together. 'How the blazes did you...?' He gave a heavy sigh, conscious of having inadvertently admitted to something. 'You're well informed, Sergeant. Yes, I did offer some ruffian money.'

'Why?'

'Isn't that obvious?'

'You needed a prostitute.'

'A reliable prostitute, if that isn't a contradiction in terms.' He paused, as if considering whether he should elaborate. 'I was assured there was such a creature. But I would have to go to her. She didn't deign to roam the streets.'

Brennan thought back to what he had been told by Seddon, the landlord of the Old Dog. He overheard Gilbert Crosby offer this unnamed *ruffian* ten pounds, only for him to refuse. No man in this town – ruffian or not – would refuse an offer of ten pounds just for pointing a stranger in the direction of a prostitute. Whatever he offered him the money for, it wasn't a woman. After the spurned offer, they'd whispered something Seddon couldn't hear. Maybe *that* was the real reason for the expense.

Which meant the hangman's brother was lying.

'Who is this chap you spoke to?' Brennan asked.

'I don't know. I met him in some flea-bitten establishment that grandiosely refers to itself as a music hall. We got to talking, as one does in places like that.'

Brennan realised he wasn't going to get much out of this man, not at the moment at any rate. He changed tack. 'How did you get on with Mrs Crosby?'

'Violet? We got on well enough.'

'And how would you describe their marriage?'

The question seemed to confuse him. 'I don't understand.'

'Did they get along?'

'Of course they did. My brother was devoted to her. And she to him.'

'Can you think of anyone who might wish to harm her?'

He shook his head. 'She was an angel, Sergeant. A veritable angel.'

The feeble smile that accompanied his words suggested the relief he felt that the questions had veered away from the awkward.

At this point, Brennan stood up and placed his hand on the door handle. 'Just a few final questions, Mr Crosby. This *ruffian* you met last night. The one who directed you to your temporary sweetheart. Did he accompany you?'

'Certainly not.'

'He gave you directions?'

Gilbert Crosby hesitated, sensing the trap the sergeant had set for him. 'No, he gave me no directions.'

'Then how did you know where to go, to call on this woman?'

'I said he gave *me* no directions, Sergeant. He did, however, tell the cabbie I hired where to go. Unfortunately, I didn't quite catch the address.'

Brennan gave a curt nod, realising that he wouldn't get more out of the man at the moment. 'It goes without saying that you and your brother, along with Mr Batsford, must remain here in Wigan for the next few days.'

'My brother has a speaking engagement tomorrow night. In Manchester.'

'I hardly think he would wish to fulfil that engagement now, under the circumstances.' Brennan was amazed at the man's insensitivity. He shook his head and left the room.

Smarmy, cold-hearted bastard, he thought, stepping into the corridor. *And a lying one, at that.*

Then his heart sank.

Captain Bell's head appeared on the stairs, quickly followed by the rest of his ascending body.

CHAPTER THIRTEEN

A group of men were standing at the bar, their occasional laughter followed by low-voiced conversations and furtive glances. They could be pitmen plotting the next strike, Evelyne reflected as he sat by the window, enjoying his fourth pint and feeling more relaxed now. Or possibly anarchists, he thought, conspiring where to commit their next atrocity. But then he smiled at the thought of anarchists meeting here in a lowly hotel in Wigan. Didn't they meet in smoky dens in London and bear Italian or French names? Besides, wouldn't the very name of the hotel – The Queen's – render the place anathema to those with staunchly anarchist views?

My thoughts are rambling. This beer must be quite a potent brew!

At that moment, the door swung open, a cold blast of air swept through the small bar and Evelyne's spirits fell: it was the one he'd seen a few minutes ago, the simpleton who'd caused the affray in King Street. There was something rather strange about the fellow, he thought. For one thing, he stood in the doorway, one foot propping the door open, and for another, he was blinking rapidly, as if he had something affecting his vision and was desperately trying to remove it. He had both hands shoved deep into his pockets.

Then one of the men at the bar shouted, 'Hey, shut that bloody door! Bloody freezin' wi' that thing open.'

The others – miners or anarchists – concurred, but the newcomer simply stood there, blinking and giving every appearance of being totally bemused by his surroundings, until Evelyne saw one of the men detach himself from the others and mutter, 'Some bugger needs a good hidin'!' before heading for the door.

Evelyne, sensing that, for some reason, he shared a bond of common purpose with the new arrival, stood up and grabbed him by the arm, at the same time kicking the offending door shut.

'Is this mon wi' thee, pal?' the miner/anarchist growled.

'No,' Evelyne replied. 'I think the fellow's got something in his eye.'

'Aye,' came the reply. 'My fist if he opens that bloody door again.'

Satisfied with the requisite guffaw from his cronies, the man returned to the bar and nodded back in Evelyne's direction, muttering something that ended with the phrase, 'Not from round 'ere, anyroad.'

Oscar Pardew allowed himself to be led to the table by the window and sat down. The blinking became less pronounced, and finally, he focused his eyes on his saviour, offering an outstretched hand in gratitude. 'I'm Oscar,' he said.

Evelyne took his hand and was surprised by the strength of the handshake.

'Thomas Evelyne.'

Then Evelyne looked down at his hand – it felt wet, gritty. His eyes opened wide when he saw the blood.

'What the hellfire…?'

'Sorry,' Oscar said. 'I cut myself on Dead Father. In the fighting.'

Evelyne stared at him for a while then took out a handkerchief and wiped his hand. It was already clear that the man was unhinged.

For an uncomfortably long time, Oscar stared back at him. Finally, he blinked a few times and said, 'I saw you earlier.'

Evelyne nodded. 'And I saw you. You caused quite a stir outside the Public Hall.'

Oscar frowned. 'The policeman tried to hit me.' Then he shook his head and said, 'But no. Not then. I didn't see you then. Not when the policeman tried to hit me. I saw you earlier.'

'Ah, you mean the meeting then? In the Market Square?'

Oscar swallowed hard and nodded. 'Yes. I was talking to a woman. She was asking me all kinds of questions. I tried to show her my father but she didn't want to see him. And my sister, of course.'

Evelyne shifted in his seat. *Perhaps I should have let the man thump him*, he thought.

'You don't like Mr Crosby, do you?'

'No,' said Evelyne. 'I don't.'

'But he hangs people, doesn't he?' Oscar began to snigger, as if suddenly he'd thought of something quite amusing.

'What's funny?'

'I was thinking of what the Thuggees did.'

'Who?'

Oscar placed a hand on Evelyne's shoulder and leaned towards him, whispering in his ear, 'They used to annoy the hangman, you see? In India. They'd stand on the scaffold and launch themselves into the noose and jump off the scaffold, and there was nothing the hangman could do to stop them. He wanted it to be slow and dignified with all sorts of things read out. But those Thuggees… they insulted the law by doing what they did. I can't see Mr Crosby letting them do that! He'd make them wait. Suffer. My sister told me that's what Mr Crosby did with…'

Evelyne pulled away as his voice grew louder. The man's breath

145

was hot on his ear and foul-smelling. He could see others in the bar watching the two of them.

'Interesting,' Evelyne said with a forced smile. 'Look, can I get you a drink?'

Oscar looked down at the empty glass on the table. 'Why?'

Evelyne shrugged. 'I'd like you to have a pint on me. Is that so strange? After what we've both been through tonight. A shared adventure and a positive outcome. You just wait here, Oscar.'

He went over to the bar, studiously avoiding the men at the far end who were giving him curious and not altogether friendly glances. He'd give the man his drink then plead tiredness and leave him to it. Once he'd been served, he carried the frothing pint back to the window table and sat down. He was surprised when his new-found companion picked up the pint and held it up to the light.

Immediately, one of the men at the bar yelled out, 'Heyup, Billy. What d'you reckon?'

The man behind the bar, evidently the one being addressed, looked across to glare at Oscar, who was still holding the glass to the light.

'Summat up wi' that pint, pal?' the man shouted.

All of a sudden the room fell silent as all eyes turned on the newcomer.

Oscar turned his gaze upon the barman and said, 'Mr Evelyne here asked me to have a pint on him.'

The barman shrugged. 'Well sup it then an' stop bein' a smart-arse.'

Whereupon Oscar leaned forward, held out his hand and poured the entire contents of the pint glass over Evelyne's head.

Evelyne gasped for air and was frantically wiping the beer from his eyes, unable to witness the barman rush from the bar and raise Oscar by the neck while one of his customers kindly held the door open as Oscar was hurled back into the cold night.

*

Brennan always felt that the chief constable's face would be put to better use as a portrait hanging in the window of a funeral undertaker, so cadaverous were his features. Now more than ever, as they stood face to face in the room where Mrs Violet Crosby had recently met her painful end, Captain Bell had the appearance more of a funeral mute than the chief constable of Wigan. His eyes were dark with hooded eyelids, and his cheekbones protruded as if the skeleton beneath the skin were trying to force its way through. But it was the way he held his lips tightly closed, with the pressure removing all colour from them, that made Brennan wonder what the man's wife must think every morning when she wakes beside him: is he asleep – or dead?

Brennan's explanation of the circumstances of finding the woman's body was met with a stern silence that only now seemed about to be broken as his superior took a deep breath.

'You had the full complement of the constabulary at your disposal, Sergeant.'

'I did indeed, sir.'

'You knew that Mr Crosby was *persona non grata* in the eyes of some in this town?'

'Yes, sir.'

'And yet the poor chap returns to his beloved wife to find her strangled in her own hotel room.'

'That is about the size of it, sir, yes.'

The chief constable swallowed hard, unsure if Brennan were being obedient or insubordinate. 'It never entered into your head that the man's wife needed protecting?'

For a moment, Brennan felt like asking the same question back, but instead, he decided to limit his responses to the plain truth. 'I didn't know she was staying behind, sir.'

'No one saw fit to tell you?'

'The men had instructions to bring Mr Crosby and his wife to the Public Hall by the route you chose, sir. And when Mr Crosby told them his wife was feeling unwell, they carried on with their instructions. Mr Batsford, the journalist, made his way to King Street on foot, again as you instructed.'

'Alone?'

'Of course not, sir. One of the men went with him.'

'I see. And you have spoken with the hotel staff?'

'Yes, sir.'

'Some of them can have tendencies, you realise.'

'Tendencies?'

'Light-fingered, some of them. If *I* were conducting the investigation, I should take a particular interest in that aspect of the case. A light-fingered bellboy, for instance, creeping into a darkened room which he thinks is unoccupied...'

He let the scenario drift away, as if in some way it would find a home in his sergeant's brain.

But Brennan was thinking along other lines.

Let me do the police work.

His superior's background was military. He doubted if the man had ever taken part in any sort of criminal investigation, certainly nothing as serious as a murder inquiry.

Captain Bell went silent for a while then said, 'Well I'm sure you know what you're doing. But this is a very bad business, Sergeant. The country's foremost executioner comes to deliver a talk on his experiences, and his wife is brutally murdered. Doesn't look good now, does it?'

'No, sir.'

To Brennan, it was clear that the man saw tonight as a slur on his reputation. He'd already failed to gain one appointment beyond the north of England. He might well be envisioning another set of interviews in another southern county and facing the inevitable observation that he was the man in charge when Mrs Simeon Crosby came to such a dreadful end.

And you expect this board to consider you a fit person to fulfil the onerous duties of our chief constable? Really!

'I will expect regular reports on the matter, Sergeant. Is that clear? Regular and detailed reports that will unambiguously record the progress you are making. Do you understand?'

'Of course, sir. Regular and detailed. As ever.'

He couldn't help throwing that last phrase in.

Captain Bell gave a sharp cough, nodded and left the room.

It's been a strange night, Brennan thought. First of all, Mrs Crosby declines to accompany her husband to the Public Hall because she has a headache. When Simeon Crosby left her in their hotel room she was in bed, presumably her nightdress, and settling down with a novel. Yet when her body was found, the woman was fully clothed.

Had she left the room? Gone down to reception, ordered something to eat or drink?

No one had mentioned such a thing, but he would be sure to ask.

And then the circuitous route Crosby had been driven to the Public Hall – a route devised by his lordship himself – had failed to avoid a violent confrontation with the protesters, who had appeared to be orderly, if a little loud, until some fool had charged down the middle of the crowd and shrieked out Crosby's name. That had been the spark to inflame the marchers and all hell had broken out.

Afterwards, once a few of them had been dragged down to the station, Crosby had given his talk and Brennan had returned with him to the Royal.

Where earlier, a woman had arrived at the hotel claiming she had an appointment to see Mrs Crosby. But there was no answer when the boy went to her room.

Who was this woman? And what was the nature of her appointment?

And then, of course, someone had hurled a brick through the hotel bar window.

Who? A local rough? Someone still smouldering from the foiled attempt to silence the hangman?

Ralph Batsford had expressed concern about the man who led the protesters tonight – Evelyne. According to the journalist, Evelyne had been scathing in his denunciation of Simeon Crosby. Had Evelyne taken his dislike of Crosby and everything he stood for several steps further? But holding views against capital punishment was hardly the spur to murder – going so far as to kill the man's wife would be hypocritical, to say the least.

And where had Gilbert Crosby been last night and most of the day? Was he enjoying the dubious delights of one of Wigan's ladies all that time, as he claimed? Or had he been somewhere else?

Brennan shook his head to disperse the thoughts buzzing in his head. He went over to the window, unlocked it and opened it wide to let the cold air swirl into the room. He wondered what Ellen and Barry were doing at this moment. Barry would be asleep, of course. He looked at his watch and saw that it was almost eleven o'clock. But Ellen. Was she lying awake, waiting for the front door to swing open? He smiled. She was used to him coming home late. She'd be asleep, too. Bless her. Bless them both.

He was about to close the window when he glanced down to the street below. He could hear the noise from the downstairs bar as the barman was in the process of urging them all to *sup up*. But across the street, he caught sight of a figure, half hidden in the shadows of a shop doorway. There was something about its actions – furtive, almost – that aroused his curiosity. He gently closed the window and stepped out into the corridor, reaching the stairs and taking them two at a time.

CHAPTER FOURTEEN

Maria Woodruff stood in the doorway of the shop facing the Royal Hotel and watched the man walk quickly down the steps of the hotel and cross the road. He seemed to be heading to her right, back towards the centre of the town when suddenly, he veered to his right and made rapid progress to where she was standing.

'Can you tell me what you are doing, miss?' he asked, pulling his coat collar close against the bitter cold.

'I beg your pardon?'

She gave him a stare of defiance. It was highly probable that this man was a police detective, she told herself. He had left the hotel where a murder had been committed, and his manner suggested someone who was used to asking questions and expecting answers. Besides, who else would ask such a thing on a foul night like this? It wasn't the usual conversational gambit spoken by a roué.

She smiled. 'I'm trying to keep warm.' Nervously she toyed with the small bag she was holding.

'And your name is?'

She appeared to give the question some thought before replying. 'I'm Maria Woodruff. I'm a journalist.'

'My name's Brennan. I'm a policeman.' He cast a quick glance back towards the hotel, where he spotted Constable Jaggery lumbering up the steps and looking none too pleased with life. 'Perhaps you'd like to continue our conversation over there? It's drier and warmer.'

'I wasn't aware we were having a *conversation.* Is it a crime to take shelter from the cold in Wigan?'

'I'd be more than happy to get my colleague over there to help escort you across. He's not much in the way of courtesy, mind.'

Realising how embarrassing such a course of action would be, she gave a shrug and walked past him, crossing the road unescorted, as it were. Within a few minutes, she was sitting facing him in a small office.

'Now, Miss Woodruff. I gather you were here earlier tonight.'

It was a statement, she realised, not a question.

'Mr Gray at the reception desk told me a Miss Woodruff had been here asking to see Mrs Crosby.'

She raised her chin and her eyes sparkled.

She's a pretty young thing, reflected Brennan. *And spirited.*

'Yes, that's true. I had an appointment to see her.'

'What about?'

'Before I answer that particular question, may I ask if the rumour is true? That Mrs Crosby has been found murdered?'

'Yes. It's true.'

The news, confirmed, seemed to disturb her. Her lower lip began to tremble, and she looked to be fighting back tears.

'I had arranged an appointment to see her tonight.'

'But she was supposed to be attending a talk given by her husband until she pleaded a headache. Which means she lied to her husband.' Brennan thought for a while then said, 'What did you wish to see Mrs Crosby about?'

'I'm writing a series of articles for a London magazine on the subject of capital punishment. Oh,' she said quickly, seeing the cynical glaze that flitted across his eyes, 'not the usual stuff, abolitionist arguments or the trenchant views of its supporters, no. These articles are about the human aspect, if you like. I've already had several articles published. One where I interviewed the wife of an executed murderer, her feelings before, during and after the trial, the morning of the execution, her struggle today to bring up three fatherless children. Many of the people I've spoken to are relatives of the victims of murder though. Earlier, in fact, I spoke with a man who seemed to me most disturbed.'

'Oh? Who was he?'

'Scruffy-looking chap. I don't know his name. But he told me his father had been murdered and that his killer was executed by Mr Crosby. I was interested and wanted to know more but then he showed me...'

'What?'

'A photograph he said he carried with him always. Of his sister with his dead father.'

'What was so strange about that?'

She took a deep breath. 'When I say *his dead father* I mean just that. Have you ever heard of photographing the dead, Sergeant?'

He nodded. 'I've heard of it. Never seen it in practice though.'

'The photograph showed his sister holding hands with his father, who was staring directly into the camera. But the photographer had actually prised open the dead man's eyes and then taken the picture. People do the same when a child dies. They sit the corpse in a chair, dressed in all his or her finery. Sometimes the photographer opens their eyes. For the grieving family, it's supposed to create a final lasting memory of a lost loved one. In my view, it's disgusting. Until that moment, I thought the man might prove an interesting source – the mourning son whose father's killer was hanged by Crosby. But after five minutes in his company, I was disturbed, to say the least. In my view, the man was deranged.'

Deranged.

The word resonated with Brennan. He would like to speak with this man who carries a macabre photograph around. But why would he want to kill the wife of the man who hanged his father's killer?

Maria gave him a look of defiance. 'But you have no wish to hear about my work, do you?'

'Tell me more about Mrs Crosby.'

'It's never been done, you see? The reflections, the sentiments of a woman whose husband is one of the select few men in England allowed to take a life. I've spoken to relatives of the murderers, relatives of the victims, but no one has ever recorded the views and feelings of the executioner's wife.'

'She was willing to share those feelings?'

Maria Woodruff nodded. 'She is quite a spirited woman, Sergeant.' She dropped her gaze and fumbled with her hands as she realised what she had just said. 'I'm sorry.'

'Go on.'

'It was actually Mrs Crosby who contacted *me*. She wrote how she had read my articles and admired them. She said I have a novelist's eye for the telling detail.'

Brennan remembered the novel beside the woman's bed.

'We exchanged letters. She asked me to write to her at her sister's address in Morecambe. It was to be kept from her husband. I think she enjoyed the thrill of it all. The intrigue. Like something from the novels she told me she loved reading.'

'Her husband is in the process of writing his own book, is he not?'

A flash of anger bolted across her face, but it vanished quickly, like lightning in a disturbed sky.

'He isn't *writing his own book*, as you say. He's merely providing the information. Someone else is doing the writing.'

'Ah yes. Mr Batsford. Another journalist. Do you know him, by any chance?'

A frown spread across her forehead. 'There are male journalists, Sergeant Brennan, a huge number of them, and there are female ones. Pitifully few of us as yet. Let's say there is a distance to travel before the two sides meet on a mutually respectful level.'

'So you know him?'

'I've met him, yes.'

From the set expression on her face, he knew he would get no further with this particular line of questioning.

'Mrs Crosby arranged to meet you tonight? At what time?'

'I was to call here at the hotel and ask to be shown to her room just after eight. By which time her husband would be well into his verbal stride. We would then have just short of an hour to ourselves. I spent the earlier part of the evening listening to Mr Thomas Evelyne address the crowd in the Market Square.'

'You've spoken with Mr Evelyne?'

A slight hesitation. 'I have. It's important to gather as many views as you can. I had intended to speak with him tomorrow, but he's leaving early.' She glanced down at her hands.

Was she keeping something back?

'Do you know where Mr Evelyne is staying?'

'The Queen's Hotel, he told me.'

He wrote the information in his notebook.

'I see. So, what happened when you came here?'

156

'I stood there at the desk, gave my name and my appointment and waited for the bellboy to return, fully expecting him to escort me to her room. But he came back and said there was no answer when he knocked. I asked him to go back. She might well have fallen asleep, I told him. I also told him to knock louder.'

'And?'

'That officious fool behind the desk told him not to. So I asked to go up myself and save the boy's legs any further trouble and then the man got quite brusque. Said it was against the rules or some such nonsense. We had words. Then I left.'

'You didn't return?'

'I did.'

Brennan's eyes widened. 'When?'

'About five minutes ago when you came across the road and dragged me back here.' The smile that accompanied her words contained not a hint of humour.

'Why did you come back here? Morbid curiosity?'

'Professional curiosity, Sergeant. I'm staying at the Victoria Hotel, near the station. I heard people talking excitedly about what had happened here and so I returned. I am, as I say, a reporter. And reporters are interested in news.' She suddenly opened the bag she was carrying and extracted a small, leather-bound notebook, holding it almost with reverence. 'The notes in here will turn miraculously into articles, to be read throughout the land.' He saw something in her eyes, a sudden shiftiness, which suggested that this woman wasn't telling him the whole truth.

'It looked to me you were hiding across there. Surely a reporter would be more… assertive?'

She took a deep breath and returned the notebook to her bag. 'In case you haven't noticed, I'm a woman. A male reporter would bluster his way into the hotel on some pretext. I was here earlier, and I don't think I'd be welcome.'

'Aren't you contradicting yourself? You come as a journalist and hide because you're a woman?'

'I was biding my time.'

'For what?'

A slight hesitation, then, 'Any opportunity to show itself. Mr Crosby out for a walk, for example.'

'Mr Crosby would be hardly likely to do that now, would he? With his wife lying dead in a mortuary.'

'True, but I was referring to Mr Crosby's brother. I believe there was some distance between him and his sister-in-law.'

'She told you?'

'I can read between the lines, Sergeant. Sometimes things unsaid speak louder than things said.'

For a second, she glanced down and examined her hands once more. 'Now if that will be all?'

Brennan nodded and watched her leave the room, one question gnawing at him.

What are you leaving unsaid, Miss Woodruff?

*

When she left the Royal Hotel, Maria Woodruff knew exactly what she had to do. She was angry at the way the policeman had spoken to her. Angry, too, at the thoughts that were swirling around her head like peevish wasps. She stormed across the road and turned left, deciding that there would be nothing to gain from staying around the hotel now, her original intentions having been quashed by her unfortunate encounter with Sergeant Brennan.

As she made her way into Market Place, where a tram was shunting its way along the reversing triangle, she caught sight of a small group of men standing beneath a large lamp in the centre of the road, clapping their hands and shuffling their feet.

Why not simply go home? It's freezing. Men are such fools!

One or two of them nudged each other and made crude comments in loud whispers. There was a burst of laughter. For a moment, Maria was tempted to make her way towards them, confront their despicable lewdness and shame them in full view of the rest of the people on the street. But she contained the impulse.

No point in making a show of myself. These men will never change. As hard and unyielding and intelligent as the cobbles they stood on. Besides, I have much to do.

She walked on, head held slightly higher, ignoring their filth. It was why she failed to notice the one who was following her, the one who had been behind her since she left the Royal Hotel.

*

Brennan recognised Constable Jaggery's mood at once. He'd appeared to be quite in his element when the trouble started in King Street – there was nothing Freddie Jaggery liked more than a good scrap – and he'd dragged several subdued offenders back to the station where inevitably he would have shown them to their overnight accommodation with great relish. Now, though, with the action presumably over for the night and with the slow and (in Jaggery's view) tedious process of investigation facing him, he looked in low spirits.

'Bit of a bugger, though,' he said as he and Brennan stood in the deserted dining room.

'What is, Constable?'

'I mean, meladdo's a hangman an' lo an' be-bloody-hold, it's his wife wot gets her neck stretched.'

'Not quite true. Though I agree with the sentiment.'

Jaggery shrugged morosely as if he felt that he'd made a contribution to the investigation by his shrewd observation and it had been disregarded.

Brennan reached into his pocket and took out his notebook. Opening it, he extracted the slip of paper that Gray had given him from Eastoe, with the names of the other two guests at the hotel. Commercial travellers, apparently.

'We have two more people to interview, Constable,' he said. 'Plenty to do yet, I'm afraid.'

He was met with a stony silence.

*

It took a while for someone to come to the door. The young man who opened it took one look at the large uniformed constable, and his face was immediately drained of colour. He looked along the second-floor corridor and quickly invited them inside. The room – number five – Brennan noted, was along the corridor, around the corner and three doors away from where Violet Crosby was found.

David Morgan was around twenty-five. He was clean-shaven, with bright blue eyes and light-coloured hair. He was quite handsome, but there was a nervousness, almost a shiftiness in the way he held eye contact for no more than a few seconds before looking elsewhere. He was wearing a dressing gown that had been hastily tied at the waist, and his ruffled hair suggested he'd had his sleep disturbed.

The room was like the others – small, compact. On the bedside table lay a gilt-edged framed photograph of a very pretty young woman.

'Your wife, Mr Morgan?' said Brennan with a nod in that direction.

'Yes,' said Morgan, casting a lingering glance at the small picture. 'I bring her with me on my travels. Silly, I know, but she keeps me company. It can be lonely in my position. I'm a commercial traveller, you know?'

'You know why we're here?'

For a moment, there was a flicker of concern on the young man's face. It vanished as quickly as it had appeared.

'I gather something awful has happened,' he replied.

'Yes. It has.' He paused and took out his notebook and pencil, opening on a fresh page.

Morgan moved over to the bed, sitting on the edge with one leg dangling in mid-air. 'I was asleep, you see – early start tomorrow – and I heard shouting. I thought I was dreaming.'

'As a matter of course, I'm asking those few residents who are staying here about their whereabouts earlier tonight.'

'Earlier? What time?'

'Any time from, say, six thirty.'

'I was here,' Morgan replied. 'Having a lie-down. Then I went down to the dining room around quarter past seven, ate my evening meal. Pork cutlets with tomato sauce. Quite delicious, too.'

'Was anyone else in the dining room?'

He thought for a while, then said, 'Mr Dodds was there. He can vouch for me.'

'He's the other guest, isn't he? Another commercial traveller?'

'Yes.'

'And you returned to this room?'

'Indeed, yes. When I'd finished my orange jelly, that is. That hadn't quite set, a mixture of jelly and soup if truth were known.' He'd meant it to be humorous, but when he saw the policemen fail to catch the humour he gave a nervous cough.

'What time did you come back here?'

Morgan thought for a few seconds. 'Just after eight, I think. I was quite alone.'

A curious thing to say, thought Brennan.

'Did you hear or see anything when you got back?'

'Such as?'

'Anything at all, Mr Morgan.'

The man thought for a moment then said, 'Nothing, Sergeant.' He glanced at the photograph and smiled. 'I just went to bed for an early night. It's my Manchester day tomorrow.'

'I beg your pardon?'

He didn't answer immediately. Instead, he stepped from the bed and reached down beneath its frame to pull out a rather large leather suitcase which he lifted onto the bed. He then flicked it open.

'Bloody 'ell!' was Jaggery's response when he saw what was inside. At the moment, he had the advantage over his sergeant until Morgan turned the case round and displayed the contents.

The case was packed full of a variety of sweets: hard-boiled pepper-mints and lemon, Turkish delight, jelly beans, peanut brittle, aniseed twists, their bright colours enhanced by the sudden waft of tangy, sugary aromas.

Forgetting for a moment where and who he was, Jaggery reached forward and pointed at a small packet. 'Them's me favourite!' he declared, his eyes shining.

'Ah yes. Everton Toffee Mints. Very popular in Liverpool, where Nobletts make them.' He reached inside and took out one of the mints, handing it to a now beaming Jaggery.

'Leave it!' Brennan snapped.

Reluctantly, Jaggery handed the sweet back.

'We also sell Brierley's Sweet Rollers and Machine Boiling Pans, though naturally, I can't carry them round in this,' said Morgan, avoiding Brennan's gaze and patting the suitcase with some pride. 'Tomorrow, I'm in Manchester, doing my usual rounds.'

'That might not be possible, I'm afraid.' Brennan's voice had suddenly become flinty.

'Why not? I mean, it's my job, you see.'

'I do see, Mr Morgan, but you must see that this is an investigation into a brutal murder, and until I have some answers, I can't allow anyone who was here tonight to leave.'

'Why not?'

Brennan gave him a meaningful look.

You're not that stupid, pal.

Morgan's shoulders slumped.

'Did you happen to call for room service at any time?'

'No. Like I said, I went to bed early. You woke me up, as a matter of fact.'

'You heard no commotion earlier? Shouting? Sounds of a scuffle on the corridor?'

The young man licked his lips and seemed flustered by the question. Finally, he said, 'I'm a heavy sleeper, Sergeant.' He nodded towards the framed photograph. 'My wife is always complaining about it.'

'Did you hear anything tonight on this floor? Any time after you came up for your early night?'

Morgan thought for a while then shook his head. 'No. The place seemed as quiet as the... It was very quiet, Sergeant.'

'I see.' Brennan looked down at his notebook and said, 'Where are you from, Mr Morgan?'

'Pardon?'

'Your home address?'

Morgan cast another quick glance at the young woman, smiling serenely behind the glass frame. 'Why?'

'Because I wish to know.'

Jaggery, who was standing by the door, shifted his stance and coughed. He recognised the sergeant's tone of voice.

Morgan swallowed and gave an address in Chester. 'It's near the cathedral,' he added in a belated attempt to be helpful.

The address was the same as the one recorded in the hotel register.

Brennan closed his notebook, reminded him of his warning not to leave the hotel – 'Manchester Day or no Manchester Day' – then bade him goodnight.

Once they were in the corridor, Jaggery said, 'He got on your nerves, didn't 'e, Sergeant?'

Brennan merely grunted and made his way to the stairs. Their next visit was to Room One on the first floor.

Another commercial traveller.

*

Edgar Dodds rubbed his eyes as if he couldn't quite believe what he was seeing. Granted, thought Brennan, the sight of Freddie Jaggery standing in your doorway was enough to alarm anyone.

Dodds was around his mid-thirties, slightly greying around the temples, his small moustache also betraying tiny wisps of grey. His expression seemed to be much more worldly-wise than David Morgan – there was a sagging to his jowls that gave him a hangdog appearance, more suited to an undertaker than a commercial traveller, and Brennan wondered how on earth this man – a commercial traveller – could speak with enthusiasm about whatever goods he was hawking around the shops. On the bedside table, a half-smoked cigar was smouldering in a tray, and the atmosphere in the room felt heavy with the lingering wisps of cigar smoke.

Notebook at the ready, Brennan asked his whereabouts earlier that evening.

'Why on earth would you want to know that?' said Dodds in a reasonable, even friendly tone.

'You're aware of what's happened here tonight?' Brennan asked.

'I've been asleep, Sergeant. I leave early tomorrow. Something woke me about ten minutes ago – footsteps, people talking. I needed some sustenance.' He pointed to the cigar.

'I'm afraid you won't be leaving tomorrow, sir. You see,' he went on quickly as the man was about to protest, 'there's been a murder.'

'My goodness!'

'And I'm asking the other guests their whereabouts earlier. Say, from six thirty to half-past eight.'

Dodds brushed a hand through his hair, giving him a more dishevelled look. 'I ate alone downstairs. Seven o'clock.'

'Did you see anyone in the dining room?'

A slight hesitation, then, 'Yes, I believe I saw Mr Morgan. He's a traveller, too, you know.'

'We've already spoken to him. What time did you get back to your room?'

'I stayed down for a cigar. Mr Morgan had left by then. Said he was having an early night. I suppose it was quarter to nine when I came up.'

'I see.' Brennan wrote something down in his notebook. 'You didn't hear or see anything untoward?'

'No, Sergeant.'

'What exactly do you sell, Mr Dodds?'

'Cigars, Sergeant.'

'You must be very popular.'

'Cigars are very soothing.'

'I like a cigar myself. Might I have a glance at your stock?'

Dodds gave a frown and shook his head. 'Oh, I'm not carrying any stock, Sergeant. There's no need, you see? I just take orders.'

Brennan regarded him for an uncomfortable length of time. Then he asked him where he lived.

'I don't see how that can be of any help,' came the rather anxious reply.

'Nevertheless, I want your home address.' Brennan's voice had suddenly adopted a harsher tone.

Dodds took a deep breath and gave him an address in Feilden Street, Blackburn. As with Morgan, the address given tallied with the one in the hotel register.

Brennan reminded him of his instruction not to leave the hotel in the morning then bade him goodnight.

As soon as they were alone in the corridor Jaggery said, 'He's lyin', Sergeant.'

'Oh I know that,' said Brennan.

'I mean, a travelling salesman wi' nowt on 'im? Should 'ave a case bulgin' wi' cigars.'

'Oh, I agree. But did you notice something else, Constable?'

'Such as?'

'When I told him there'd been a murder, he didn't ask the obvious question.'

Jaggery kept quiet, not willing to admit that the obvious question wasn't obvious at all.

'He didn't ask who'd been murdered,' Brennan explained patiently. 'Doesn't that strike you as strange, Constable?'

Jaggery had to admit it did.

'There was something else he said – or didn't say – that was strange. Did you notice it, Constable?'

Jaggery, who felt increasingly that he was undergoing some sort of test, shook his head. There was only so much thinking you could do.

Brennan didn't elaborate. Instead, he placed a friendly hand on his constable's shoulder, causing his heart to sink. Whenever the sergeant did that, it meant something unpleasant.

'And now I need you to find a Mr Thomas Evelyne. Do you think you can do that?'

Jaggery glowered. 'Which room is he in then?'

'Oh, he's not staying here.'

'It's past eleven, Sergeant.'

'It is.'

'I've been on me feet since half bloody seven this mornin', Sergeant.' It seemed ages since he'd smelled that rancid fish in the station yard. 'There's some smart constables outside, Sergeant.'

'I don't want a smart constable, Constable. I want you.'

Rebellion seemed to be about to break out on his lips, but he bit them. 'Who is he, this Evelyne bloke?'

Brennan told him.

'So where's he stayin' like? Or do you expect me to charge round every doss-hole in Wigan askin' for some bloke called Evelyne? Sergeant?'

Brennan gave his constable his basilisk glare. 'If I order you to swim the canal and dredge the bottom for dead bodies you'll do just that. Is that clear? Constable?'

Jaggery let out a deep breath. At least he'd got his mutinous feelings off his chest.

'You'll go to the Queen's Hotel. Ask him to accompany you to the station. I'll be there in half an hour. And if for some reason he isn't there, leave word that he must under no circumstances leave town until he has spoken with me. Can you remember all that, Constable?'

Jaggery tapped his head with his forefinger. 'It's already stored.'

Brennan sighed and added, 'And when you're done, you get yourself off home. You must be exhausted, poor chap.'

Always does it, the bugger! Jaggery reflected. *I always end up feeling grateful when he throws me a bone.*

'Thank you, Sergeant,' he mumbled and left the room.

*

It was almost midnight when Brennan arrived back at the station. He was completely drained of energy now, and the prospect of a further interview, this time with the rabble-rousing Mr Evelyne, made him groan with distaste. Still, if the man had told Maria Woodruff he was planning to leave early tomorrow, then it was essential he be spoken to beforehand. He'd organised the march earlier, and the ensuing commotion and stirred-up feelings might well have contributed to the night's tragedy. It had meant that most of the borough's constables were tied up with the disorder in King Street. Was the disturbance used as a distraction for someone to make their way to the Royal?

Brennan gave a heavy sigh and approached the front desk, where the duty sergeant was seated, reading what appeared to be a Penny Dreadful. He could just make out the title: *The Boy Detective, or The Crimes of London.*

'We could do with a couple of boy detectives round here, Sam,' said Brennan, startling his semi-recumbent colleague.

'Bloody 'ell, Mick. Nearly shit meself!'

'Well, you wouldn't be short of paper, eh?' He indicated the volume in his hands. 'Where's my guest?'

'Who would that be then?' The duty sergeant carefully folded the corner of a page and placed the book on his now vacant chair.

'Thomas Evelyne.'

'Oh aye. Constable Jaggery called in on his way home. Said I was to give you a message.'

Brennan's heart sank.

'Said he'd been down to the Queen's like you asked, but the owner told him Evelyne had gone out.'

'Out? Where, at this time?'

His colleague shrugged. 'Jaggery just said he asked the bloke to go up to his room and make sure, and the bloke refused so Jaggery grabbed him an' threatened him with all sorts – gamblin' on unlicensed premises, after-time boozin', you know the routine.'

Despite his growing sense of frustration, Brennan smiled. He could easily imagine the scene, with an already unhappy constable rendered even more dejected by the information the landlord gave him.

'Anyroad, he took Jaggery up to the chap's room an' it was empty. When he got back here, he wasn't in the best of moods. Said he'd done all he could and he was – now, how did he put it? Ah yes, said as how he was *only made of flesh and bloody blood*. Then said he was off to his bed.'

'Fair enough,' said Brennan, a note of resignation in his voice. 'Well, I suppose I'll be off an' all. Goodnight. I'll let you get back to London.' He nodded at the book on the chair.

'Sod off, Mick,' came the good-humoured reply.

As Brennan stepped away from the station, he pulled his greatcoat close to his neck. The roofs of the buildings on King Street were now coated in ice, and the tram rails glistened in the freezing cold. A cold wind blew along the street, where only hours earlier a mass brawl had taken place. At the top, he turned left into Wallgate, and there, he met the full blast of wind, sharp and piercing. He caught his breath.

To his left, a small curved entrance led to the rear premises of *Wm. Livesey, Saddler and Harness Maker*. He barely gave it a glance, imagining only that the entry offered some meagre respite from this damnable cold, before making his way down past the station and underneath Wallgate Bridge.

If he had chanced to break his journey and take shelter in Livesey's Yard, it would have taken him a lot longer to get home.

But the body would lie undiscovered for another seven hours.

CHAPTER FIFTEEN

William Livesey arrived at his shop on Wallgate earlier than usual. His young assistant, Andrew, had been given strict instructions to be there for seven o'clock, for today was a most significant day in the shop's history. The usual displays of saddles and harnesses had to be put outside the shop, of course, as they did every day, but what rendered the day special would be arriving by wagon at eight o'clock, and everything had to be made ready for then.

The central area of the shop, for instance. That had to cleared of all manner of clutter – saddles, stirrups, bridles, hackamores, headcollars, reins – all had to be rearranged and placed in their proper areas so that there was nothing to interfere with the new arrival's pride of place.

The New Horse Action Saddle.

With glowing testimonials from HRH The Princess of Wales herself, this wonder of the equine age, this cure for dyspepsia, this stimulator of the liver, was about to make its debut appearance in the north of England and in William Livesey's shop in particular. This remarkable machine, that simulates the moving action of a horse without actually having the expense of owning and grooming one, would bring him customers from far and wide and establish his reputation as the foremost saddler in the north.

Young Andrew slouched through the door at a minute past seven, his cheeks flushed and his nose a deep scarlet from the chill of the morning. Such a pity the boy didn't share his enthusiasm for the imminent arrival, Livesey reflected as he watched the boy remove his cap, coat and muffler and place them behind the counter.

'You're late,' Livesey snapped.

'Parish church clock says I'm on time,' came the surly reply, accompanied with a demonstrative yawn to the accompaniment of the dying notes of the church bell.

'We'll have none of your cheek today, my lad. We've an hour to get ready.'

'For what?'

Livesey sighed. Why was it the little devil couldn't share his excitement? Or had he simply not been listening yesterday when he shared the great news with him?

'Never mind for what. Take those old saddles out back. We need to make room.'

Young Andrew sniffed and shivered, muttering, *Bloody freezin' out yonder!* under his breath. Still, he did as he was told, lifted one of the saddles from the stand by the counter and shuffled his way through the back room where he unlocked the door that led to the small yard. Then he made his way outside, the saddle held high in front of his face.

A few seconds later, William Livesey heard an unholy crash, followed quickly by the sound of his young assistant uttering a foul curse.

The young fool's dropped the saddle! If he's damaged it in any way I'll damage his head.

But before he could move to the back of the shop to discover what damage had in fact been done, he was met with his young helper, who had suddenly transformed into a trembling child.

'Tha'd best come!' he said, breathless and scared. 'I tripped over it. Tha'd best come *now*!'

*

At that moment, not fifty yards from William Livesey's establishment, the LNWR Wigan Station was experiencing its own excitement. David Gilchrist took his role as lad porter seriously. Although only seventeen, he had high hopes of becoming Head Porter once Mr Douglas moved on, then rising to the giddying heights of Stationmaster one day, so he too could parade around the station, with his gold braid glistening to proclaim his status, and accept the servitude of others with a stern magnanimity, just like Mr Powell, who even now was overseeing the clerks in the booking office. But at present, part of Gilchrist's duties was to make sure the oil lamps in the lamp room were filled, the wicks trimmed and the paraffin holders checked.

This morning, however, he found that the door to the lamp room had been forced open. At first, he wondered if there had been a break-in during the night and some of the lighting equipment stolen, but when he saw the curled up shape on the floor of the room, heard its rather loud snoring and saw the dishevelled state of its clothing, he realised that the culprit was nothing more threatening than a vagrant. Confident of his ability to deal with such an intruder and aware that his firm response to such an eventuality would stand him in good professional stead, he quietly approached the slumbering figure and gave him a resounding kick in the ribs.

Oscar Pardew was immediately awake. His first thought was he was in the process of being trampled to death by a Brahmani bull – he'd seen some huge and angry examples of those beasts during his time in India, whose malevolent glances were rendered more menacing by their peculiarly hard-boned shoulders – and he curled himself into a ball, crying out, 'Jao! Jao!'

Gilchrist saw the wild-eyed terror of the man and thought about locking him in the lamp room until he could go and get some help, but then he turned and saw the lock hanging askew from the door.

'This is the property of the London and North Western Railway,' he said grandly. 'You shouldn't be in here.'

The information had no visible impact on Oscar, who merely blinked, saw that the Brahmani bull had slipped back into his mind-shadows and that this creature seemed a few sizes too small for the livery he wore. He stood up, holding out a hand coated in what looked like rust.

'Don't you leave this room!' Gilchrist ordered, in what he hoped was a voice of command. He thrust the intruder's hand to one side.

'You just said I didn't belong here,' said Oscar with a quiet reasonableness. 'So why have I to stay? It doesn't make any sense.'

'You're trespassing. I have to report you. You can't just break into railway property like this.'

'I'm waiting for a train.'

The response threw the young porter. 'We've a bloody waiting room for that.'

'It was all locked up as well. And it was cold. Very cold.'

Why am I talking to him like this? Gilchrist thought. *Mr Douglas needs to be told.*

'Just you wait here,' he said. Before Oscar could respond, the boy turned round and left the lamp room.

Oscar shouted after him, 'It's a single to Newton-le-Willows. I've got the money here!'

*

Brennan had been on his way to the police station that morning when he noticed what appeared to be a large commotion halfway up Wallgate, with several constables standing in front of Livesey's Saddlery, keeping an excited and curious crowd at bay. They'd seemed very relieved when he got near, and once he'd been informed of what had been found in the covered yard behind the shop, he immediately took charge.

It was only when he looked at the body for the first time, at the congealed mess of blood beside the head, that he felt a wave of nausea almost overcome him, despite his melancholy experiences in the past.

Now, half an hour later, he waited for the police surgeon to conclude his examination of the body.

'There's no doubt it's murder,' the surgeon, Dr Harrison, told him. 'Post-mortem will tell you more.'

'How was she murdered?'

Dr Harrison placed his hands against Brennan's throat and pushed him none too gently backwards. 'There's bleeding at the back of the head and marks around her neck. First indications would suggest she was grabbed by the neck and forced back against that wall.' He indicated the wall flanking the shop, where Brennan could see traces of blood glistening in the brickwork. 'My guess is that whoever did this used great force to slam her head back against the brickwork. It's sharp and uneven, see?'

He reached up and pointed at the jagged surface of the wall.

'Her last minutes would not have been very pleasant, Sergeant.'

He noticed the pallor that had spread across Brennan's face. 'You knew the poor creature?'

Brennan nodded. 'Only met her last night. Hard to believe that such a...' He gave a small cough and shook the thoughts away.

'What was her name?'

'Maria Woodruff. She was a journalist.'

*

Captain Bell had marched into Brennan's small office, swinging the door open with some violence, and now stood facing his detective sergeant who had quickly got to his feet. It was a visit he had been expecting ever since he had returned to the station. And it was a speech he had been expecting since he stared down at the lifeless form of Maria Woodruff.

'I am fully aware, Sergeant Brennan, that murder – any murder – is the fault of the perpetrator and not the detective whose task is to bring such a fiend to justice. But it becomes the duty of said detective to do what his role suggests and that is to *detect*. Last night, you had one woman dead at your feet, and not twelve hours later, you have another. It might well be that if you had been more energetic in your enquiries, your latest acquisition might still be alive! Well?'

Brennan allowed time for his own anger to subside. If he said what he felt at that particular moment, he would be summarily dismissed. He felt bad enough to have been in the presence of a second victim; he felt even worse when he recalled the animated sparkle in that young woman's eyes, the flash of anger, the flush on her cheeks…

Not twelve hours ago.

Finally, he spoke. 'I'll be doing all I can to find out who did this, sir. You can rest assured.'

'*Rest?* How the blazes can I rest when the wife of the country's executioner and a young female journalist lie side by side in the blasted mortuary? How can I be *assured* that you'll not only find the blackguard who committed these heinous crimes but that you'll do it before you add another one to your morbid collection of cadavers?'

'I shall do my very best, sir.'

The chief constable looked on the verge of providing another gloss on his sergeant's words, but instead, he glared for a few seconds then wheeled round and stormed out of the office, slamming the door behind him.

Under less fraught circumstances, Brennan would have shared with his superior some of the things that were gnawing at his brain concerning the murder of the young reporter. When he spoke to her, she had been carrying a small bag, from which she had taken out a leather-bound notebook, holding it before him as if it contained all the wisdom of Solomon. Yet neither her bag nor the notebook was found near the body. It could mean nothing, of course. She could have returned to her hotel and simply left them there. He had ordered Constable Corns to the Victoria Hotel, where she'd told him she was staying, to make sure the poor woman's room remained locked until he could examine it, which he intended to do forthwith.

Brennan wrote down a few notes and was preparing to leave for the Victoria when there was a knock on his door.

'Come in!' he shouted and took a deep breath.

The door opened and Constable Jaggery peered in.

'His Lordship looks as though he's seen his own arse, Sergeant.' Jaggery nodded behind him at the figure of the chief constable retreating down the corridor.

'What is it, Constable?'

Jaggery came in and closed the door behind him. 'First of all, Sergeant, I've come to apologise, like.'

'Apologise? What for?'

Jaggery cleared his throat. 'Last night. I were out of order. Bit snappy, like. When you told me to go an' find that Evelyne chap.'

'Forget it. He wasn't in his room, was he?'

'No, Sergeant. Landlord said as 'ow Evelyne had been in a bit of a row wi' some bloke.'

'What bloke?'

Jaggery shrugged. 'Didn't say. Only that the bloke seemed a bit off, like.'

'Off?'

'In his head. Said as how he poured a full pint over Evelyne's head an' all.'

'Why?'

'Dunno. They must've 'ad words. Bloody criminal though. Wastin' good ale. Landlord said he went up to 'is room cursin' like a pitman then come back down in dry clothes an' went out. Reckoned 'e was after blood.'

'Did he now?'

Jaggery coughed as he realised what he'd just said. Or suggested, at any rate.

Brennan thought for a while. It might mean something or nothing. He'd already sent a constable down to the Queen's to bring Evelyne to the station.

'Oh, I nearly forgot!' said Jaggery, as if that were a most unusual occurrence.

'What?'

'You've got a visitor, Sergeant. At the front desk.'

'Who is it?'

Jaggery smiled. 'Says he's left his rats at home, in case you're wonderin'.'

Brennan shook his head, felt his heart sink. He knew exactly whom Jaggery meant.

*

Breakfast at the Royal Hotel was a melancholy affair. By now, of course, everyone was aware of what had taken place the previous night. Servants, waiters, cleaners, chef, each with his or her own version of events.

For the two men who sat in the dining room this morning, there was none of the animation they'd shown yesterday. They dined in silence, concentrating on their bacon and eggs and kidneys and mushrooms as if each item of food held a particular fascination. They glanced up only occasionally, their eyes on the door as if expecting someone to enter at any moment. A quick glance back at their plates avoided the need for any sort of conversation.

A solitary waiter stood by the small entrance to the kitchen area looking bored. He was somewhat surprised, therefore, when he saw Gilbert Crosby make an entrance. *The hangman's brother!* He stood in the doorway, ignoring the waiter, and surveyed the room with an expression of curiosity and boldness, almost daring the other two diners to make a comment. He made his way to a table in the centre of the room and stood there while the waiter scurried across and pulled back his chair. Gilbert grunted and sat down.

A few minutes later, as he was being served, the door once more opened and Ralph Batsford walked in. David Morgan and Edgar Dodds, the other two diners, gave each other a curious gaze, and the older one leaned forward and said something. The waiter, who was waiting to see where Mr Batsford would choose to sit, caught sight of the younger guest, Mr Morgan, shaking his head sharply. Mr Dodds, who had by now finished his breakfast, dabbed his mouth with his napkin.

Batsford saw Gilbert about to tuck into his breakfast and made his way over to him, the waiter following. As he passed the only other occupied table, he heard Mr Dodds say, *Nothing to worry about.*

179

The waiter drew back a chair for Mr Batsford.

'There you are!' Batsford said.

Gilbert held his fork mid-air. 'Who do you think I am? Doctor Livingstone?' He put the fork to his mouth and began to eat. 'Where did you think I'd be at this time?'

Batsford seemed about to give some retort but thought better of it. Instead, he sat down and faced the hangman's brother, resting both arms on the table. He gave the waiter his order and watched him walk away, noting how the chap approached the nearby table and asked the two men sitting there if everything was to their satisfaction.

'Did you sleep well?' Batsford asked, a hint of accusation in his voice.

'Tolerably. Under the circumstances.'

'I thought you might have called in to see Simeon this morning. Before breakfast, that is.'

Gilbert frowned. 'If I know my brother, he'd like to be left alone. With his thoughts. You've spoken to him?'

'I have. A few minutes ago. He hasn't slept, you know.'

'I find that hard to believe, actually. He may have slept fitfully and laid awake for hours but I'm sure he dropped off some time. Everyone does.'

Batsford leaned forward, his voice an urgent whisper. 'Gilbert? Where were you? All yesterday? The night before?'

Gilbert skewered a piece of kidney and forced it into the yolk of his egg. Then he said quietly, 'I had a stroll on the moon.'

The journalist snorted.

'How old am I, Batsford?'

The question appeared to throw the journalist. 'Thirty?'

'Thirty-one. Old enough to do what I wish, when I wish, and with whom I wish. Now I believe that should answer your question.'

'It doesn't answer Simeon's question.'

'What?'

'It was the first thing he asked me when I went to his room this morning. It's evidently been playing on his mind. So. I shall ask again. Where were you?'

Gilbert waited, lifted the kidney, dripping with dark yellow egg yolk, and placed it in his mouth. He began to chew and for a second, closed his eyes to savour the blend of tastes. Then he said, almost in a sing-song voice, 'My dear Batsford, you can go to blazes. Do you hear me?'

*

Brennan had escorted his visitor to the small room they used for interviews. The last time he had taken him to his office, the stench had lingered for days. It wasn't so much the tattered and filthy clothes the man wore, although they had a unique aroma that wouldn't be out of place in a badly kept dairy. It was more his breath. Brennan hadn't smelt anything like it. It was obvious from the foul smell and the brown teeth that the man had never seen the need to use toothpaste or carbolic tooth powder, not even salt and bicarbonate of soda. However, the reason for the foul odour lay more in what he did rather than didn't do.

He made money (when he wasn't stealing, that is) by going round the public houses in Wigan and district and providing the entertainment reflected in his nickname.

In a leather-lined pocket, Rat-Yed would bring a live rat into the pub – normally the vault, where only the men would be drinking – collect a sizeable sum to ensure his performance, put the rat's head in his mouth and bite it off. The men would cheer, and the women – if he put on his show in the lounge of the pub – would cover their faces and struggle to keep down the bile fast rising to their throats.

Now, as he sat opposite Brennan, he gave a wide, brown-toothed grin and placed both hands across his threadbare jacket.

'I've not got all day,' said Brennan. 'What is it?'

'I've getten a bit o' news, like.'

'What news?'

'I heerd a young wench got done in last night.'

Brennan sat forward, interested despite the proximity. 'Go on.'

'Dost know, Micky lad, I've not 'ad a butty for a while. An' as for a pie, well…'

Brennan reached into his pocket and pulled out a sixpence. He placed it on the table between them.

'A tanner?' said Rat-Yed, unimpressed.

'I've had a flat week.'

Rat-Yed sneered. 'Bugger off. Bobbies get overtime like dogs get fleas. Can't avoid it.'

Brennan took out another sixpence and placed it next to the first one. 'Well? About the young woman.'

Rat-Yed lunged forward and scraped the two coins into his hand. 'I got told she were pretty.'

'She was.'

'Aye. She looked pretty an' all.'

'What do you mean? You saw her?'

'I did. Last night. I were stood under t'Big Lamp.'

The Big Lamp was a well-known meeting place in the town, near where the trams took on water in Market Place.

'There were a few of us. An' this bonny wench comes strollin' past. You know what some of 'em are like. Nasty buggers with their mouths, they are.'

There speaks an expert, thought Brennan.

'How do you know it's the woman who was found this morning?'

'Lennie Lawson were with us last night. An' he sneaked a peek at the lass's body this mornin' in Livesey's Yard. The lad who works there were tellin' every bugger what 'e'd found when he'd sent for you lot. Place were full o' folk before your lads turned up.'

'Go on then. You say she walked past you last night?'

'Aye. Anyroad, she ignores what some of 'em were shoutin', sticks her nose in th'air an' walks on. Only some bugger were followin' 'er.'

Now Brennan was very much interested. He paused then said, 'How do you know he was following her?'

'Because she gets to t'top o' Wallgate an' turns round fast. I thought she were gonna give him a bloody driver smack around 'is chops, she looked that angry. But she didn't. The chap starts talkin' an' she starts arguin' an' shakin' 'er 'ead an' shoutin' an' then she turns round and buggers off. Bloke turns round an' goes t'other road.'

'Where did he go?'

Rat-Yed shrugged. 'Dunno. We buggered off ourselves then. Bloody freezin', it were. He just went back the way 'e'd come.'

'Towards the Royal?'

'Aye. Might be.'

'What did he look like?'

Rat-Yed frowned, and for a moment, Brennan thought he might ask for further remuneration. If he had done, he would have found himself downstairs in a cold, damp cell. But the man might well have read Brennan's mind, for he said, 'It were dark. But 'e were dressed smart. Not from round 'ere, anyroad.'

'His build?'

Rat-Yed shrugged. 'Didn't take much notice. Like I said, it were dark.'

It was exasperating, but Brennan gave a sigh and stood up. 'Well, thanks for coming in. It helps a little.'

At the door, Rat-Yed turned round, flashing his row of brown teeth. Brennan, closer to the man now, was put in mind of a badly kept cemetery and headstones warped out of the perpendicular.

'Shit an' sod it!' he exclaimed. 'I nearly forgot!'

'What?' Brennan moved his head to one side as a waft of foul air headed his way.

'When the lass shouted at that chap. She said summat we all heard.'

'What was it?'

'She said, *You get back to your golden goose. I'll get back to mine.*'

'That it?'

'It's all I heerd. What the bloody 'ell's a golden goose, eh, Micky? Th'only goose I've ever seen is white.'

*

Brennan was glad to see – or, more accurately, smell – the back of his visitor as he escorted him to the front entrance to the station. As he stood on the top step, breathing in some of that lovely, cold and refreshing Wigan air, he watched two constables walking towards him, a curious-looking fellow between them. He had an overcoat that had obviously seen better days, and his boots were scuffed and filthy. Watching Rat-Yed depart and this bloke arrive, he wondered if some mischievous spirit were testing him.

'What have we got here then?' he asked the constables.

'We've got a right one 'ere, Sergeant. Broke into the lamp room at Wigan Station and got his head down for the night. Then when he's found, he demands a ticket for Newton-le-bloody-Willows. When the young lad refuses, this feller starts getting all worked up and threatens every man and his dog. So we invited him along for a bit of a chat, like.'

Brennan stepped to one side. 'Be my guest,' he said.

Oscar Pardew stretched out his right hand and offered it to Brennan. 'I saw you last night, sir, did I not?'

Brennan looked down and saw streaks of caked blood covering the man's hand. Several thoughts, none of them pleasant, swept over him. He knocked the hand to one side. 'Last night?' he asked mechanically. Then he realised this was the madman who'd charged all the way down King Street yelling out Simeon Crosby's name. Once the trouble started, he'd somehow vanished from view.

Was this Maria Woodruff's blood?

Was this the 'scruffy-looking fellow' she had been talking to last night – the one with the photograph of his dead father?

'He doesn't have a framed photograph on him, does he?'

'Bloody 'ell, Sergeant!' one of the constables exclaimed. 'How the 'ellfire did you know that?'

'I have powers you've never dreamed of, son.' Brennan enjoyed seeing the awe on the young constable's face.

'It's tucked inside his coat,' said the other, older one. 'We've got rid of the bits o' glass. Says we broke it, little sod. No 'arm in lettin' 'im keep the photograph itself though, eh, Sergeant?'

'None at all. Now get him inside.'

As they walked past him, Brennan scratched his head.

It was going to be a very long day.

*

There was something dreadfully sad about Miss Woodruff's hotel room. It was small, nondescript and was almost adjacent to the platform at the nearby station. But it was the things she'd left behind – three sets of clothing hanging in the wardrobe; a pair of white laced boots beneath the window; a hat with elaborate trimmings; and, much to the embarrassment of Constable Corns standing in the doorway, a scarlet corset draped over the bed – that gave a forlorn sense of loss to the place.

Brennan went over to the small chest of drawers, but in each one, there was nothing of interest, only an array of silk handkerchiefs and stockings.

Of her black leather-bound notebook there was no sign.

It was as he was closing the top drawer that something nestled among the handkerchiefs caught his eye. It was a piece of paper. He took it out, unfolded it and quickly read its contents.

'Found something, Sergeant?' Constable Corns asked.

'Yes, Constable.'

As Brennan refolded the paper and slipped it into his pocket, Constable Corns couldn't help feeling a little resentful. After all, the bugger could've told him what was on the piece of paper.

Secretive sod.

CHAPTER SIXTEEN

Thomas Evelyne didn't take too kindly to being summoned from his room, where he had packed his case with the intention of leaving the town as quickly and as unobtrusively as possible. When he'd returned to the hotel the previous night, the landlord had given him the message left by the constable – that he was to make himself available to the police first thing in the morning – and had delivered the message with a look of distaste that implied how badly Evelyne had sullied the hotel's good name.

If he hadn't gone out seeking revenge on the lunatic for drowning him in beer... such a pity he hadn't found the fool.

When he awoke this morning, therefore, he was irritated beyond measure to hear the sharp knocking on his door and the flinty, contemptuous voice of the landlord informing him that a police constable was waiting for him in the bar, and would he be so good as to settle his account before being taken to the station.

The walk from the Queen's Hotel had taken Evelyne and the constable past the saddler's shop, where another constable was standing in the entrance to the yard and keeping the curious at bay, not that there was anything now for them to see – the body had been removed and

William Livesey had been most anxious for them to take a look inside his establishment, where they could see for themselves something that would astonish them.

Evelyne had asked what all the interest was around the shop, only to be given a single word response from his constable companion.

'Morbid.'

Once he arrived at the police station, the constable took him along a musty smelling corridor to a small office at the end. There, Detective Sergeant Brennan introduced himself and offered him a seat.

'You caused quite a stir last night, Mr Evelyne,' was Brennan's opening comment.

Evelyne looked at him questioningly. 'You dragged me here to tell me that?'

'If I'd wanted you dragged here, Mr Evelyne, I would have sent a quite different constable. Still, you're here, and that's all that matters. You came to Wigan to cause trouble, didn't you?'

'I came here to protest against the presence of Simeon Crosby.'

'You dislike the man or his profession?'

A slight flush spread across Evelyne's face.

'Both, I suppose,' he said after a thoughtful pause. 'Is this some sort of belated arrest? I wasn't responsible for what happened last night, you know.'

Brennan leaned forward. 'What exactly are you talking about?'

'Why, the violence outside the Public Hall. That wasn't caused by me. It was that madman who tore through the crowd, screaming like a wild animal.'

'Ah yes. The *madman*.'

'And he came to my hotel last night and assaulted me.'

'Really?'

'Yes. I took pity on him; he came into the place and seemed in a distressed state – his hands were bleeding. I presumed from the trouble outside the Public Hall. So I offered to buy him a drink. When I did so, he poured the whole damn pint over my head.'

'I see. What did you do then?'

'They threw the devil out, but I admit I was blazing mad. I went to my room, dried off and unfortunately let the incident seethe inside me. You know the feeling? You let the resentment build up so much that… well, I stormed downstairs and left the hotel in search of my assailant.'

'With what purpose?'

'Why, to treat him to a fish supper. What do you think?'

'You didn't find him?'

'Fortunately for him, no.'

'What time did you get back to the Queen's?'

Evelyne frowned. 'Look. Just what is all this about?'

Brennan sat back. 'I sent a constable to the Queen's Hotel last night, and you weren't there.'

'So? I told you, the trouble in that street was not of my doing. Am I being held responsible for the action of a madman who later tried to drown me in beer?'

'Certainly not. But I sent the constable because I wanted to ask you some questions about last night.'

Evelyne blinked. 'But I've already told you…'

'You know that Mrs Crosby was found murdered last night?'

'What?' The man's eyes opened wide.

'I'm sorry. I thought you knew. Word spreads fast in Wigan.'

'I'm not from here.'

'Where are you from?'

'Bolton.'

Brennan took out his notebook. 'Whereabouts?'

Evelyne blinked several times. 'Why?'

'Because I want to know.' It was Brennan's usual response to an unwilling witness. He knew it riled them, and it was intended to.

Evelyne shook his head at the folly of the police but gave him his address. He then added, 'Not too far to come to protest against Crosby, is it? Mind you, I've travelled further.'

'You must have firm convictions.'

'I have.'

'At any rate, Mrs Violet Crosby was found murdered when Mr Crosby returned from his talk at the Public Hall.'

Evelyne looked down. 'I see. That must have been dreadful for the man. Whatever my feelings towards him…' His voice trailed off.

'I wonder if you could tell me where you were last night? After the brawling I mean?'

A flicker of concern flashed across the man's face.

'Why?'

'*Why*? Because at the risk of repeating myself, I want to know, Mr Evelyne. That's *why*.'

Slowly, Evelyne raised his left hand and placed it on the top of his head.

'Sergeant. Would you be so kind as to feel my head?'

Brennan frowned. 'I beg your pardon?'

'Please. Won't take a minute.'

Brennan gave a theatrical sigh and stood up. He walked around his desk and stood behind Evelyne. Then he rested his hand on the spot indicated. Through the thick hair, he could feel a sizeable lump sprouting from his scalp. 'That must be painful,' he said, quickly withdrawing his hand and returning to his seat.

'It was put there by one of your overly enthusiastic constables, swinging his truncheon like a windmill on a gusty day.'

'Doing his duty.' Brennan's voice was a blend of defiance and defence.

'That depends on your point of view. My point of view was the sight of a wooden implement crashing down on my skull.'

'It doesn't really answer my question, does it? Where were you after the trouble?'

'I found myself staggering up the street like a drunken man, if you must know. Then I must have blacked out because the next thing I know I'm waking up in some church doorway and there's a priest standing over me. I thought I'd died.'

Brennan reached for his notebook and pencil. 'Which church?'

Evelyne shook his head. 'Blowed if I know. It was past the station though. Under the bridge there and to the left.'

He put his pen down. He knew which church he meant. St Joseph's, in Caroline Street. The church he attended every Sunday with Ellen and Barry.

'Would the priest be Father Clooney?'

Evelyne shrugged. 'No idea. But the man took me into his home and gave me a small glass of brandy. Then I left.' He smiled. 'The man gave me his blessing.'

He would, thought Brennan. Father Fergal Clooney was a veritable saint. He would need to speak with the good father to corroborate what Evelyne had just told him.

'What time was this?'

'I really have no idea, Sergeant.'

Brennan shifted in his seat. 'When you were out seeking revenge on the man who soaked you with beer, did you happen to see a young woman, alone?'

'What sort of woman?' Evelyne's tone suggested he'd put a less than respectable meaning to the sergeant's words.

'I mean the young woman who attended your gathering last night on the Market Square. Miss Maria Woodruff.'

'Ah. You mean the female journalist? She came to see me yesterday afternoon, as a matter of fact. Seeking my views on Crosby and his work.' He paused. 'Why do you ask?'

'Did you see Miss Woodruff last night when you left the Queen's?'

Evelyne shook his head. 'No. And again, why?'

Brennan told him.

'My God! And only yesterday… What in God's name is going on in this town?'

'You saw her speak with anyone at the Market Square?'

Evelyne thought for a moment then said, 'As a matter of fact, I did. She was standing towards the back of the crowd – she was the sort of young woman it's hard to miss – and I saw her talking to someone.'

'Who?'

'The madman who tried to drown me. She was engaged in what seemed to be a deep conversation with him last evening. I don't think it ended well.'

Brennan stood and dismissed Evelyne, instructing him not to leave Wigan until he gave permission.

'I've been away for too long, Sergeant,' said the man.

Whether he'd meant it as a warning that he would be leaving with or without official permission, or as a plea for understanding from one married man to another, Brennan couldn't be sure.

Nor could he give a damn.

*

It came as something of a shock to Ralph Batsford when Simeon Crosby entered the dining room and sat down between him and Gilbert. The man's eyes were red-rimmed, and he wondered what demons had assailed him in the darkness of his room. Somehow, his fleshy features seemed to have shrunk, become greyer, with none of the animation he was wont to show. Now, he sat and stared at his brother. No word was spoken, and a heavy silence hovered around them like mist in a graveyard.

Morgan and Dodds, still seated at their table, looked at each other; both nodded and stood up. It looked as though Morgan, the younger of the two, was intending to approach the latest arrival, but Dodds grabbed his arm and whispered something in his ear. Both then left the dining room.

Gilbert, for his part, was studiously trying to ignore his brother, concentrating instead on his breakfast and dragging his fork around the plate for the crumbs that were left. Finally, after ensuring it was now clear, he quietly placed knife and fork on the plate, dabbed his mouth with a napkin and looked across the table at his brother for the first time.

Batsford couldn't quite make out the nature of the mute exchange between them. Certainly Simeon's expression was almost without any feeling whatsoever, only a glimmer in the bloodshot eyes from time to time denoting some faint hint of hostility. Gilbert, on the other hand, had adopted a pose that was devoid of confrontation, his features gradually developing a softness, a show of concern.

'Simeon,' he said in a voice not much above a whisper. 'If there's anything I can do...'

'There is,' came the sudden reply that appeared to startle his brother, who had clearly expected more of a negative response.

'Oh?'

'You know the police, especially that detective sergeant, won't allow you to leave the town until certain matters are explained to his satisfaction.'

Gilbert flashed a quick glance in Batsford's direction.

'Nor,' Simeon went on, 'will he allow any of us to leave.'

'How can I be of help?'

'You can explain where you were on Monday night and all day yesterday. That's what you can do.'

'I have already given Sergeant Brennan that information.'

Simeon slowly shook his head. 'What did you tell him?'

Gilbert scowled. 'I sought company. That's all you need to know.'

'I see.' Simeon turned to Batsford and said, 'Ralph? If you don't mind?'

With a sharp glance in Gilbert's direction, Batsford nodded and left the table. When he reached the door, he cast a final glance in their direction and left the room.

'Now,' said Simeon, waving a hand around the room, which was now empty. 'You forget, dear brother. I know you well.'

Gilbert shifted in his seat, lifted up the knife from his plate and balanced it in the palm of his hand. 'Your point?'

'My wife was murdered last night. I'm not in the mood for confrontation. But the truth will come out sooner or later. Let me be the first to know. I know you're lying through your teeth. And so, I suspect, does Sergeant Brennan. Tell me the truth. Before it's too late.'

*

The cells at the Wigan Borough Police Station were below ground level. The only glimpse of daylight, for anyone unfortunate enough to occupy one, came through a narrow gap at the top of the wall farthest from the door. And even that meagre light was often blacked out by the feet of passers-by or the shunting, rattling tram labouring its way along King Street.

Oscar Pardew, his hands now covered in bandages, courtesy of the police doctor, sat facing such a gap as Sergeant Brennan sat down on the iron-framed bed beside him. Having ascertained his name from the front desk – which Oscar had given without demur when the charge of breaking and entering had been put to him – Brennan gave a nod of recognition.

Only that morning, the duty sergeant had received word from Haydock Lodge that one of their inmates, an Oscar Pardew, had taken flight and was last seen at Newton-le-Willows Station catching a train to Wigan. When the aforementioned lunatic had been conveniently brought in by two constables, it had considerably lightened his day, for the arrest would go down in his report as a fine example of rapid police work, even in the face of a double murder inquiry.

Now, Brennan sat next to Pardew rather than facing him across a desk. No telling how lunatics would respond, of course, but giving an appearance of friendliness would be far better than confrontation.

'How did you cut your hands, Oscar?' Brennan asked.

'I explained all that to those policemen.'

'Explain it to this policeman.'

Oscar sighed heavily. 'Your men smashed my father's photograph. I reached inside and cut my hand on the sharp pieces of glass. Have you ever cut yourself on a sharp piece of glass? It hurts, and blood comes.'

His hands had indeed been cut, consistent with broken glass. In fact, the doctor who'd dressed his wounds told him he'd picked out a few *nasty-looking slivers.*

'Do you remember last night, Oscar?' he began. 'When you went to the Market Square to hear Thomas Evelyne speak?'

Oscar gave a brief frown then nodded.

'You spoke to a young woman there, didn't you?'

Again, a frown then a more vigorous nod.

'What did you speak about?'

Oscar looked beyond Brennan's head, to the feet passing by above them. 'She asked me why I was there.'

'And what did you say?'

'I wanted to see Mr Crosby. And I heard that everyone who wanted to see Mr Crosby was meeting on the square. So I asked people where it was, and they told me.'

'Yes, but what did you say when the young woman asked you why you wished to see Mr Crosby?'

'I wanted to shake his hand.' He held up his bandaged hands.

It was Brennan's turn to frown. 'But the meeting was for those people who disliked what Mr Crosby did.'

Oscar took a deep breath. 'Mr Crosby is a good man. He killed the man who killed my father.'

'What happened?'

'Oh, Mr Crosby put a rope around his neck, and he dropped straight through a trap door.'

Brennan held up his hand. 'No, I mean what happened when your father was killed?'

'He was playing cards, and a man was cheating, and Father told him and told everyone, and the man didn't like it so he waited for my father after the card game and stabbed him there, and I was away in India.'

He raised a finger and pressed it against Brennan's chest, to mark the spot where his father had been fatally stabbed.

It took Brennan a while to recover his composure. Oscar had spoken with such vehemence, such s imple anger that he could almost feel the point of a knife against his breast.

'What did the young woman say to you?'

Oscar swallowed and took another deep breath, as if the questions he was being asked were causing him some confusion. Then he said, 'She asked me did I believe in hanging, and I told her I did, most definitely. Mr Crosby hanged my father's killer.'

'Anything else?'

'She told me she'd come here to write a story, and she'd leave here writing another.'

Brennan tried to keep the urgency from his voice. 'What did she mean by that?'

Oscar gave a shrug. 'She didn't say. I told her I'd been in India. Worked there for a while till I got word about my father and had to come home. I was ill on the ship, you see. And it was all because of the curse. I was sick. Father was stabbed. All because of the curse.'

Brennan saw the man's eyes begin to glaze over, his mind apparently adrift on an ocean of its own. He felt it best not to enquire into the nature of the *curse*.

'And I told her about all that, and she said it was very interesting, but she'd never been on a ship and never been to India and had no intention of doing so.' He leaned towards Brennan, whispering, 'She'd heard how they treat women, you see.'

'Just a few more questions, Mr Pardew, then I'll leave you alone.'

Oscar gave a small nod. He seemed disappointed that his new friend would be leaving him soon.

'Why did you run through all those people last night? When the trouble started?'

Oscar closed his eyes tightly shut, replaying the scene in his head. Then he opened them and said, 'I wanted to shake his hand. Mr Crosby's, I mean. And I saw him going into the hall, and I had no ticket. Then those policemen stopped me and hit me. That big brute of a man frightened me.'

'Where did you go after the trouble in King Street?'

Again he closed his eyes then spoke softly. 'It was foggy.'

Brennan frowned. 'No it wasn't.'

Oscar pointed to his head. 'In here I mean. Gets like that sometimes. It gets foggy, like I'm in a thick cloud. And I can't remember things.'

Brennan sighed. No alibi then. But was it feasible that this poor bugger was capable of sliding into the Royal Hotel and finding his way to Mrs Crosby, strangling her and leaving unseen? Furthermore, why would he do that?

He stood up and moved to the cell door. 'Someone will see to you soon,' he said kindly. By now, the duty sergeant would have sent Haydock Lodge a telegram letting them know their escapee was now under lock and key. For the moment, however, the man was going nowhere.

Once he was back in his office, he took out the piece of paper he'd found in Maria Woodruff's hotel room. He read through the short telegram he held in his hand:

Inconvenient and unprofessional. Need more. Who is the man?

The telegram was sent from The Strand, London, and the sender was someone named L Townley, whose position, according to the transcripted section on the telegram, was Editor, *The Graphic.*

But who was the man she'd evidently referred to? The murderer? Or someone quite unconnected to the case?

The one person who could offer an explanation was now lying in the infirmary mortuary.

CHAPTER SEVENTEEN

On his way to speak with Ralph Batsford, Brennan paid a visit to the General Post Office, whose rather grand building took pride of place on Wallgate. He told Constable Jaggery to stand beside him and say nothing, yet look menacing – two things he had no trouble at all in fulfilling.

He asked to see the manager, who at first, was quite adamant in his refusal to allow the detective sergeant to be given access to their file of telegrams that had been despatched. But then Brennan pointed out that he was investigating a double murder, and the telegram he sought might well provide a crucial clue in apprehending the villain, and further, that if he were obstructed in any way from carrying out his duties, then the murderer might well strike again, and who would want that on his conscience for goodness' sake? It would, indeed, be unfortunate if the manager's recalcitrance were to find its way into the letters page of the *Wigan Observer*, or indeed the chief constable's monthly report to the Watch Committee.

Finally, a young clerk was sent to retrieve the telegram sent by Miss Woodruff. When he returned (with a quick glance at his superior and a look of quiet triumph on his face), Brennan held the original in his hand. Miss Woodruff's elegant handwriting reminded him once more of the lively looking woman she had been.

The telegram ran:

Found a man living a lie. Need to delay article. Maria

Brennan folded the paper and placed it in his pocket, despite admittedly half-hearted protests from the Post Office manager.

A man living a lie.

The phrase puzzled him, for it begged the obvious question – which man? And that begged another question: what was the lie he was living? That, of course, led inexorably to the third, most crucial question of all: was the lie potent enough to bring about the murder of two seemingly innocent women?

Of course, the two murders could be completely unconnected, but he didn't believe in coincidences. Two women, who had arranged to meet in secret, found murdered on the same night?

Ralph Batsford was about to leave the hotel when he caught sight of Detective Sergeant Brennan approaching, with the lumbering constable alongside him. When the policemen reached the steps of the Royal, Batsford gave them a wave of acknowledgement.

'Any news, Sergeant?' he asked.

Brennan suggested they go inside, but to his surprise, the journalist politely refused.

'To be honest, Sergeant Brennan, I'm feeling rather claustrophobic at the moment. I know you said we hadn't to leave town, and of course, that's perfectly fine. But there are times when I feel the need for some fresh air. Simeon and Gilbert aren't exactly on speaking terms. The atmosphere in the breakfast room is decidedly unfraternal and frosty. I thought I might take a stroll around town.'

'What's the matter with the Crosby brothers?'

Batsford gave a small shrug. 'Obviously, Simeon is completely destroyed by what happened. Gilbert should be supporting him. But...'

'Are they close, would you say?'

Batsford began to walk down the steps. 'Look, why don't we walk around the town? You can ask me anything you like.'

A few minutes later, the three of them – Constable Jaggery labouring to keep up with their pace and remaining silent during the conversation – were walking down Market Street towards the Market Hall.

'I think,' said Batsford, 'that Gilbert Crosby sometimes feels annoyed because of his brother's… is *fame* the right word? He's been coming with us on this small tour, and I have the feeling he's waiting for Simeon to put a foot wrong – so he can gloat. Sibling rivalry and all that, I suppose.'

'What does Gilbert Crosby do to earn his living? Or is he of independent means?'

Batsford smiled. 'Certainly not. Gilbert was the pride of the family, according to Simeon. Went to university – the Victoria University in Leeds, as a matter of fact – and was set fair for a career in the civil service. But then he got sent down.'

'Kicked out, you mean?'

'Yes. He fell in with a bad crowd, and his studies took very much second place to other pursuits.'

'Such as?'

They entered the Market Hall, and the noise immediately grew louder, with stallholders yelling out their wares to all and sundry (*Good job the Inspector of Nuisances isn't here,* thought Brennan, knowing full well that raucous shouting like this was strictly against the council bye-laws.)

'Perhaps we should leave the market for another day, Mr Batsford,' said Brennan. 'It's quite loud in here.'

Batsford shook his head. 'Oh no, Sergeant. The place is teeming with life. And those smells! I'm perfectly happy to wander around the place while you continue your interrogation.'

Brennan saw the expression in the man's eyes. *I'm no fool,* they said.

After a few moments adjusting to the sounds, Batsford said, 'Well, Gilbert was sent down from Leeds ultimately, for gambling. He had many debts, and word spread. Missed lectures and tutorials and all sorts of deadlines for his work. They had no choice really.'

'Is that how he got his scar? Trouble at university?'

Now Batsford laughed out loud. 'Gilbert likes to tell the story that the scar is an old duelling wound. From his time at university in Germany.'

'I thought you said…'

'Sergeant. Gilbert Crosby has never been to Germany in his life. He got his scar in some other place.'

'Where?'

Another hesitation. Then, 'Prison. Gilbert served three months a few years ago. He was arrested in a police raid on a notorious gambling club in London – the Bedford Club. Gilbert was fined – it wasn't the first time, by the way. He's an inveterate gambler. But, of course, he couldn't pay. He asked Simeon for the money, as was his wont, but poor Violet persuaded him to refuse.'

'Why did she do that?'

'She was very protective of Simeon's reputation. Said she was tired of Gilbert continually bringing shame on his brother's name and that perhaps he needed a sharp lesson in the realities of life. Violet had a rather strictly moral way of looking at things. Simeon agreed, and Gilbert was sent down once more, as it were.'

Brennan cast a glance at Jaggery, who had temporarily left their company and was engaged in conversation with a butcher.

'He got the scar in prison?'

'Indeed. He told Simeon that he was attacked by a fellow inmate who'd sharpened the handle of a spoon.'

'Why?'

'Simeon told me it was the gambling again. And if you gamble in those hellish places and become indebted…'

Brennan thought about what he'd been told. It was certainly food for thought.

Jaggery caught up with them, clumsily trying to conceal a small paper parcel, from whose shape, Brennan suspected, contained several large sausages.

'Mr Batsford, are you aware that there was another murder last night?'

Batsford stopped and looked at Brennan closely.

'I don't know anything about that. Who was the victim?'

'A fellow journalist. A Miss Maria Woodruff.'

'What?' Batsford's face took on a pale, stony expression. Then he swallowed hard, and for a second, Brennan thought the man was about to faint.

'Are you feeling all right?' he asked as Jaggery fetched up beside the journalist, just in case.

Batsford stretched out an arm and leaned against the counter of a hardware stall. 'Miss Woodruff? But that's not possible.'

'You knew her then?'

Batsford took a deep breath. 'How did she die?'

'There was a wound. To the back of her head.'

The journalist stared at the floor for a long time.

'Mr Batsford?'

The man looked up. 'Yes, Sergeant. I knew her. She was my wife.'

*

The three of them sat around a small table in the cramped confines of the Market Hall office. Upon seeing the distressed state Ralph

Batsford was in, the hall manager had immediately offered his sanctuary to Detective Sergeant Brennan, whom he knew well, and had miraculously reappeared five minutes later with three steaming hot mugs of tea. He then left them, stating his intention to *take his hourly promenade.*

After a few minutes, during which time Batsford cradled his mug, more for the warmth it gave than the sustenance it contained, Brennan spoke gently.

'I'd like to ask a few questions, Mr Batsford, but you can take all the time in the world to answer them.'

'I understand.'

'I assume you and your wife were separated? The names…'

Batsford took a sip from his mug, glanced quickly at the mute, stern-faced constable beside him then held Brennan's gaze. 'Yes. She left me six months ago. Reverted to her maiden name.'

'Can I ask why?'

Batsford looked over the rim of his mug. 'You're a direct one.'

'I'm sorry. Sometimes I have to be.'

'We held different views,' Batsford began. 'About several things.'

'Such as?'

Again, Batsford gave Jaggery a quick glance. To Brennan, it seemed he was more apprehensive about the constable's large and menacing presence than facing the questions he was asking. As usual, Jaggery showed no emotion other than sternness, like a statue hewn from granite.

'The profession she had decided to pursue, for one thing.' Despite the grievous news he had just been given, the man couldn't keep traces of bitterness from his voice. 'It was ludicrous.' His tone immediately grew softer as he added, 'I wanted one thing and she wanted another.'

'What did you want?'

'A family.'

The answer surprised Brennan. His early impressions of the man had been that he was detached, mercenary in his arrangement with the hangman, but here he was showing a side to his character that Brennan could recognise in himself. For Brennan, the family – *his* family – was the most important thing in his life.

Batsford went on. 'She had this insane ambition of becoming a journalist.' He smiled bitterly. 'She wasn't content even with that. Once she gained a position with a magazine, she quickly expressed dissatisfaction with the assignments she was being given. She would be asked to describe a New Year's Eve ball or a short piece on the German custom of decorating children's graves on Christmas Eve. *It isn't real reporting!* she'd say. She flatly refused to contemplate motherhood. To me, there is nothing more unfeminine than that. And so we agreed to a separation.'

'Do you know why she had come to Wigan?'

Brennan watched the man's reaction closely. He, of course, knew the reason – Maria Woodruff had explained to him outside the Royal that she intended to conduct an interview with Violet Crosby, getting the wife's perspective on being married to the hangman. But if Batsford was aware of that, what impact, if any, would that have had on his work as Simeon Crosby's biographer?

And there was also the puzzling comment she had made to Oscar Pardew: that *she'd come here to write a story, and she'd leave here writing another.*

Batsford drained his mug and placed it gently on the table. 'I'm afraid I have no idea, Sergeant.'

'Did you speak with her? Here in Wigan?'

Batsford gave Jaggery another look. Then said, 'We were hardly on speaking terms, Sergeant.'

'That doesn't really answer my question, Mr Batsford.'

'Then no. I never spoke to her.'

Brennan frowned. He recalled what the malodorous Rat-Yed had told him, of an encounter between Maria Woodruff and a well-dressed man in Market Place on the night she was murdered. What was it he had heard her shout?

Get back to your golden goose.

Was the man Batsford? And if so, then the *golden goose* would be Crosby, whose story Batsford was chronicling. It made sense. What didn't make any sense, if it were true, was why Batsford would lie about having seen his wife. Unless Batsford were telling the truth and hadn't seen his estranged wife here in Wigan. In which case she met someone else last night. Who could that be? Simeon Crosby? His brother Gilbert? Unlikely to be the hangman, he reasoned, for he *was* the golden goose, wasn't he? Besides, he'd just discovered his wife had been murdered. He wouldn't have left the hotel to argue with a journalist, would he? Unless…

It could, however, have been Gilbert Crosby – perhaps he, too, is benefiting from his brother's celebrity? In the past, he'd certainly benefited from his generosity.

Brennan shook the thoughts away for the time being.

Batsford began to stand up. 'I thank you for the concern you've shown me, Sergeant Brennan. I'd better return to the hotel.'

Jaggery looked at Brennan for guidance. *Should I drag the bugger back down into his seat?* But Brennan shook his head.

As Batsford opened the office door, he turned and said, 'I presume I am to remain here? In Wigan?'

'I'm afraid so, Mr Batsford. There'll be the inquest, for one thing. And my investigations, for another.'

Batsford sighed. 'In that case, I suppose it's my duty to send a telegram.'

'To Miss Woodruff's family?'

'Oh no. She has no family to speak of. No, I meant her employers. She works for a prestigious London magazine, you know. *The Graphic.* You may have heard of it?'

'Oh yes, Mr Batsford. I've heard of it.'

*

As they walked back to the station, Brennan spoke his thoughts out loud.

'You saw the telegram she sent to the editor in London. Who's this man living a lie?'

'Dunno, Sergeant.'

Brennan smiled. Constable Jaggery often failed to understand the nature of a rhetorical question. 'I think it's time I sent a telegram of my own.'

'Who to?'

'Our friend, the editor.'

'I thought meladdo back yonder were sendin' him the bad news?'

Brennan shook his head. 'I'm after information. Might be clutching at straws, but it's worth trying. Wouldn't you think?'

Jaggery merely scowled and mumbled, 'Never sent one o' them buggers in me life. Wouldn't know where to start.'

As they passed the General Post Office, Brennan asked Jaggery to wait while he sent his telegram. A few minutes later, he reappeared, and they crossed the road.

They reached the Minorca Hotel, on the corner of Wallgate and King Street. Further down Wallgate, he saw a small group of children pushing each other near the entrance of the yard where Maria Woodruff's body had been found a few hours earlier. Little sods should be in school, Brennan thought, not daring each other to enter what they'd inevitably rechristened the Haunted Yard.

'Couldn't be Simeon Crosby,' Jaggery suddenly said.

'What?' said Brennan.

'Livin' a lie. I mean, we all know what that bugger does. Or did. Everybody knows of 'im.' His brow creased in thought. 'I reckon same thing applies to that brother of 'is. Bein' the hangman's brother.'

'Who's served time,' Brennan added. 'That might lead to a lie or two.'

Jaggery rubbed his chin. 'Aye.'

'There's Batsford, of course. A journalist.'

'But they just report stuff, don't they? I mean, they write what's in the newspapers.'

'A journalist isn't just a journalist, Constable. Just like a hangman isn't just a hangman. They have good points and bad points.'

'Just like policemen, eh, Sergeant?' Jaggery was beaming as if he'd just scored an important debating point.

After a short silence, during which time they were halfway down King Street and nearing the Public Hall, Brennan said, 'Maria Woodruff told Pardew she'd come to Wigan to write one story and would leave the town writing another. What exactly did she mean by that? The story she came to write was an interview with Crosby's wife, which Crosby knew nothing about.'

'What if Crosby found out, Sergeant? Lost his temper and felt betrayed by his missus? Killed 'er an' then saw off Miss Woodruff.' Before Brennan could respond, Jaggery began shaking his head. 'Can't 'ave done, though. His wife were alive when they left the hotel, weren't she? An' when he got back from 'is speech-makin' she were dead. It's what 'appened between them times that counts, I reckon. It's a puzzler, Sergeant.'

Brennan gave a thoughtful nod. It certainly was.

*

He was sitting at his desk, going through the various notes he had made concerning the case, when he heard a timid knock on the door.

'Come in!' he shouted.

Slowly, almost reluctantly, the door opened. Constable Palin peered round. The young man looked nervous, hesitant, his youth emphasised rather than concealed by the thin wisps of lip-hair that could never be described as a moustache. Constable Jaggery had laughingly referred to the hairs as *arse-fluff* in the station canteen, much to the poor lad's embarrassment and the rest of the constables' amusement.

'What is it, Constable Palin?'

'Sorry to bother you, like, Sergeant, only—'

'—Spit it out. I'm busy.'

'Only I've summat to tell you.'

Brennan sighed and indicated a chair.

'I'll stand, Sergeant. Not take a minute.'

'Well then.'

The young policeman bit his lip. 'Last night, when I was on duty…'

'Go on.'

Brennan could see his face flush and waited for what he suspected was assuming all the hallmarks of a confession. He'd heard plenty in his time.

'Well, I forgot to tell you summat. I don't reckon it must be owt important but… anyroad, I were supposed to escort that Mr Batsford down to the Public Hall.'

'I thought you did escort him? I saw you myself walking down King Street.'

'Oh aye. It weren't that. It were earlier, when he left the hotel and Mr Crosby got put in his carriage.' He took a deep breath. 'Well, Mr Batsford went back inside.'

'Inside? You mean back into the hotel?'

'Aye, Sergeant. Said he'd forgot his notebook. Had to go back upstairs an' fetch it.'

Brennan sat upright. If Batsford had gone back to his room, he'd had the opportunity to knock on Mrs Crosby's door…

'I didn't think it were important, Sergeant. But I've thought about it an' thought about it an'… I reckon it might be.'

Brennan stood up. Constable Palin stepped back and actually flinched.

'Well done, lad,' said Brennan.

'What?'

'You showed initiative. There's not many would have seen how important such a detail was. But you did. Well done!'

Constable Palin's chest suddenly thrust forward proudly. 'Thank you, Sergeant!' he said with a smile that was a mixture of pride and relief.

'And now I want you to do something for me.'

'Sergeant?'

Brennan reached into his desk drawer and pulled out a sheet of paper with a list of names. 'These people are guests at the Royal. I want you to take Constable Johnson with you and speak to each of these guests. The Crosbys. Batsford. Morgan. Dodds. I want to know where they were last night from eleven o'clock.'

The young constable frowned. 'But wouldn't they all've been in their rooms? After you'd left the place?'

'Highly likely. And the problem with that is there'll be no alibis to speak of. But I'll need it confirming, all the same.'

'You can count on me, Sergeant! I just fancy a bit o' detective work!'

With that, he turned around and marched out, head held a lot higher than when he came in.

When he'd gone, Brennan stood there for a while. He knew exactly what the statements would say: everyone in their rooms, as Constable

Palin had said, no one with an alibi. It would simply be a waste of his time to conduct such negative interviews. Especially if they were dealing with someone *living a lie*.

Still, it gave the lad something to get his teeth into.

*

Walter Anders had been a missionary for the Wigan Temperance and Rescue Mission for over ten years. During that time, he had seen many unfortunates struggle pitifully against the vagaries of those hateful foes to contentment: Unemployment, Sickness and Death. Families had been rent asunder by them, and his heart had been affected when he was confronted with the results – children in rags, fathers with racking and sinister coughs and mothers with their faces wan, all ravaged by hunger and despair. Such circumstances had never been an excuse for straying from the law, however. As long as those in receipt of the mission's beneficence realised that Salvation could brook no deviation from the straight and narrow path to God, then he would be there to offer what support and succour he could.

This morning, as he walked briskly along St Patrick Street, he was carrying a large parcel wrapped in brown paper. It contained some bed sheets that had been donated to the mission, and he was looking forward to seeing the expression on Mrs Dowling's face when he presented this tangible example of relief to her and her family. Her husband's sickness had lasted eight weeks, and his enforced absence from his job as a hewer down the pit had the unfortunate consequence of rendering his young son Terence, twelve, unem- ployed as well. Terence had worked as his father's drawer down the pit and so when the sickness came, both father and son were forced to remain at home.

Home was in Higham Street, in Scholes, just round the corner from St Patrick's Roman Catholic Church. Scholes was Walter's least favourite and most visited district, its rough-and-ready reputation giving it a most unsavoury name. He couldn't help feeling that some people looked on him with suspicion, a few with downright hostility. Whether it was because of the way he was dressed – suit, tie, polished shoes – or because he was known as a member of the mission and therefore a dispenser, some felt, of charity or (even worse) an advocate of the Pledge, he wasn't sure. On more than one occasion, he had attempted to bring succour to degraded and fallen women of the area, his efforts greeted with mixed results. But, as he often told himself, he was a missionary, and although his duties took him no further than the boundaries of the town, he saw it as his moral purpose to bring what relief he could. At least they didn't blow poison darts from crocodile-infested rivers.

It was with some surprise, therefore, that he was greeted with the most delicious aroma – a rich beef stew, by all accounts – when Mrs Dowling opened the door to let him in.

'Something smells good!' he said heartily.

'Aye. First time we've 'ad a stew since Adam were a lad.'

He entered the tiny front room and nodded to young Terrence, who was seated by the fire and peering over the heavy pot that rested on the range. His thin features seemed less skeletal today, the flames from the fire giving his face a ruddy glow.

'And how's Mr Dowling?' he asked.

'Oh still badly, though 'is chest's not as bubblin'.' She cast a quick glance at the ceiling.

Walter coughed and handed her the sheets, which she took with an expression of gratitude and shame.

'Thanks,' she said.

He walked over to the pot and breathed in the smells of meat, onion and vegetables. 'It seems there are many kind souls in Higham Street, Mrs Dowling,' he said with a benign smile.

'What d'you mean?' There was a hint of resentment in her voice.

He nodded to the pot. 'All this food. It gives one a warm feeling.'

'How d'you know? You've not tasted it.'

He smiled. 'You misunderstand me. I meant it's a good feeling to know that your neighbours have contributed to—'

'—They've give us nowt.'

He frowned. He knew full well that the Dowlings had no money and relied on the mission for what little relief they were given. Before he could make a discreet enquiry, young Terence Dowling spoke up.

'It were me,' he said, giving him a defiant look and thrusting his chest out proudly.

'You've left the pit? Got another job?'

'No.'

'Well then?'

Before the boy could answer, his mother gave him a warning glance. *Say no more.*

But Terence had more to say. 'I did a job for some bloke.'

'What sort of job?'

'He give me three pounds if I did what 'e asked. He said two at first but I towd 'im it were three or 'e could whistle. So 'e give me three.'

Walter Anders felt his heart sink. A variety of possibilities played out in his mind like some devilish phantasmagoria. He looked at the boy then at his mother. There was no appearance of shame in either of them, Mrs Higham seemingly resigned to the boy's admission now that the cat was out of the bag.

With some apprehension, Walter asked his next question. 'What did this man ask you to do, Terence? No matter how painful it is to answer, answer you must if we can begin to seek forgiveness and redemption.'

Terence looked at his mother. She reached over the pot, took a ladle from the hooks beside the range and gave the contents a stir.

'Might as well tell 'im now,' she said.

'I just did what 'e wanted me to. I weren't bothered.'

'But surely you know that such things are wrong, Terence?' Walter said.

The boy shrugged. 'It were only the bar in t'Royal. They're all stuck up buggers anyroad what stay there.'

Walter's eyes grew wide. 'A man staying at the Royal took you to his room?'

Terence gave a harsh laugh. 'Bugger off!'

His mother lifted the ladle, dripping with stew juice and pointed it menacingly at their charitable visitor. 'What sort o' boy d'you think our Terry is?'

'I was simply pointing out…'

Terence frowned. 'You've allus told us pubs were evil places anyroad. So it can't be wrong, can it? Besides, it were only a brick.'

'What?' said Walter, confusion creasing his brow.

'What I threw. It were only a brick. Straight through the bloody winder. An' I got three pounds for it from that bloke. Daft sod, eh, Mr Anders?'

His mother gave a proud nod towards the pot bubbling on the range.

*

When the young constable had left the hotel, proudly patting the notebook he'd brought with him, one of the guests he'd just spoken to watched him walk briskly down the steps and turn to his left, heading back to the station.

Cocky bastard! the guest thought. But no match for me.

His thoughts quickly reverted to the events of Monday night. He'd never done that sort of thing before, but by God, it had felt good. He felt truly liberated for the very first time. But now, he told himself, now was the time to be extra vigilant. He'd heard of too many instances where overconfidence had led to misjudgement, and misjudgement had led to blunders. Then, inevitably, arrest.

He just needed to tread very carefully, do nothing to attract attention.

Then everything would be all right.

And then he could do it again.

CHAPTER EIGHTEEN

Detective Brennan's Notes

Violet Crosby Murder

1. Last seen alive 6.30 p.m. Monday 29th November. Husband, Simeon Crosby, spoke to her as he left. Overheard by Ralph Batsford. (Crosby says she was in bed, reading. If she were seeing Maria Woodruff later, against her husband's wishes, wouldn't she be undressed at that point? Did he know what she was planning? Motive enough to kill her?)

2. Ralph Batsford excused himself from Constable Palin and went back into hotel 'to get his notebook'. Genuine? Or was there a darker reason? Did he go up to Crosby room, knock on door and strangle Violet? (But this was minutes after her husband left. If she were still alive then and undressed – to fool her husband – would she have dressed so quickly? Possible – but likely? Again, what was the motive?)

3. If she were still alive when both men left... what time was she murdered?

4. Someone threw a brick through the window of the hotel bar. While everyone was at the Public Hall, Miss Woodruff went to the Royal and asked to see Mrs Crosby just after eight. Then, according to the receptionist, Gray, who'd gone outside to catch the culprit, Miss Woodruff was standing at the desk waiting to see Mrs Crosby. (Did she throw the brick? Pay someone to throw it? If so, why? To give her time to kill Mrs Crosby? But what possible motive did she have?) No response when George the bellboy went upstairs. Was she already dead at that point?

5. Who was the man George, the bellboy, bumped into on the stairs, going down, according to the boy? A guest, he reckoned. Knew George by name. Morgan? Dodds? Couldn't have been Simeon C or Batsford – they were at Public Hall. But Gilbert Crosby?

6. Where was Gilbert Crosby from Monday night to Tuesday night? Reappeared after body found. Motive? Violet Crosby urged her husband not to pay his fine for gambling. Sent to prison. Got his scar in a prison brawl. Bitter?

7. Thomas Evelyne. Despises what Simeon Crosby stands for. Says he was attacked by police in King Street. Woke up on steps of St Joseph's. Where was he from time of disturbance in King Street until Fr Clooney roused him? Is his stand against capital punishment a strong enough motive to murder Violet Crosby? Hypocritical, to say the least, if so. Besides, why her and not Simeon himself?

8. Oscar Pardew. Escaped lunatic. Says he merely wanted to shake Crosby's hand after hangman executed the murderer of his father who was killed in a gambling row. Is he a realistic

suspect, considering his state of mind? Would he have the cunning sense to enter the Royal, persuade Mrs Crosby to open her door and then not only kill her but make his escape? Would he then make such a show of himself by assaulting Evelyne in the Queen's? Unlikely suspect!

9. The two travelling salesmen, Morgan and Dodds. Morgan was evasive when asked where he came from. Chester. Dodds – travelling salesman with no wares. No interest in who was murdered. Why? Also, Dodds said he was downstairs having cigar after evening meal until around 8.45. Why didn't he mention the brick smashing the hotel window? He was downstairs at the time. Or was he?

Maria Woodruff Murder (including interviews with Constable Palin)

1. Simeon Crosby. In his hotel room, grieving over his wife's death. Did he leave the hotel? Not seen by anyone, but that doesn't mean he didn't venture out. Motive? Resentment because of her involvement with his wife? Enough to kill? Potentially, twice?

2. Gilbert Crosby. In his hotel room. Could have left, as per Simeon above. Motive? Any connection with Maria Woodruff?

3. Ralph Batsford. In his hotel room. As above. Denied seeing Maria Woodruff in Wigan yet admits she was his estranged wife. Secretive buggar. Motive for killing her? Professional jealousy towards her success as journalist? Her involvement with Violet Crosby? Or something else?

4. Who was the man Maria Woodruff was seen arguing with in Market Place? When she told him to get back to *his*

golden goose? Batsford? Gilbert Crosby? More than likely Batsford. No love lost between them. But the second part of what Rat-Yed heard her say: *I'll get back to mine.* What – or who – did she mean by that? Who was *her* golden goose? The man *living a lie*?

5. Morgan and Dodds. In their hotel rooms. No alibis. No apparent link with either of the two victims. No reported sightings of them with VC or MW. Innocent or careful? Nervous when asked where they came from. Check addresses! (Palin says Dodds was aggressive when questioned.)

6. Oscar Pardew. He spoke to Miss Woodruff Monday night in the Market Square. Did she find something interesting or peculiar about him? Is it likely he killed her for whatever reason and then let himself be found following morning in a railway station lamp room? Motive for murder? Unclear.

7. Thomas Evelyne. Not in his hotel room when Constable Jaggery called Monday night. Where was he? Says he was out seeking Pardew after trouble in Queen's. Did he meet Maria Woodruff on his travels? Kill her? Motive? Unclear.

8. Maria said *she'd come here to write a story and she'd leave here writing another.* What did she mean by that? What was her new story, and how did it link with the murder of Violet Crosby?

9. Who was the man she described as *living a lie*? Is he the double killer?

CHAPTER NINETEEN

Summons for a Witness

Whereas, I am credibly informed that you can give evidence on behalf of our sovereign lady the Queen, touching the death of Violet Crosby, now lying dead in the parish of Wigan, in the said county of Lancashire. These are, therefore, by virtue of my office, in Her Majesty's name, to charge and command you personally to be and appear before me at the Wigan Borough Police Court in the said parish of Wigan at six of the clock in the evening on the day of Friday 23 November, then and there to give evidence and be examined on Her Majesty's behalf, before me and my inquest, touching the premises.

Hereof fail not, as you will answer at your peril. Given under my hand and seal this day of 21 November, one thousand eight hundred and ninety-four.

A Milligan, Coroner

The formal inquest into the death of Violet Crosby, under the jurisdiction of the coroner, was to be held at the Wigan Borough Police Court on Friday. This meant, of course, that all the people involved, however remotely, would need to present themselves at the inquest if requested. The following Monday had been set aside for the second inquest, into Maria Woodruff's death.

It was a requirement of the proceedings that the jury and the coroner view the body – though not necessarily at the same time – at the first sitting of the inquest, after which the coroner would take the jury into a private room, call over the names of the jury and explain to them the object of the inquiry – namely to ascertain by what means the deceased came by her death. He had already made a proclamation for the attendances of witnesses, and Detective Sergeant Brennan was given the notices to serve on the relevant witnesses.

Failure to appear at the inquest would prompt the coroner to issue a summons for contempt, which would involve arrest and enforcement of the summons.

The inquest would, of course, bring in a verdict of murder. It had the authority to imply guilt, and that would result in the accused's immediate arrest after the inquest closed.

But I'll have the bugger before that! Brennan promised himself as he patted the swathe of summonses in his inside pocket and approached the Royal Hotel.

He had been busy that morning.

First, he'd made use of the station telephone. It was an instrument he didn't really like using – he liked to see people's faces when he spoke to them – but these calls were a matter of urgency. He rang the police stations in Chester and Blackburn, asking for urgent verification on the two addresses he'd been given by Morgan and Dodds. In both instances, he was given assurances that they would check on them immediately. Then he continued on his route away from town and headed for St

Joseph's Church in Caroline Street, where he spoke with Father Clooney, who confirmed Evelyne's story of being found unconscious on the steps of the church bar one possibly significant detail.

'Sure the poor fella had a lump on his head the size of a rugby ball,' said the priest. 'And shaped like one too!'

'What time was this, Father?'

'Let me see now. I'd just got back from visiting poor David Vose. The man's not long for this world, Michael.'

Brennan knew David Vose, who lived in Fowden Street, round the corner from where he himself lived. He was, at one time, a bantam cock of a bloke, wiry and muscular with a chirpy sense of humour. He'd worked down the pit most of his life. Now, on the increasingly rare occasions he saw him on the street, the man had lost his cheerful swagger, and his body seemed wizened, the muscles wasted and the gaunt look in his sunken eyes speaking silent volumes.

'It must have been after nine o'clock when I heard a faint knocking. Sure, I thought it was the ragamuffins who sometimes stand in the nave and yell during the mass. They think playing knock-and-run on a church door is hilarious.'

Brennan thought of his young son, Barry, whose friend had only recently been trying to persuade him to join in a similar game. He suppressed a smile. He'd done much the same himself, a sin he always under-confessed the following Saturday morning when he described it as *talking and playing in church. That is all I can remember, Father.* He often worried if lying in the confessional were a mortal or simply a venial sin.

'Anyway,' said Father Clooney, breaking into his thoughts, 'I took him in and gave him a little something to bring him round.'

When Brennan left Caroline Street, he reflected on the comparative severity of lying to a priest and lying to a policeman. Which was worse?

Depends on the reason, he thought. *And we both deal in confessions.*

At the Queen's Hotel, he found Thomas Evelyne seated at a solitary table in the vault, the plate of bacon and livers barely touched. He sat down opposite him and handed him a summons. He had several more in his possession.

'I don't understand,' said Evelyne when he'd read the document. 'What has Mrs Crosby's death to do with me?'

Brennan spread his hands palms down on the table. 'Because you're a witness, Mr Evelyne. It's quite possible that the trouble in King Street Monday night helped whoever killed Mrs Crosby.'

'Helped? How?'

'It created a diversion,' said Brennan with a smile. 'While all hell broke loose, the killer might well have sneaked away and carried out the murder.' He made no mention of another possible diversion – the hurling of a brick through the hotel bar window.

Evelyne sighed. 'I've been away from my wife for too long, Sergeant.'

'And you'll be away from her a bit longer, I'm afraid.' He nodded down at the summons and shrugged. *Out of my hands, pal.*

He shivered as he made his way back up Wallgate and headed for the Royal Hotel. The temperature had dropped even further, and he could see the way people almost hugged themselves to keep warm.

Ellen had urged him to wear his muffler to keep out the cold. He had refused. As usual, she was right, and he was stubborn.

He focused on what he needed to do. He was determined to get to the bottom of where Gilbert Crosby had been from Monday to Tuesday night. If need be, he'd arrange for Constable Jaggery to drag him down King Street and into a nice, cold cell. He hoped it wouldn't come to that, though. Simeon Crosby was in mourning – as indeed was his brother Gilbert – and the last thing Brennan wanted was to cause the family more upset.

But he needed some answers.

When he arrived at the Royal, he was informed that Mr Gilbert Crosby had left the hotel some fifteen minutes earlier, expressing his intention to *take some much-needed air.*

'If you ask me,' said Mr Gray on the reception desk, in an air of professional confidence, 'there's bad blood between them two.'

'Which two?'

'The brothers, Sergeant. They came down those stairs in a right how d'ye do. The hangman's face was flushed red, and that scar-faced brother of his kept shrugging him off and sayin' he was tired of bein' told what to do. As Mr Gilbert was makin' for the door, his brother called out, *Have you no sense of shame? Even now?* Made no difference. Out he went.'

'He wasn't carrying a suitcase?'

Gray shook his head. 'Oh no, Sergeant. I reckon he'll be back once he's had his fill of Wigan air.'

Brennan bit his lip. Gilbert Crosby was beginning to annoy him. The sooner he placed the summons in his hands the better.

He made his way upstairs and knocked on Simeon Crosby's door. It was Ralph Batsford who answered.

'Any news, Sergeant?' he asked. 'Simeon has been sharing some of his fond memories of poor Violet.'

As Brennan entered the small room, he saw Crosby standing by the window, gazing out.

'I'm sorry to interrupt, Mr Crosby. I wished to speak with your brother, but I hear he's gone out.'

He noticed the man's shoulders tense for a moment at the mention of his brother then slacken as he turned round to face his visitor.

'What did you wish to see him about?'

Brennan shrugged. 'His whereabouts since Monday night.'

Simeon Crosby glanced at Batsford. 'He won't say. I've asked him and urged him to speak with you. My brother's a fool, Sergeant, but I'm sure you've already come to that conclusion yourself.'

'I think he's foolish,' Brennan said carefully. 'But perhaps you might have some idea. He has told me merely that he was with, shall we say, loose company?'

Simeon Crosby gave a bitter laugh that seemed hideously incongruous in this room of mourning.

Brennan's next words were spoken with some caution. 'I gather you and he had strong words in the past. When he was sent to prison.'

For a moment, Crosby flashed a glance at Batsford. It was a look of pure anger that vanished, to be replaced by a slow nod of acceptance. 'He was on a path of self-destruction,' he said finally. 'If I had paid his fine, as he begged me to, then within a week, he would have been back at the tables, and the whole thing would have started again. I had much on my mind back then, as my wife well knew.'

'Such as?'

The hangman gave a small cough and looked once more at Batsford before continuing. 'Because of my brother's indiscretions, I'd become distracted and I had started to make mistakes. In my work.'

'What mistakes?'

'Once, I misjudged the drop, and the prisoner struggled at the end of the rope for a few minutes longer than was acceptable. And once, I found the gallows equipment must have been faulty, even though I'm sure I checked it, and so one lucky prisoner was allowed to serve a life sentence instead of swinging at the end of the rope. To make matters worse, the villain escaped from prison, but once he was recaptured, we renewed our acquaintance, shall we say? Another time, I made the mistake of arguing with a female prisoner who'd drowned her child, while the chaplain stood by tut-tutting and telling me to show some consideration. I must admit that made me laugh! The chaplain reported me to the governor.' He sighed. 'All this because of Gilbert and his... troubles.'

'It was your wife who persuaded you to withhold the payment of the fine?'

'Yes. It was the only way to cure his addiction.'

'Did it work?'

'I doubt it very much.'

'Oh, before it slips my mind,' Brennan said, reaching into his coat pocket and extracting the summonses. 'A formality, of course, but a necessary one.'

He handed each man his summons. Batsford read it through and looked at Brennan, a frown creasing his brow. 'This means I have to stay till Friday?'

'Yes, Mr Batsford. Does that cause a problem for you?'

'No, Sergeant. Not at all.'

'And, of course, you'll be summoned for your wife's inquest. That will be on Monday, though the coroner hasn't issued those yet.'

Batsford was about to say something but thought better of it.

Simeon Crosby simply looked at the summons and shook his head.

'I have one here for your brother, Mr Crosby. Will he be back soon?'

'I should imagine so.'

Suddenly, there was a knock on the door. When Batsford opened it, the bellboy, George, was standing there.

'Sergeant Brennan? Mr Eastoe says you've to come down at once.'

'Oh? And why is that?' Brennan asked lightly.

'He says 'e's got somebody responsible for what 'appened Monday night. Got 'im in 'is office and you're to come an' arrest 'im.'

*

When Brennan walked into Eastoe's office, he was somewhat taken aback to be presented with a young boy, standing beside the manager's desk with Eastoe himself seated behind it and a third person, whom Brennan didn't recognise, sitting in a chair facing the desk.

'Ah, Sergeant Brennan,' said Eastoe with a satisfied smile on his face. 'May I introduce Mr Walter Anders, who, among other things, is a senior missionary for the Wigan Missionary and Rescue Mission.'

Anders shook Brennan's hand – a firm grip, thought Brennan. He was immediately struck by the man's height – he must be well over six foot, he reflected, with the narrowest set of shoulders he'd ever seen. He wasn't thin exactly, but there was an austerity about him that put Brennan in mind of some of the more ascetic monks he'd encountered back in Tipperary.

Brennan turned his attention to the boy, who stood with his head bowed, twisting his cap in his hands tightly, the way you'd squeeze out the last drops of rain if it were damp. He snivelled occasionally, but whether that was through some winter cold or the accompaniment to recently shed tears, he had no idea.

'What's this about catching who did it?' Brennan asked. 'And who did what, exactly?'

Eastoe sat back and held out his right hand, palm upward. 'This is the wretched vandal who threw a brick through my hotel window,' he said sharply.

Brennan frowned and addressed the boy. 'What's your name, lad?'

'His name is Terence Dowling,' Anders said before the boy could respond. 'He lives in Scholes,' he added in a tone that carried dark but unspoken implications.

Eastoe said, 'Mr Anders here has told this miscreant that he must apologise to the hotel and work off the cost of what he damaged. Namely, one window and a valuable set of beer glasses. My inclination is for the boy to be arrested and charged with criminal damage.'

'I visit the family regularly, Sergeant,' Anders went on as if the manager hadn't spoken, 'and both father and son haven't worked for two months. When I discovered what he'd done, I warned his mother that if young Terence here didn't accept his responsibilities and confess, then the mission cannot continue to provide the support we have given ever since her husband was laid off with sickness.'

For a few moments, Brennan stared at young Terence, whose head had remained bowed throughout these opening comments.

'Right,' Brennan said, 'I think I can manage from here, thank you.'

Both Eastoe and Anders stared at him, Eastoe expressing what they both seemed to feel.

'You're asking us to leave?'

'I am indeed.'

'Might I remind you, Sergeant Brennan, that this is my office?'

Anders chipped in. 'And I should remain here with the boy to make sure he does admit to everything he did. Without my witnessing a confession I don't think I could recommend...'

Brennan raised a hand. 'You've shown great public spiritedness, Mr Anders, and I'm sure the chief constable will make mention of it in his report to the Watch Committee. I can assure you the boy will tell me what I wish to know. And spend time here in the Royal to work off what he owes. But in the meantime, I need to speak with him alone. I greatly appreciate your support. Gentlemen?'

He stood aside and waited until both men, grudgingly and with stern glances at young Dowling, had left the room. Then he went over to the boy and placed a hand on his shoulder. 'You can look up now, lad,' he said in a gentle tone.

Terence Dowling raised his head. The rims of his eyes were a dark red with weeping, although there were no tears now. Brennan could see tiny specks of coal dust that appeared to be ingrained in the boy's eye sockets. It was a common symptom of working down the pit, no matter how long they'd been away from the coalface. He was small, with a painful-looking rash around his mouth. A few of his teeth were missing, whether through decay or fighting, it was impossible to tell.

'How old are you, Terence?'

'Twelve.'

'You work down the pit?'

'I did. Till me dad got sick.'

'I see. Why were you in town Tuesday night?'

The boy looked quickly away, then returned Brennan's gaze. He'd already admitted the crime, his expression suggested. No point denying anything.

'I were sellin' newspapers. An' I were bloody frozzen.'

Brennan knew that the practice of young boys selling newspapers on the streets at night had come to the attention of the Watch Committee. The Wigan branch of the Newsagents' Union had objected to such a trade after nine o'clock.

'Why did you throw a brick through the window?'

The boy shrugged. ''Cos I wanted to.'

'Why?'

His shoulders sagged. Whatever it was he might be holding back had lost its strength.

'Some bloke asked me to.'

Now Brennan was alert. 'What bloke?'

'I dunno. Never seen 'im before.'

'He asked you to throw a brick through the window and you just did it?'

'Offered me some money. Two quid. Told him to piss off. Then he offered three so I took it. Like I say, I were frozzen.'

'What did he look like?'

Again the boy shrugged. 'Dunno. It were dark.'

'Tall? Short? Fat? Thin?'

'One o' them, aye.'

'Well then, how did he speak?'

Terence Dowling looked at the policeman as if he were weak-minded. 'With 'is mouth. How else?'

'I mean, the way he spoke? Was he from Wigan or somewhere else?' The boy's blank expression forced him to elaborate. 'Was he from another town?'

'Dunno.'

Brennan bit his lip in frustration. 'You must have got some look at his face. You must have seen that, at least.' He could feel his heart racing. If Terence Dowling could recognise the one who paid him to hurl the brick – obviously a distraction so whoever it was could gain access to Violet Crosby's room unseen by the receptionist, Gray – then it wouldn't take Brennan long to extract a confession.

But the boy shook his head. 'I told yer, it were dark. An' even when he stepped out o' t'shadows after he'd paid me it were no good.'

'Why not?'

''Cos I already told you, it were cold. He had 'is face wrapped in a muffler. Couldn't see nowt but 'is eyes an' I didn't see them proper like.'

Inwardly, Brennan cursed. The man, whoever he was, had gone to great lengths to hide his features from a young boy he would probably never see again.

Now, why would he do that?

*

Once the boy had left, under the stern gaze of Mr Anders, Brennan made his way to Room One, but there was no answer when he knocked. Brennan's brow creased. There had been no one in the breakfast room or the hotel lounge – he'd checked when he first arrived to deliver the summonses – and if Dodds had left the hotel without informing anyone, then he wouldn't be pleased. There was nothing to stop anyone leaving the hotel, of course. He could hardly keep them prisoner in the place, but it did give him some anxiety not to have people where he wanted them. As he climbed the stairs to the second floor to deliver the summons to David Morgan, he would ask if the younger salesman had any idea where Dodds had gone.

But he found, when the door was opened by Morgan, that he had no need to make such an enquiry.

Edgar Dodds was there, sitting by the window and smoking a cigar.

'This is a stroke of luck!' Brennan declared as Morgan ushered him in.

'Sergeant Brennan. What can I do for you?' asked Morgan, his tone slightly nervous. He glanced across at Dodds, who inhaled slowly and deeply on his cigar.

'I wanted both of you, actually.' He reached into his pocket and drew out the two remaining summonses, handing one to each of them.

The younger man read through the document quickly. The colour drained from his face. 'A summons?' When he spoke, his voice was faint.

'It's nothing to worry about, Mr Morgan. A formality, really. Once you've given your evidence you'll be free to leave.'

'*Evidence?*' The word seemed to hold untold terrors for David Morgan.

Then Dodds, casually perusing his own summons, came to his rescue. 'My dear Morgan, it's a matter of form, that's all. The *evidence* will simply be your statement of what you saw on Tuesday night. And as you didn't see anything at all, I should think your time in court will be quite a short one.'

The words appeared to have a soothing effect. Morgan nodded and placed the summons on the table by the window. He caught Dodds' eye and the older man said, 'You'll be able to have your Manchester Day on Saturday instead.'

Morgan nodded and turned to Brennan. 'Will that be all, Sergeant?'

'I think so, Mr Morgan. And I appreciate your co-operation. It's an imposition, I know, but best to turn up and get the inquest over with, eh? You wouldn't want the court to issue a warrant for your arrest, would you?'

He'd spoken gently, with some humour, but his words had the opposite effect.

'Warrant?' said Morgan, swallowing hard.

'Oh, it's just what we say to reluctant witnesses. Won't be necessary in your case.'

'Isn't a warrant for arrest overdoing things a bit, Sergeant?' It was Dodds who spoke.

'It's all in the coroner's hands, Mr Dodds. We're just his servants. Anyone – what's the phrase? Ah yes. Anyone *wilfully and absolutely refusing to give evidence* will be put in gaol until such a time as he or she agrees to do so. It's a tedious business, tracking such people down. But I don't think we'll have any trouble with two such respectable persons as your good selves. And now I've got many things to get through, as you can appreciate.'

Brennan took his leave of the two travelling salesmen and headed back to the station.

*

On his return, the desk sergeant hailed him.

'Summat's come for you, Mick.' He reached down and lifted up a telegram, which Brennan accepted eagerly. In the solitude of his office, he opened the telegram and read its contents.

It was from the editor of *The Graphic*.

Devastated to hear of M. Woodruff's death. Gifted writer. Wrote article July last year re Crosby's Victims. Suggest read edition 1 July. No idea of her proposed new article.

Editor, The Graphic.

Brennan looked up and smiled. He knew exactly where he could get his hands on a copy of the magazine. Why, if he walked back down the corridor, stood on the steps of the Wigan Borough Police Station and looked across Rodney Street, he would see the very place.

*

The Wigan Free Library was built in 1878, and a few years ago, an extension to the building – generously paid for by Lord Crawford himself – had been warmly welcomed by the town. Detective Sergeant Brennan was a member, although his visits were infrequent. And as far as he knew, the only time Constable Jaggery had set foot in the place was in response to a complaint, by the chief librarian, of several books being damaged by a few unsavoury youths. Jaggery had lain in wait, despite patience not being one of his virtues, and eventually caught two ruffians who were tearing pages from books and coughing to conceal the act. Jaggery's subsequent manifestation and apprehension of the culprits – a loud and messy business involving the collapse of at least one fully-loaded shelf – had given the chief librarian cause to regret reporting the matter in the first place.

Now, as he entered the library, accompanied by his scowling constable (*takes me all me time to read the bloody roster 'is lordship makes us read*

had been his response to the invitation), Brennan passed the new Boys'
Reading Room on his left and approached the large oak table that served
as the administration desk.

The assistant librarian – a pleasant-faced young man, smartly dressed
in suit, collar and tie – listened to the sergeant's request and directed
him to the reference room.

'You'll notice the large table in the reference room, Sergeant, with a
sign that reads *Ladies Table*. You might as well ignore it, as it's underused
to the point of redundancy. Our ladies prefer the company of the general
public. They're missing so much, you know. If you've time, you'll find
the latest pamphlets on current political and social topics. Sir Francis
Sharp Powell is a most generous donor to the reference library. And,' he
almost whispered it in confidence, ignoring the impatient sigh from the
lumbering constable, 'I can let you have a glimpse at our most recent
acquisition. A rare copy of Martin Luther's tract *Contra Henricum Regem
Angliae*. Mr Folkard tells me not even the Bodleian possesses a copy!'

'Thank you. It's something Constable Jaggery here is most keen to inspect.'

'Really?' was the young man's surprised reaction.

A phlegmy cough was Jaggery's.

A few minutes later, with Jaggery standing a few feet away, staring
incomprehensibly at the ranks of periodicals, magazines and pamphlets
on the shelves, Brennan sat at the aforementioned Ladies Table and
opened the first July copy of *The Graphic*.

The front cover depicted an exciting, dangerous scene – a lifeboat was
being lowered into violent seas, and the caption read *A Man Overboard*.
As he went through the pages, he was struck by the superb quality of
the illustrations: one page showed HRH the Prince of Wales unveiling a
memorial panel, the next a remarkably detailed portrait of a *Gladstonian
Member for Swansea*, while another was an actual self-portrait of an

illustrator – Seymour Lucas A.R.A. – in the process of drawing scenes from a new story by H Rider Haggard.

'Them's bloody good drawin's!' came a voice from close to his right ear. Constable Jaggery had somehow – miraculously – stolen up behind him and was staring at the pages in wonder.

'Yes, they are.' Brennan felt a slight irritation but continued to turn the leaves until he came to page fourteen.

'Bloody 'ell!' Jaggery exclaimed, causing Brennan to flinch.

'Why don't you nip out and get a megaphone? Didn't quite catch that, Constable.'

As a rule, irony was wasted on Jaggery, but even he understood the sergeant's annoyance.

'But, that's meladdo, ain't it?' he said, this time almost whispering.

'It is, indeed,' said Brennan.

The article, headed *THE MURDERER'S UNSPOKEN VICTIMS*, was emblazoned across the top of the page, while underneath, in much smaller print, lay the name, *M. Woodruff*. Halfway down the page, covering two columns of print, was an uncannily accurate drawing of the hangman himself, Simeon Crosby, the wisps and strands of his hair and beard, distinct and separate.

Brennan began to read the article. Its focus wasn't on the condemned men and women who paid the ultimate price for their crimes. Nor was it on their relatives, the ones they left behind and about whom Miss Woodruff had told him she'd written. This particular article concerned the families of those murdered by the condemned.

Maria Woodruff had a hauntingly simple style of writing, he thought. She reproduced the thoughts and feelings of those whose loved ones had been taken from them, while steering away from the more lurid aspects of the murders themselves. It focused more on how they were now coping with life, the impact of losing a wife, a husband, a daughter, a sister, a brother, a parent and how they were facing the future, especially those with young children to look after.

There was very little dwelling on the feelings of hatred, of revenge, of satisfaction that the one who did this to their lives had now paid the ultimate price. It seemed to be an unspoken thread running through the article, reinforced by the almost overwhelming sense of loss.

One elderly woman, Alice, spoke of how she had never told her young son about what happened to his father, how she moved away from the neighbourhood where she had lived since a child herself so that no one would speak to him about it, nor would anyone know of what she called *the blemish on her name.* As if she herself had had something to do with her husband's murder. The one who had committed the murder had sworn his innocence, supported by his family, especially his son who even tried, unsuccessfully it transpired, to provide his father with an alibi. They blamed her for the verdict, even railing against the hangman for carrying out the orders of the state.

Her son thought his father was away at sea. A number of years had passed, and the boy had grown into a man, his questions about his father fading with his childhood.

I pray every day that Alfred, my handsome, happy son, remains in ignorance, but I dread the day he discovers the truth. What would that do to him, miss?

Maria, obviously affected by the experience, went on to describe how Alfred, the son, was indeed a fine-looking chap, resplendent in the naval uniform he wore in the photograph taking pride of place on the mantelpiece.

Another woman described how her cousin, a young woman barely twenty, had been beaten to death by her husband, how he had left their son, five years old, battered and unconscious and how the horror of one death was swiftly followed by the horror of another, for the victim's mother – the interviewee's aunt – had succumbed to her grief and taken her own life, leaving her poor husband distraught.

Imagine a pool of blood, Miss Woodruff had written. *Imagine a stone dropped in its centre. See the ripples of blood flow outwards, disturbing even the calmest of places! That is the common theme with all of these acts.*

One case Brennan recognised, despite the absence of names. A woman had been murdered by her husband, whose execution was mishandled by Crosby. She left two brothers who had been arrested outside the prison on the morning of the failed execution when they heard the news that their beloved sister's killer had somehow escaped the noose. Miss Woodruff had written of their intense grief, of how their lives were now bereft of meaning. Earlier, Crosby had spoken of the incident as a simple *mistake* caused by his brother's gambling debts.

One man, a frail, elderly sort, spoke sadly of his son, whose wife was murdered by an escaped prisoner who had broken into her home. The poor fellow came back from work to find his dear wife lying dead, their home ransacked. What made it worse was the fact that the poor woman was with child. It was little consolation, said the old man, to hear that the murderer had died on the gallows. For understandable reasons, thought Brennan, his bereaved son had flatly refused to speak with the journalist, who merely added that his photograph showed a handsome chap whose stern expression held no hint of the tragedy that would befall him.

Yet another – a man this time, by the name of Stephen – had talked of how he relied on the good nature of his neighbours once his wife had been stabbed to death, a victim of a brawl in a gambling den that left several people injured. His wife had been serving drinks and simply got in the way. If it weren't for the help provided by his neighbours, his children – all five of them – would even now be living in some workhouse or orphanage. The one who killed her had never been caught, he told her. No one had been hanged, no one had paid the price, and it was only the thought of his dear children that prevented him from scouring the land and finding out the identity of the one who'd wielded the knife. Maria Woodruff had described his tale as *in some ways the saddest story of all. Those poor children, innocent victims of an evil act. And yet the poor man blamed himself for allowing his wife to work in such a place of sin and evil.*

The thread that linked them all, she wrote, was the overwhelming sensation of helplessness, a silent raging against a future that bore no resemblance to the one they had foreseen before a murderer struck.

She had been careful not to mention any surnames.

Brennan closed the magazine.

'Anythin' of interest, Sergeant?' said Jaggery.

'I'm not sure,' came the reply. There was a look of disappointment on his face. He had hoped that somehow the face of the murderer would present itself on the page, that it would then be a simple matter of identifying the guilty one and slamming him in a cell, confession pending.

As he thanked the assistant librarian and left the building with Constable Jaggery in tow, Brennan was deep in thought. There were certain things that niggled at him, like an itch that you couldn't quite scratch.

'Bloody musty in yonder, Sergeant,' said his companion, misreading the cause of Brennan's silence. 'Comes of all them books, I reckon.'

There was something... he thought. Something that didn't quite fit. But for the life of him, at the moment, he couldn't think what that something was.

CHAPTER TWENTY

It was two o'clock in the afternoon when Gilbert Crosby presented himself at Wigan Borough Police Station and asked to see Detective Sergeant Brennan. Within minutes, he was seated in Brennan's office, his hands clasped on his chest and a satisfied smile on his face.

'My brother tells me you have something for me, Sergeant.'

Brennan reached into a drawer and took out the summons, which he handed to his guest. Crosby perused the letter and folded it before placing it in his pocket. 'Not quite the kind of summons I'm used to,' he said with a twinkle in his eye.

Brennan leaned forward. This wasn't the aggressive witness of last time.

'You left the hotel this morning.'

'Indeed I did.'

'When I'd asked you to stay there.'

'I value the open, the fresh air. Even though this town seems to be smothering itself with all manner of dust.'

'It's honest dust,' Brennan replied. The town's mills inevitably gave off tiny specks of cotton, and the coal mines issued their own particular type of dust. So, too, did the iron and steel works. If the air was less than pure, it at least was the product of honest toil.

'Well,' said Crosby, making to stand up. 'If that's all, I'll get back to my grieving brother.'

'You'll sit down,' snapped Brennan.

'I beg your pardon?'

'You heard me. I have some questions for you, and you won't be leaving this police station until you answer them.'

Suddenly, Crosby's air of affability vanished. His expression grew dark, menacing, but he had enough sense to sit back down.

'Now, Mr Crosby. Simple answer to a simple question. Where did you go on Monday night? And all day Tuesday?'

'I've already told you.'

'No, you haven't.'

Crosby was about to say something but remained silent.

'I'll ask again. Where did you go on Monday night?'

'I went to enjoy the services of a lady.'

'Which lady?'

Crosby sighed. 'They don't spend time introducing themselves.'

'In my experience – as a policeman who's brought more than one of these ladies in, might I add – in my experience, they don't spend much time doing anything other than what they're paid to do.'

'Well then,' said Crosby with arms spread outwards.

'It's also my understanding that once the – shall we call it the *transaction*? – has finished, you both go your separate ways.'

Crosby shrugged. 'Not necessarily.'

'Oh?'

'If a – shall we call him a *customer*? – pays handsomely enough, why, the transaction can go on for as long as the payment is valid. Rather like a train journey. You can buy a ticket for a short trip – Lancaster to Bolton-le-Sands, say. Or you can stay on board as far as Carlisle.'

Brennan saw the man's scar gradually developing a deeper hue. His expression, his eyes, even the contours of his mouth, exuded a calm self-control, but the jagged curve of his scar told a different story.

'It doesn't much matter how long you stayed – you are, after all, a free man.' He laid emphasis on the final phrase, a subtle hint that, if he carried on in this uncooperative vein, he wouldn't be *free* much longer. 'But I'm conducting a murder inquiry – two murder inquiries actually – and I need to be able to place the whereabouts of everyone involved with Mrs Crosby in any way. You're her brother-in-law. That makes you involved.'

Crosby held Brennan's gaze for a few seconds, evidently weighing up whatever odds he had playing out in his head. Finally, he sat back, shook his head slowly and said, 'I can't tell you where I was on Monday night. I don't know the address, as I told you the last time we spoke. I know enough about police procedure to be sure that you need nice, strong evidence before you can arrest and charge someone. You don't have any nice, strong evidence because I know full well I am innocent of any murder. So I'm afraid I won't be answering any more questions. You can do your worst, Sergeant Brennan.'

Brennan nodded, stood up and went to the door. 'Stay there,' he said.

'What are you doing?' Crosby asked, shifting in his chair.

'My worst, Mr Crosby. We'll get you nice and arrested and nice and charged and then you can enjoy the delights of a nice little cell. As I said, stay there.'

*

After Brennan had seen Gilbert Crosby escorted down to the cells, he made his way upstairs to the chief constable's office.

Might as well get it over with, he told himself.

Arresting the hangman's brother – not for murder but for refusing to provide information relevant to the inquiry – wouldn't be very well received by Captain Bell, who might be expecting more substantial progress in the two cases, but at least the chief constable could claim that an arrest had been made when he next reported to the Watch Committee.

I'm clutching at straws, thought Brennan as he knocked on the great man's door.

Once he was admitted, he got the bad news out of the way first. Then Captain Bell, leaning in his chair behind the large table, listened as he went through the progress of his investigations so far. When he'd finished, his superior said something quite unexpected.

'As far as the arrest of Crosby is concerned, I don't think you could have done anything else, Sergeant, given the circumstances. Well done.'

'Thank you, sir.'

'Nor can I find fault with the way you have directed your inquiries.' He invited his detective sergeant to sit down. 'Now, this escaped lunatic – Pardew?'

'Yes, sir.'

'You tell me he was in the thick of the action in King Street?'

'Yes, sir. It was actually Pardew who caused it in a way.'

'How?'

'He was at the back of the crowd as they entered King Street, then as the ones at the front got near to the Public Hall, he suddenly started running, pushing his way through and yelling out Simeon Crosby's name.'

Brennan watched as Captain Bell reached forward and peered at something that lay on his table. It seemed to be a telegram, a rather long one at that, but as to its purport, he had no idea. After apparently reading it for a while, the chief constable gave a satisfied grunt and leaned back again.

'Would you say that the disturbance was deliberately caused by the madman?'

Brennan thought for a time. 'I'm not sure, sir. It did *cause* the disturbance, there's no doubt about that. But as to whether Pardew intended it to be the consequence, I can't say. He is, as you say, an escaped lunatic.'

Again, Captain Bell leaned forward, this time lifting the letter from his table and placing it to one side. Brennan saw there was something else lying beneath where it had been. It was another telegram.

'Mr Flynn, the medical superintendent at Haydock Lodge Lunatic Asylum, from where Pardew made his escape, has sent me a most interesting telegram concerning the man. The place is a private asylum, you know, and Pardew's family are paying six guineas a week – *six guineas!* – to help care for him and hopefully restore him to his senses.'

Brennan wondered what this was leading up to.

'According to Mr Flynn, Pardew has shown most encouraging signs of improvement. He was in the Indian Civil Service, you know?'

Brennan nodded. This was getting close to the matter. Captain Bell had served in India, and sometimes to hear him talk, there was almost a mystical attraction to the place.

Captain Bell gave a small cough. 'In your preliminary report, you have written that the man had apparently cut himself that night.'

'Yes, sir. His hands had been bleeding.'

'Surely not from the murder? The poor woman was strangled or choked with a rope, was she not?'

'Indeed, sir. But Maria Woodruff, the second victim, had her head smashed against a brick wall. A lot of blood, sir.'

'According to the police surgeon who bandaged the fellow, his wounds were filled with glass. Something about a framed photograph.'

'Pardew says that when he was in King Street, he was attacked by one of our constables and it smashed the glass frame of a photograph he always held close to him. It was a photograph of his father's corpse.'

Captain Bell's eyes widened. 'Dreadful practice. Nothing but morbid nonsense. And some people have the nerve to sneer at the customs of the sub-continent!'

'Yes, sir.'

'So there's really no reason to keep Pardew here in the cells any longer, is there?' said the chief constable, as though his statement flowed logically from what they had just been discussing.

Brennan moved awkwardly in his chair. 'I'd rather keep him here for a while, sir. He's still a suspect. And he can't tell me where he was immediately after the skirmish in King Street.'

'But the man's a lunatic, Sergeant!'

'Lunatics have murdered in the past, sir.'

'Yes, but surely both of these murders suggest a cunning, a… an intelligence? Paying some lower-class urchin to hurl a brick through a window? Entering the hotel unseen? Tapping gently on the poor woman's door and persuading her to let him in? Making good his escape once the deed was done? Then, instead of escaping from the town where he'd committed such foul murder – twice if we accept the second murder was by the same hand – he goes and breaks into the Lamp Room of the Railway Station and sleeps there until woken in the morning? Really, Sergeant!'

Brennan wasn't really paying attention. His eyes had drifted to the first telegram that lay on the chief constable's table, placed askew now so that he could read at least some of what was written there. He could make out a few phrases:

...eternally grateful if you could... no wish to impose such a burden on our friendship... pray for the day poor dear Oscar is returned to... only the fondest memories of your kindness in Limerick...

The wily fox knew the family! They'd sent the message as soon as Pardew had been found in Wigan. The asylum had been quick in letting them know and the family even quicker writing their telegram and making pointed references to a past acquaintance.

'I'm sure we're close to solving the murders, sir. It wouldn't look good for the police force if we released someone who has no alibi while at the same time incarcerating another man for exactly the same reason. Would it, sir?'

Captain Bell pursed his lips. His eyes had suddenly narrowed. He'd been outfoxed.

It was only when he got outside the man's office that Brennan felt that familiar sensation tugging at his brain. Something the chief constable had said in there had been of some significance, something that needed to be investigated. But now it was out of his grasp.

If only he'd been paying more attention when the man had launched into his staunch defence of the lunatic!

*

Brennan, who didn't believe in coincidences, was forced to accept that the incident that followed his meeting with Captain Bell might well be designated as such.

Ten minutes after he'd returned to his office, he heard a commotion from down the corridor. Some shouting, the sound of boots clattering in haste down the steps that led to the cells, a door slamming.

When he stepped out and followed the sounds, he saw three constables standing in the doorway of an open cell door, looking inside at whatever was taking place there.

'What's going on?' Brennan asked the constable nearest to him.

'That bloody looney, Sergeant.' He nodded and stepped aside so that Brennan could get a clear view of what was happening.

The desk sergeant was kneeling beside Oscar Pardew, who was lying on the damp cell floor, writhing in apparent agony, his eyes wide open and staring wildly around the cell.

'Get a doctor. Quick!' said the desk sergeant. 'I think he's havin' a bloody fit!'

The constable beside Brennan immediately turned and ran back upstairs.

'You!' the desk sergeant shouted at the constable closest to the door. 'Get in here and grab a hold! He's all over the bloody place!'

The young constable did as he was told. Brennan, too, rushed in and grabbed hold of Pardew's legs, which were thrashing around as if he were drowning in some imagined sea-storm.

After several seconds of such convulsive horrors, the man's agitations gradually subsided, and finally, he lay still, his eyes tightly closed as though the anguish of the convulsions was now continuing inside his head.

Twenty minutes later, after the nearest doctor to the station, whose surgery lay in Darlington Street a quarter mile away, had tended to him and recommended he be transferred immediately to Wigan Infirmary for close supervision, Brennan stood on the steps of the station and watched the horse ambulance begin its journey through the streets and up the incline towards the infirmary to the north of the town. Pardew had remained in his semi-unconscious state, and it had taken two constables to lift his dead weight and place him on the bed inside the ambulance. He had insisted on Jaggery accompanying the patient in the ambulance, despite the big constable's mumbled objections that seemed to offer a dark diagnosis of demonic possession.

'At least with Freddie Jaggery beside him, there'll be no shenanigans, eh, Mickey?' the desk sergeant had whispered in Brennan's ear as they watched the horse ambulance turn right into King Street. 'Pardew might be daft, but he's not stupid.'

The desk sergeant was wrong.

*

It started as the ambulance negotiated the turn from King Street into Wallgate. Not only was it a sharp turn, the road also suddenly began to rise as it led towards Market Place. Jaggery, keeping a keen eye on the still-slumbering prisoner, held onto the side of the ambulance as it took the right turn. He leaned down to peer through the gap in the side of the carriage, and when he returned his gaze to Pardew, he saw, with some astonishment, that the man's eyes were now wide open and staring at him with such intensity, it caused him to swallow nervously.

'What the bloody 'ell's up wi' thee?' Jaggery asked. He was afraid of no man, but having a wide-eyed lunatic glaring at him wasn't the most pleasant of experiences.

Pardew licked his lips then pressed them together, billowing his cheeks out as though he were desperately trying to whistle but no sound was forthcoming. He lifted both hands to his throat and his eyes bulged, giving every appearance of choking.

'Bloody 'ell!' Jaggery clambered towards the front of the ambulance and called up to the driver. 'You'll 'ave to pull in. Meladdo's chokin'!'

The driver called back, 'I can't. I've a bloody big tram up me arse!'

Before Jaggery could offer a response, Pardew leaped up from the bed, spread both arms wide before a thoroughly alarmed constable and roared like a lion before hurling himself through the rear of the ambulance, evading both the front of the Wilkinson engine pulling the bogie car behind it and the curses of the tram driver whose arms were flailing as wildly and as violently as his language.

Jaggery followed and was met with the same response, this time augmented by the yelling of the conductor who referred to him as a 'Mad fat bastard!'

But Jaggery, who under normal circumstances would have dragged the conductor from his platform and given him a thick ear, was more concerned with chasing the escaped prisoner, who had by now disappeared from view.

*

It was, Constable Jaggery admitted later, the worst moment of his time in the force. He'd scoured the streets for over an hour – Market Place, Standishgate, Wallgate, Crawford Street, all the alleys nearby, even checking the graveyard by the Municipal Offices in the hope that the damned lunatic might be crouched behind a headstone. But he found nothing. When he stopped people in the street and told them he was looking for a scruffily dressed idiot who might have run past them, they shook their heads and regarded him as if *he* were the idiot. One even suggested he try the workhouse in Frog Lane if he were that desperate.

Finally, he'd been forced to make the short trudge back down King Street and face the music.

Sergeant Brennan, he was relieved to discover from the desk sergeant, had left the station a few minutes after Jaggery had left in the ambulance.

'We'd best let everybody know,' said the sergeant after spending several minutes tearing into the forlorn constable for being, among other things, *a bloody stupid waste of a uniform.* He'd hastily gathered together as many duty constables as he could, urging them to spread the news about the escape but keep it among themselves for the time being.

'If his bloody lordship upstairs finds out,' he warned the small gathering in the canteen, 'Constable Jaggery's out on his arse. Let's find the looney little sod before it gets to that, eh?'

They'd all patted Jaggery on the back as they left, commiserating with his predicament while at the same time silently acknowledging that there but for the grace of God…

*

Sergeant Brennan, meanwhile, oblivious of the gross error perpetrated by Jaggery, had made his way to The Squirrel in Upper Morris Street, Scholes. He knew full well that his quarry would be ensconced in the vault of the public house, his favourite watering hole where he and his cronies would meet, drink and discuss the possibilities for the night, which would be spent either drinking or thieving or a combination of the two.

Rat-Yed was less than happy to see him. It wasn't something he liked the others to know about: the rare occasions he offered information to the detective sergeant never involved them or their nefarious activities, yet the very fact he was helping the police would have gone down very badly indeed.

Brennan, fully aware of the man's feelings, approached the table where another two of his associates were sitting and spoke sternly, making it clear that Rat-Yed was under suspicion for a wholly imaginary theft from a shoe warehouse the previous night.

Once they were outside, Rat-Yed gave full vent to his feelings. 'Not a fuckin' good idea, Mickey, lad. Makes me look bad, that does.'

'Don't worry,' Brennan replied. 'I can give you a thick lip if you like, remove any suspicions they might have.'

Rat-Yed shrugged off the idea. 'Anyroad, what dost want now?'

'I want you to take a walk with me. Up to the Royal.'

'Why? They'll not let me anywhere near the place. I'm barred.'

'I'll unbar you. Temporarily. I just need you to identify someone, that's all.'

'Who?'

'Remember the man you say spoke to the woman who was murdered? Argued with her in Market Place Tuesday night?'

'Aye.'

'Somebody I want you to look at. Tell me if it was him.'

'I already told you. It were dark.'

'You recognised her all right. Or at least your mate did, the one who saw her in Livesey's Yard.'

'No bloody choice then, have I?'

They both set off along Upper Morris Street, turned left into Greenhough Street and walked the short stretch to the Royal Hotel. Mr Eastoe, the manager, made a strong protest when he saw who Brennan's companion was.

'This creature devours vermin!' he said, pointing a finger at Rat-Yed.

'There tha wrong!' declared the latter. 'I don't eat the buggers. I just bite their heads off. It'd be disgustin', swallowin' a rat's head, now, wouldn't it?'

After a few minutes' negotiation, during which Brennan agreed to take his friend to the hotel's rear entrance, Mr Eastoe went off to ask both Simeon Crosby and Ralph Batsford to join the detective and help him with his inquiries.

After what Brennan thought was an unconscionably long time, the manager opened the rear door and stepped out, his face ashen white.

'What is it?' Brennan asked, sensing immediately that something was wrong. 'Where are Crosby and Batsford?'

Eastoe shook his head. 'Mr Batsford is nowhere to be found, and Mr Crosby… I really have no idea how he got in.'

'What? Who do you mean?'

Eastoe cleared his throat. 'The man. Upstairs.'

'Which man?'

'I have no idea. But he's with Simeon Crosby, and the door is locked, and I could hear someone singing a song about a headless corpse. Mr Crosby sounded quite alarmed. He said there was blood everywhere, and the man had something in his hand.'

Impossible! thought Brennan. *It can't be Pardew. I'd left him under the care of…*

Jaggery!

'Stay here!' he said to Rat-Yed. 'If you move, I'll make sure you can't bite the head off a dandelion, never mind a rat.' He turned to Eastoe. 'Come with me!'

Before the manager could object, Brennan had pushed past him and vanished into the dark interior of the hotel.

Barely half a minute later, both of them were standing outside Simeon Crosby's room. When Brennan tried the door, he found it was still locked.

'Mr Crosby?' he called out. 'It's Detective Sergeant Brennan.'

'Thank God!' came the response from beyond the door.

'Oscar? Is that you?'

Brennan, with Eastoe at his side, tugging nervously at his collar and looking around the landing in case he needed to offer some explanation to other guests, spoke in as friendly a tone as he could muster.

'You stopped me last time!' was Oscar's response. His voice was strange, husky as if he'd been crying. 'But you can't stop me now!'

'Why don't you just unlock the door, Oscar, and you can tell me all about it?'

'I made a promise to Dead Father!' Oscar said with a sob. 'And my sister. I told her what I wanted to do.'

'And what was that?'

'But he won't! After I've come all this way, on the train and the march and even Dead Father's frame. Smashed! And that youth kicking me at the station! All because I wanted to do what I'd promised to do.'

Brennan turned to Eastoe and whispered, 'Do you have a passkey?'

Eastoe at first looked puzzled. 'There's one in my office downstairs.'

'Then please go and get it,' he said urgently. 'And be quick!'

Eastoe turned around and headed for the stairs.

There was a pause and then Simeon Crosby called out, 'His hands, Sergeant! They're dripping with blood!'

'Oscar? Can you do something for me?'

'What?'

'Whatever weapon you have in your hand, just put it on the bed and then perhaps you won't make Mr Crosby so nervous.'

When Pardew didn't respond, it was Crosby who yelled out, 'He doesn't have a weapon, Sergeant Brennan. He has a photograph, and it's covered in blood.'

When Eastoe arrived with the key, Brennan inserted it into the keyhole but found it wouldn't turn. The other key was still in place.

So, to Mr Eastoe's consternation, Brennan kicked the door down.

CHAPTER TWENTY-ONE

'I only wanted to shake his hand,' said Oscar Pardew as Brennan placed him under the charge of the two constables he'd sent for.

When he broke into the room, he saw Simeon Crosby standing with his back against the window, staring at Pardew's hands with some trepidation. It was apparent that he'd reopened the jagged wounds when he made his escape from the horse ambulance – a fact he proudly admitted, adding that he could never forgive himself if the man who hanged his father's killer left the town without him shaking his hand. The offer of an outstretched hand, dripping with blood, had been enough to render Simeon Crosby fearful for his life.

'I thought it was Batsford returning,' he told Brennan when Pardew had left the room. 'So I just opened the door without thinking.'

'Where is Mr Batsford?' Brennan asked, wondering if Rat-Yed was still at the hotel's rear entrance. It had been some thirty minutes now since he'd left him there.

'We talked about Miss Woodruff, Sergeant. His estranged wife. It seems Batsford and myself share some malignant fate, with both of our wives lying cold in a mortuary, the victims of some madman.' He gave a curt nod in the direction of the door now hanging loosely from its hinges, through which Pardew had not long been taken. 'He told me he would go to see his wife. She is at the infirmary mortuary. He should be back any time now, I shouldn't wonder.'

'You decided not to go with him? To see your own wife who lies up there?'

Crosby shook his head. 'I've no desire to see a mere shell, Sergeant. I've seen enough dead bodies to know that whatever is left is mere dead flesh and stagnant blood. It will never flow again.'

Brennan looked at him curiously. It was a strange, detached thing to say. Here was a man unwilling to view the remains of his late wife, and there was Oscar Pardew, who carried around with him a bizarre photograph of his late father, eyes forced open and holding his daughter's hand. And now Batsford had gone to see his own wife, from whom he was separated and who spoke so harshly about him when Brennan last saw her.

'My brother went to the station earlier. Is he still there?' Crosby asked, deftly changing the subject.

'He is.'

'Still silent on his whereabouts on Monday and Tuesday?'

'Yes, unfortunately.'

'You know he doesn't wish to incriminate himself?'

Brennan frowned. The hangman had said it calmly, without any rancour.

'What exactly do you mean? *Incriminate himself?* If you think he had anything to do with your wife's—'

'—Oh no, Sergeant. Nothing of the sort. Gilbert wouldn't dream of harming poor Violet. They got on so well.'

'That isn't quite true, though, is it?'

Brennan recalled what Batsford had told him when they spoke to him in Wigan Market Hall, how Violet Crosby had urged her husband not to settle his brother's fines anymore, which resulted in him going to prison and suffering a violent attack, with the vicious scar on his face the outcome. That might indeed give him some sort of motive for revenge. Murder even. But what of Miss Woodruff? What had she done to deserve her fate?

Still, if Simeon Crosby wasn't referring to the murder of his wife, what exactly was he referring to when he said his brother had no wish to incriminate himself? Of what? Paying to visit a prostitute? Was the wish to avoid a petty fine stronger than providing himself with an alibi, someone who could vouch for his whereabouts on the night of the murder?

'I don't know what you mean.' Crosby spoke sharply. 'Now I'm feeling rather exhausted, Sergeant. I haven't been sleeping, and the horror and the sadness of the last few days have weakened me more than I can say. If you don't mind?'

'Remember the inquest tomorrow evening, Mr Crosby. Another ordeal to go through.'

'Of course.'

As Brennan was taking his leave, two workmen suddenly appeared at the door, armed with a bag of tools and scratching their heads at the damage recently done to the door.

'Whoever done this wants stringin' up,' said one of them.

'Have they never heard of knockin'?' said the other.

It was that final comment that caused Brennan's heart to flutter.

I wonder, he thought. *I bloody well wonder.*

*

When Brennan reached the rear entrance of the Royal Hotel, he was somewhat surprised to find Rat-Yed still standing there, shivering and blowing into his hands to keep them warm.

'Bloody 'ell fire, Mickey!' was his greeting as Brennan appeared. 'I'm freezin' me bollocks off out 'ere. What've you been doin'? Havin' a three-course meal?'

'Good of you to wait,' said Brennan, ignoring the sarcasm. 'Now, if we move quickly, we might just manage what I brought you here for.'

'But that bugger won't let me in, will 'e?' Rat-Yed gave a curt nod towards the interior of the hotel.

Brennan grabbed his arm and began to pull him along the street towards the front of the hotel. 'We don't need to go in. From what I've just been told, the one I want you to look at is even now on his way back from the mortuary.'

Rat-Yed stopped. 'He's not a bloody ghost, is 'e? I draw the line at ghosts.'

'Don't be stupid! Now come on. He should be back any minute.'

With a gloomy shake of the head, he allowed himself to be escorted round the corner towards the steps that marked the entrance to the Royal.

They stood there for no longer than five minutes, during which time Rat-Yed had tried to explain for the umpteenth time that the entertainment he provided for the public house regulars the length and breadth of Wigan was, above all, a public service, for who else in the town took such active steps to rid the place of the vermin that infested every alleyway and ginnel?

'You deserve a medal,' said Brennan, whose eyes were fixed on the lower part of Standishgate. That would be the direction Batsford would come from if he were travelling from the infirmary.

Sure enough, a hansom cab trundled its way up the incline and stopped outside the Royal, Batsford clambering down and paying the cab driver. He seemed out of sorts, his eyes downcast, and for a moment, he stood on the pavement, staring at his feet as if he were in some doubt as to which direction he wanted them to go.

Brennan nudged his companion and nodded at Batsford. 'That him?'

Before Rat-Yed could reply, the object of their interest seemed to have made up his mind, for he climbed the steps of the hotel with almost funereal slowness.

'Oh aye, Mickey. That's the bugger. Him an' that lass were 'avin' a right go at each other. That's the one right enough.'

Brennan gave him a shilling and told him he was free to go. He then stood there, looking at the now closed doors of the hotel entrance, and tried to put his thoughts into some sort of order.

People have been lying, he told himself.

Slowly, he was beginning to see.

It was still obscured, just like the world outside a bedroom window when the frost was on the inside of the glass. You scrub away until the ice begins to fragment, giving you just a glimpse of the scene beyond. But you have to scrub and scrub at that window, breathe on it and spit on it until all the ice has gone and you can see clearly for the first time.

Why did Batsford lie to him? Why did he tell him he hadn't spoken to or seen Maria Woodruff while she was here, in Wigan?

Why is Gilbert Crosby so steadfast in his refusal to say where he was on the night of the murders? Is it because he has no alibi? Or is the alibi itself incriminating?

More incriminating than a murder charge?

There's another lie needs nailing down, too, thought Brennan.

He turned to his left and headed across town and back to the station. But first, he would call in at the Post Office, aware that they'd be regarding him as something of a regular now. He needed to send another telegram. This time, to a friend of his.

*

Constable Jaggery was nowhere to be seen when Brennan got back to the station, where he was told of the circumstances of Pardew's escape. His absence was hardly surprising since there were some hard words to be said. He would take no pleasure in giving the big man the mightiest of reprimands: somewhere deep inside him, he had a soft spot for Freddie Jaggery, whose sheer brute strength had on occasion more than compensated for his limited (some might say *stunted*) intelligence, and he knew that there had been some sadness in his life, something he had found out only recently when Jaggery had confided in him about losing his young daughter years ago. Still, to allow a prisoner under escort to escape from a horse ambulance – in full view of a tram full and a pavement full of Wiganers – a bloody lunatic as well! That wasn't to be borne.

He shuddered to think what Captain Bell would make of it all.

In a perverse sort of protectiveness, he needed to punish Jaggery before the chief constable could.

'Tell the big oaf I need to see him as soon as he sets foot in this station,' was Brennan's comment to the duty sergeant, who nodded his understanding before giving Brennan the keys to the cells below ground.

When he entered the narrow corridor that led to the cells, he could hear a low, sad keening from the cell next to Crosby's. He glanced through the tiny iron grille in the door and saw Oscar Pardew seated on the bench beneath the tiny gap of daylight above his head, rocking to and fro, his hands freshly bandaged and his eyes closed.

Brennan shook his head and moved along to the door to Gilbert Crosby's cell. He was immediately struck by the difference in his prisoner.

The man now seemed fidgety, perspiring heavily and he was pacing the narrow confines of his cell with his hands clasped together. The scar, too, seemed a deep red. *It must be throbbing*, Brennan thought. And *painful*.

It's the close confinement, he realised. The awful sensation that the walls of the cell are slowly closing in. He'd seen this reaction before, in those who'd served time in Her Majesty's prisons and couldn't get the experience out of their system. A prolonged stay in a Wigan police cell wasn't something to be desired. And he remembered what Ellen had told him, about Gilbert Crosby's discomfort in the train carriage. It must have been the confined space that disturbed him.

The perfect time to strike, thought Brennan.

'And how are you feeling, Mr Crosby? Room service to your satisfaction?'

'This is outrageous!' came the heated reply. 'To be held here with absolutely nothing to suggest I was involved in any way in my sister-in-law's death. I will speak to my lawyer!'

Brennan sighed and turned round, one hand on the cell door.

'Where the hell do you think you're going?' Crosby's eyes were almost bulging from their sockets.

Brennan made a great show of looking at his fob watch. 'In an hour or so, I'll be off home. My wife's got a potato pie for tea. Should be just slapping the pastry on. Now, if you need anything, just ring up and one of the servants is bound to hear you. Goodbye. We'll speak again tomorrow.'

Before he could open the door wide enough to leave, Crosby said, 'All right. Damn you! All right.'

All defiance had gone. He slumped onto the wooden bench beneath the aperture, high in the wall and put his head in his hands. 'I'll tell you what you need to know.'

Brennan closed the door once more and stood before the prisoner.

'Good,' he said. 'Just simple answers to simple questions, Mr Crosby. Then you can go back to your brother. Where were you on Monday night and all day Tuesday?'

Crosby leaned his head back and placed it against the bare brick of the wall. 'Monday night, I stayed with friends. And on Tuesday, they took me to a meeting.'

'Who are these friends? What was the meeting about?' Brennan wondered what sort of friends the man had made in so short a time. And why be so secretive about it?

Gilbert Crosby cleared his throat and explained.

CHAPTER TWENTY-TWO

'A gambling den?'

Captain Bell's face was flushed with anger and embarrassment.

Over the last few months, he had faced considerable pressure from the members of the Watch Committee for the proliferation of illegal gambling that seemed to have spread throughout the borough like smallpox. It took several forms: the street-based *three card trick, pitch-and-toss,* the more out of the way *cockfighting* and *dog racing,* to the card games of various kinds which were played out in the intimate confines of public houses, of which there were many, often for large sums of money. This illicit vice, in the opinion of the Watch Committee, led inevitably to vices of other kinds, for losing one's wages and being burdened with indebtedness rendered the victims more liable to violence. Inevitably, it was the family back home that bore the brunt of it all.

And that, in turn, increased not only the work of the constabulary but also the figures in the annual list of indictable offences.

'I thought we'd taken steps to get rid of that abominable practice.'

'We have indeed, sir. Four raids after hours in the last week alone.'

'Well then. How can Gilbert Crosby have been to a gambling den when he knows no one in the town? Do they advertise in the *Wigan Observer?*'

'He tells me he went to a billiards match on Monday night. At the Ship.'

'Go on.' Captain Bell's tone became ominous at the mention of the Ship, a public house he would gladly have scuttled.

'And there he wagered some money.'

'At a *billiards match*?' The prospect was outrageous.

'Apparently, he lost his money.'

'To whom?'

'Benny Liptrot.'

'I might have known.'

'When he later paid the Empire Music Hall a visit, he was seething with the feeling he'd been cheated by Liptrot.'

'What else did he expect?'

Brennan ignored the question. 'Later, he paid someone for information. He'd heard a whisper that Liptrot was holding a late-night gambling session at a local pub.'

'Which one?'

'The Gibraltar Inn, sir. At the top of Scholes.'

'Scholes! If I had my way…'

Brennan knew full well what the chief constable would do to the area. But he himself had been born in Scholes, still had many friends – as well as a few enemies – in the area and decided to interrupt the outburst before he found himself defending it.

'The choice of the Gibraltar is quite a clever one, being far from the centre of town. Crosby says he went there to try to win his money back.'

'Surely he didn't stay the night in that godforsaken pit?'

'He says he did, sir, having little sleep and much to drink. Apparently, after some initial distrust, he and Liptrot got on well.'

'Kindred spirits, I suppose?'

'Indeed, sir. And on Tuesday, his luck having held firm during the card games, he was invited by Liptrot to accompany him and some friends to the races at Liverpool. Crosby told them of certain practices he'd heard of that might cheat the course bookmakers out of their money.'

'Disgraceful! And his brother a respected national figure! He spent all day Tuesday at the races?'

'It's what he says, sir. Of course, I'll need to verify that. But if Liptrot supports his statement, then he might be off the hook as far as being a suspect in his sister-in-law's murder is concerned. According to Gilbert Crosby, his train got back from Liverpool after nine. By which time Violet Crosby was dead.' He paused and added, 'Although Gilbert Crosby, along with all of the others, has no alibi for Maria Woodruff's murder.'

Captain Bell glared at him, still simmering at the fact that another gambling den had eluded his notice. Brennan knew that the Gibraltar Inn's days (or nights) of intimate card games were numbered.

'I trust you'll treat the matter with the utmost urgency, Sergeant?'

'Of course, sir.'

'Then don't let me keep you from your duties.'

'No, sir.'

*

Jaggery knew he had to face the music sometime. The one relieving factor was the good news that the lunatic, Pardew, had been brought back into custody. The bad news, of course, was that the one responsible for the man's return was Detective Sergeant Brennan.

He'd made his required patrols of the town, lingering to speak with people he didn't normally speak with, entering premises he didn't normally enter – anything, in fact, to keep his return to the station as far away as possible. But time has a way of moving faster when you don't want it to and so he had walked back to Rodney Street and was now sitting in the canteen at the table furthest from the door, nursing a grievance and a mug of hot tea. The other constables had left him alone once he'd made it clear he had no use for their company, and carried on with their game of snooker or their huddled conversations. Then the door opened, and immediately the canteen fell silent. Those playing snooker, those idly chatting at nearby tables, all suddenly realised they should be out on the streets and making sure the good people of the town were safe and well. With barely a glance at the morose figure by the window, they acknowledged the new arrival respectfully.

Once they'd all left, Sergeant Brennan approached the forlorn figure hunched over his mug of tea.

'You at a loose end, Constable?' he asked quietly.

'I've just got back, Sergeant. Been on patrol.'

'Very conscientious. If only all our constables took their duties as seriously, eh?'

Jaggery said nothing. Even he recognised the quiet sarcasm.

'If you feel able to carry out just one more duty before you leave for the day…?'

Jaggery looked at him for the first time. 'Sergeant?'

'We're going to take a walk. Speak to someone. Do you think you can manage that?' His voice was so low Jaggery could hardly hear what he said.

'Yes, Sergeant,' said Jaggery, more despondent than ever.

'Very well.' Brennan started to move towards the door. 'I presume you've done with that tea?'

'Aye, Sergeant,' said the big man, standing up.

The sergeant's quiet tones were far worse than any raising of the voice. As Jaggery followed like a sulky schoolboy, he wished the bugger had bawled him out. He could have just about coped with that.

*

Bailey's Court was a small area in Hallgate, not far from the Crofter's Arms, Brennan's favourite watering hole. Benny Liptrot's Pawnbroker Shop was situated in the middle of a row of shops, which also included a butcher's, a grocer's and a wine and spirit merchant. It had always struck Brennan as repugnant that Liptrot should own such a place – many of his customers would be forced to seek his support on a weekly basis just because of his other interests. It was common knowledge that he had a finger in several gambling operations throughout the borough and indeed beyond it. The problem was catching the little sod. Brennan knew that some of the constables frequented the Gibraltar Inn, the Ship and other places Liptrot was involved in. He knew also that they indulged in the card games and the dice games and other attractions and ended up out of pocket. Which meant one or two of the more inveterate gamblers among them owed Liptrot, who sometimes accepted not cash from them, but information.

When they reached Bailey's Court, they saw a small queue outside Liptrot's shop – it was nearing the end of the week, and money was running out. He noticed some of the women queuing were clutching bundles of clothing, while others held pairs of shoes, boots and even clogs.

Brennan glanced at the dingy window, and read the day's forfeited list: *Gent's serviceable umbrella: 3s 11d; Gent's solid gold signet ring, real stone: 4s 10d; First-class breech-loading double-barrelled gun, fine twisted barrels: £4 11s; Capital pair of field glasses, long range, with case and strap complete: 10s 6d; Sweet-toned violin, bow and case, suit learner: 16s 6d...*

Each item told its own sad story, he reflected, and silently expressed the hope that he would never be in such a dire position as to rely on money from this particular leech.

Ignoring the sour glances from those in the queue, Brennan and Jaggery entered the shop and saw Benny Liptrot leaning on the shop counter, engaged in some financial squabble involving a silver-plated clock.

A woman, whose threadbare coat hung loosely on her shoulders, held the clock to what little light there was in the shop. Beneath her head-scarf, Brennan could see dry, greying hair, her cheeks pale and pinched.

'But it plays a tune every hour,' she was saying.

'What tune?' Liptrot asked, winking at Brennan whom he saw standing by the door.

'How the 'ell should I know? A tune's a tune.'

'As long as it plays *Come into the Garden, Maude*, you can have twelve bob.'

'It doesn't bloody well play that!'

'Well then. Ten bob it is. Take it or leave it, Mrs Findley.'

The woman gave an angry nod of defeat and held out her hand. Once she had gone, Brennan stationed Jaggery with his back to the door so no one else could enter. Then he took his place at the counter.

'Sergeant Michael Brennan, as I live and breathe!' Liptrot had a smile on his lips, but there was no warmth there.

Brennan asked him about Monday night and Crosby's insistence that he spent it gambling in the Gibraltar Inn.

'Whoever this chap was gambling with, it weren't me,' he said with a shrug of the shoulders.

Brennan expected nothing more. He didn't pursue the matter – it really held no concern for him what Gilbert Crosby was doing on Monday night. It was Tuesday night – the night of Violet Crosby's murder – that he was interested in. 'He must have been mistaken.'

'Must have.'

'He did say, though, that he was in your company on Tuesday. He travelled to Liverpool with you and your acquaintances. To the races at Aintree.'

Brennan could almost hear the man's brain whirring round to assess whether admitting it might harm him.

Finally, Liptrot said, 'If you mean a bloke wi' a bloody big scar running down 'is face then aye, he were with us. Tagged along, you might say.'

'And what time was he with you till?'

Again, Liptrot gave it some thought. 'Till we got back to Wigan.'

'And what time was that?'

Liptrot shook his head. 'We'd been boozin' all day, Sergeant. By the time we got back local, I didn't know me arse from me elbow. Might've been seven, eight, nine o'clock for all I know. Now is that it? Only I've a queue of regulars out yonder an' it's hardly th' height o' summer is it, poor souls.'

With the man's concern for his fellow creatures ringing in his ears, Brennan took his leave.

'Where does that leave us, Sergeant?' Jaggery asked as they left Bailey's Court.

'That little bastard knows full well what time they got back to Wigan,' said Brennan bitterly.

'Then why not tell us?'

'Because he's peeved at Gilbert Crosby for telling us about the gambling at the Gibraltar. It's the little weasel's way of getting back at him. And it leaves us as we were before. Gilbert Crosby has no alibi for his sister-in-law's murder.'

*

George, the bellboy at the Royal, stood to attention, as he always did when Mr Eastoe personally asked for him. Normally, that would have been a good feeling, a mark of his importance in the general run of things in the hotel. This afternoon, though, as he stood before the reception desk and waited for the hotel manager to give him his orders, he couldn't help glancing occasionally at the other boy standing there. He, too, wore a uniform, dark blue with grey trousers and a cap with a scarlet band – nothing as smart as George's, of course, but he did have a metal badge stuck on his lapel. What George didn't like about the boy was the smirk on his face when he surveyed George's own uniform, especially the trousers which, he well knew, were too long for him. The Telegraph messenger boy was holding a sealed yellow envelope with the heading *Post Office Telegram* and a name that George couldn't see.

'You are to show this boy the way to Mr Batsford's room. Room Six.'

There was more than a touch of annoyance in the manager's voice, and George knew it was directed at the other boy rather than himself. Perhaps he'd refused to hand over the telegram?

'This way, boy,' said George, establishing his authority as soon as they left Mr Eastoe's presence.

The telegram boy made a sort of snorting laugh. George refused to rise to the bait, though, and he kept his eyes straight ahead. As they turned the corner to the stairs leading to the first and second floors, George heard the telegram boy say, 'Mind tha doesn't trip up. Are them thi dad's pants?'

It was more than George could bear. He turned round and was about to tell the arrogant sod to bugger off when he suddenly found himself being pushed to one side.

It was one of the guests. And he was in a hurry.

The messenger gave a hearty mocking laugh, but George took no notice. As he watched the guest move quickly down the corridor and past the reception desk, he realised that the man was the same one he'd bumped into on the night of the murder, the one who'd called him *George*.

He must tell Sergeant Brennan, he thought. Although he hadn't seen the guest's face that night, he'd just remembered something.

It was the smell that he'd forgotten about.

*

There seemed no point in keeping Gilbert Crosby in the cell any longer. His alibi was dependent on one of the most devious rogues in the town, and Brennan knew he'd get nothing more from Benny Liptrot. He'd sent Gilbert on his way with a dire warning to stay close to the hotel, reminding him that the inquest was due to take place the following evening.

'I shall do my duty,' the hangman's brother had declared as they parted company on the steps of the police station.

He'd been in his office only a few minutes when there was a knock on the door, and a constable appeared.

'Young lad at the front desk, Sergeant. Says it's important.'

When Brennan saw that young George the bellboy was standing there nervously looking round, he invited him back to his office and sat him down.

'Now then,' he said, leaning back in his chair. 'Playing truant?'

'No, Sergeant.' The boy's eyes had widened, not realising Brennan was joking. 'I told Mr Eastoe an' he said I were to come down 'ere an' tell you.'

'Tell me what?'

'I remembered. 'Bout that bloke I bumped into on the stairs. Y'know, Tuesday night.'

Brennan sat forward. 'Go on.'

Before the boy could say anything further, there was another knock at the door. Brennan could hardly contain his annoyance when the same constable poked his head around the door.

'What?' Brennan snapped.

'Duty Sergeant told me I were to give you this, case it were urgent, like.' He ventured gingerly into the room clutching a single sheet of paper in his hand. He gave it to Brennan and quickly withdrew.

Brennan quickly read the contents and gave a low whistle. He placed it face down on his desk and leaned forward once more. 'Well then? You were telling me about the bloke you bumped into. The one who was on his way down from the second floor.'

George nodded. 'I were. I'd forgot, see? About the smell.'

'What smell?' Brennan had a nightmare vision of Rat-Yed rushing around the hotel like a trapped rat.

'Cigar smoke,' said George. 'I'd forgot that's what I smelt when I bumped into 'im. It come to me 'bout 'alf an hour ago an' I told Mr Eastoe.'

'Who was it?' Brennan asked, casting a glance at the paper on his desk.

'It were that Mr Dodds. Room One.'

A slow sigh escaped Brennan's lips. He showed no surprise. It merely confirmed what was stated on the sheet of paper before him. Or rather, what was not stated.

'Thing is,' the boy went on, 'I saw Mr Dodds just now, an' 'e were lookin' like 'e were in a hurry.'

'What do you mean?'

'Well 'e just brushed past me an' went past the reception desk an' through the main door. Before Mr Gray could say owt, 'e'd gone down the steps an' legged it. Had a little case with 'im an' all. I don't think he'll be comin' back, Sergeant.'

Brennan was filled now with a sense of urgency. He stood up and thanked the boy. 'Tell Mr Eastoe I'll be there as soon as I can.'

Once George had gone, Brennan picked up the sheet, a reply to the telephone enquiry he'd made earlier, informing him that the address he'd asked the Blackburn Police to check for him turned out to be a false one:

Message from Det. Sgt. Moore. Blackburn Borough Police.

No Mr Dodds living at 16 Feilden Street. Occupant never heard of him.

Muttering a curse, he grabbed his coat and flung the door open.

CHAPTER TWENTY-THREE

'But I can assure you, Sergeant Brennan, I've only just met the fellow.'

'You both checked into the hotel on the same day, didn't you?'

'We're commercial travellers. Tend to use one town as a base. It turns out we both had the same idea. Wigan's central to several towns and cities. Liverpool and St Helens in the west of the county, Manchester and Bolton in the east…'

David Morgan's voice trailed off when he saw Brennan's brow somehow darken, become more severe.

They were sitting in Mr Eastoe's office. Brennan had sent Jaggery upstairs to Room Five to bring him down, surmising rightly that the fearsome sight of the largest constable in the Wigan Borough Police Force would quickly ensure not only his attendance but also his compliance. The confectionery salesman had, therefore, entered the manager's office looking suitably cowed. He'd denied any knowledge of Edgar Dodds' disappearance from the hotel.

'According to Mr Eastoe, you dine together. You spend time in each other's company. When I delivered your summonses for the inquest, Mr Dodds was in your room, smoking a cigar. Do acquaintances develop quicker among commercial travellers?'

Morgan gave a nervous cough. 'As a matter of fact, they do. We live the same nomadic type of life, you see. We've common ground, as it were.'

Brennan gave Jaggery, who was standing by the door looking his usual menacing self, a meaningful glance. But as usual, its meaning was lost on the constable.

'His room is empty. Mr Eastoe says he hasn't paid his bill, but he was seen leaving with a case.'

'He's a salesman. Perhaps he was carrying his samples. My suitcase is filled with—'

'—Yes, we know. But Mr Dodds told me he had brought no samples with him. Do you have any idea why he should suddenly just leave like that?'

'Absolutely none, Sergeant.'

'The address he gave me is a false one. During your meetings with Mr Dodds, did he mention where he came from?'

'He told me Blackburn.'

Brennan sighed. The fact that he'd given a real address – Feilden Street – suggested he was at least familiar with the town. It was highly likely that he did, in fact, live there somewhere.

'As I say, Dodds had no samples with him. Is it usual for a commercial traveller to make his calls on premises without samples of his wares?'

Morgan shrugged.

'You realise this sudden absence – not to mention absconding without settling his hotel bill – suggests he has something to hide?'

Morgan held his gaze for a few seconds then looked away. 'What are you suggesting, Sergeant?' His voice now seemed tremulous. He looked down at his hands, which were clasped together.

Brennan remained silent, waiting for Morgan to speak again.

'I trust you've found that *my* address is as I've stated, Sergeant.'

'The Chester police haven't yet replied to my enquiry. Until they do, I should expect you to stay within the hotel. Mr Eastoe would be very annoyed if another guest were to leave without paying what he owes.'

'Does that mean I can go back to my room?'

'It does, Mr Morgan. We'll speak again soon.'

Once Morgan had left, Brennan looked over at Jaggery. 'Well, Constable? What do you think of Mr Morgan?'

'Shit scared, Sergeant.'

Brennan smiled. Sometimes, Freddie Jaggery hit the nail on the head.

*

Although he telephoned the Blackburn Borough Police with Dodds' description, Brennan held no high expectations of an early arrest. He might well have travelled elsewhere, and even if he did come from Blackburn and returned there, the description could fit many men of similar age.

The question, of course, was why the man had left so suddenly. Brennan was convinced the imminence of the inquest the following evening played a large part in his motive: by giving a false address, he had run the risk of exposure in the coroner's court. Giving a false statement there would have serious consequences, and the man must have known the information he'd given them would be recorded and checked.

But had he given a false address because he was guilty of two murders?

People lie about such things for a number of reasons, and Dodds' reason might be unconnected with the double murder he was investigating. He suspected that David Morgan knew more than he was letting on. But on his return to the station, he'd been informed that Morgan's address was a valid one, the man's mother and sister (with whom he apparently lived) confirming that he did indeed live there.

Several trails of thought presented themselves to Brennan. If Dodds were mixed up in the murders of Violet Crosby and Maria Woodruff, then what was his motive? He'd been discovered in one lie – his false address – so was he the man who was *living a lie*, according to Maria Woodruff? She surely hadn't been referring simply to his address. For one thing, how would she know?

There was also the problem of David Morgan. If he knew Dodds more intimately than he was admitting to, was he, therefore, an accomplice to the murders? Or was he guilty of one and Dodds guilty of the other? What, though, was their motive? He shook his head to clear it.

Jaggery was right, though: Morgan was *shit scared.*

And in one particular instance, the young salesman had lied to him.

The door to his office opened and Captain Bell walked in. 'Sergeant Brennan,' he began. 'In the matter of Mr Pardew.'

Brennan inwardly cursed. 'Yes, sir?'

'Since our discussion on the matter, I gather from the duty sergeant that he became ill, was being transferred to the infirmary, somehow escaped, accosted Mr Simeon Crosby in his room, was recaptured and even now is languishing down in the cells once more. Is that an accurate picture that I paint?'

'Faultless, sir.'

'How did he escape? Your fellow sergeant was most vague on that point.'

'I think the horse ambulance was involved in an accident,' came the reply.

'Who was with him?'

'I'm not sure, sir. I'd have to check the roster.'

'Do so.'

'Yes, sir. Will that be all?'

The chief constable gave a spectral smile. Always a bad sign.

'It seems painfully obvious now, does it not, that the man Pardew is of unsound mind? Might it not be a kindness to have the fellow taken back to the asylum?'

There was a part of Brennan that wanted to tell the man to leave the police work to him, that Oscar Pardew had been somehow involved, if only accidentally, in the events of Tuesday night. He'd been seen talking to Maria Woodruff in the Market Square; caused the trouble in King Street by rushing towards Simeon Crosby; gone missing after the trouble, claiming his mind was in a fog; poured beer over Evelyne's head; burst into Crosby's room – and all for what? To shake the hangman's hand?

Was he truly insane? Or was he someone else who was *living a lie*?

There was another part of Brennan, though, that had to admit some truth in what the chief constable was saying: Oscar Pardew had all the indications of madness, and sometimes what you see is what you get. If the man was lying, then he was the best liar – nay, the best *actor* – Brennan had ever met. Besides, sending him back to the asylum would be one way of keeping him locked up. He felt sure the authorities at Haydock Lodge would be keeping a very sharp eye on their escapee in the future.

'You may well be right, sir,' said Brennan finally.

'Excellent!' came the response. 'I'm glad you agree, and I felt sure you would. Which is why I took the liberty of telephoning the Medical Superintendent at Haydock Lodge a few hours ago, to arrange for two of his finest attendants to come here forthwith and ensure his safe transfer by train. They are waiting by the front desk even now. I'm sure they'll take greater care of the poor fellow than the blithering oaf who allowed him to escape earlier. Good afternoon, Sergeant!'

As he left the office, Brennan cursed once more, but not inwardly this time.

*

There were a few flakes of snow falling as he made his way home that night. Brennan ignored them, for several things were playing on his mind.

He needed to go back to the night of the murder. When was the last time Violet Crosby was seen alive? Around six thirty, when Simeon Crosby was leaving their hotel room, when he spoke to her about reading and her headache. This was verified by Ralph Batsford, who was present at the time.

Later, when Crosby was leaving the hotel for the Public Hall, Batsford had told Constable Palin that he needed to go back upstairs to his room to retrieve his notebook. Did he knock on the door of Violet Crosby's room, to see how she was?

Something else struck Brennan then. Something that had been there, just out of reach. Something that didn't quite fit. Something very trivial.

A man living a lie. And a knock on a door.

When he got home, Barry was tucked up in bed.

'He's warm as toast,' Ellen said, kissing Brennan on the cheek and helping him take off his overcoat. 'I put a brick in earlier.'

He smiled. A brick, warmed by the fire for a couple of hours then wrapped in cloth and placed in their son's cold bed, would help take the chill off the sheets before he went to bed. On a night like this, with the snow coming thicker now, Brennan knew his son would relish the warmth and the snugness of the bed. Later, of course, he would patter across the landing and get into bed with them, and the three would snuggle together to keep the chill at bay.

Once they'd finished their lamb chops and potatoes, Ellen sat at his feet before the fire, her head on his knee. She looked at him curiously.

'You've had that little smile on your face ever since you came in,' she said, running her fingers along his knee in front of the blazing coals. 'What's put it there?'

He leaned forward and kissed her. 'Oh, nothing,' he whispered.

She shook her head. 'Work,' she said resignedly before resting her head on his knee once again.

CHAPTER TWENTY-FOUR

The following morning, Ralph Batsford looked in low spirits. When Gilbert Crosby entered the breakfast room, he saw the expression on the journalist's face and decided to sit as far away from him as possible. He didn't take much to the fellow – he'd been hanging around Simeon for a while now, making notes and holding what seemed like secretive meetings to which he wasn't invited.

Working on the book, was all that his brother would say as if he were Charles Dickens. No, Gilbert reflected with a wry smile. *Anthony Trollope, more like!* The only book of Trollope's he'd read – or tried to, he'd abandoned it halfway through – was *He Knew He Was Right, a*bout a jealous husband and an innocent wife who, from what he could recall, was quite stubborn. Things didn't end well there, either.

Well, damn them both!

The waiter took his order, and he sat gazing through the window which overlooked the main thoroughfare. It had been snowing quite heavily, he noticed, and he was quite amused as he watched the towns-folk taking cautious steps to avoid falling.

He'd done that all his life!

He looked around the room and saw only one other diner, the

young man whose regular eating companion, the older man, was nowhere to be seen. He gave the fellow a nod of acknowledgement and felt slightly miffed when it wasn't returned. Is misery catching? he wondered.

Once he'd finished his breakfast, he sat back in his chair and took out a cigar, lighting it with care. It surprised him when the young man glared at him and slapped his napkin down on the table. He then left the room with such abruptness that even Batsford, gloomily contemplating his cold kidneys, looked up and gave Gilbert an inquisitive look.

'He mustn't like the smell of a good cigar!' Gilbert shouted across the room.

But the journalist had already turned his attention back to the congealing contents of his plate.

*

David Morgan stood on the top step of the Royal Hotel and breathed in the cold air of the morning. Somehow, all these people, making their ungainly way to whichever place of work that employed them, seemed to him nothing more substantial than wraiths; shapes that had crept from his nightmare of the previous hours and taken on human form. He could hear their shouts, their self-abashed laughter at some stumble or slip in the snow, could see their breaths billowing forth like minuscule chimneys belching smoke, yet the reality of them, their humanness, eluded him.

He watched two young boys throw snowballs at each other, while another group further down the street hurled snowballs at the tram windows, eliciting curses and threats from the conductor who leaned forward, one hand on the platform pole, and raised a gloved fist.

The boys shouted some obscenity and scurried off down an alleyway when the conductor abandoned his post and began foolishly to chase them.

To think, not ten years ago I was just like those urchins, before...

But he didn't want to think of before.

He pressed his lips together as if he were afraid of the words spilling from his mouth. Then he turned round and went back inside the hotel, just as Sergeant Brennan had instructed him to.

*

For Ralph Batsford, the cold, fragmented kidneys were a symbol. Where once upon a time, in their warmth and their succulence, they had tempted his palate, he now left them untouched (or rather, partly touched and half-heartedly tasted). Nothing but cold, dead offal.

He slowly dragged his fork through the thickening mix of gravy and grease, watching narrow, curving patterns form then gradually blend back into one morass as the liquids slid back together.

He'd made an unholy mess of things, hadn't he?

Violet Crosby hadn't taken any notice of him, almost laughing in his face that day in the Pavilion Café in the park. He'd tried to warn her, but her mind had been made up.

What else could he have done?

And Maria...

Once, they'd had such plans! But those plans, that had seemed so straight and clear, became blurred, congealed, and they had gone their separate ways. There, too, if only she had listened to him...

His thoughts turned to the inquest later. He would get through that, of course, spend some time supporting Simeon and trying to keep that obnoxious brother of his from making his usual insensitive remarks. If only Sergeant Brennan could find some reason to throw the blackguard back into prison.

He shook his head. No. The next inquest, into Maria's death, would be worse. Far, far worse.

*

Thomas Evelyne was also eating breakfast in the rather less salubrious surroundings of the Queen's Hotel. His mind was on the inquest, to which he'd been called as a witness that evening. There really wasn't much he would be adding to the evidence the coroner would be seeking. As for Simeon Crosby, he wondered what that man would be feeling right now. He hated Crosby with a venom, and he felt little guilt in that as he thought of the ones who had been killed and the hangman's role in it.

But now, there would be no more protests, no more marches. He would go back home to his wife.

*

For Simeon Crosby, those first few moments of awakening had been glorious. He'd been filled with such a joy that he'd turned to Violet to share with her this strange euphoria. But that had lasted merely seconds once the cold reality of where he was, and who he was, struck him. He contemplated the empty space beside him, the smooth, undented pillow. Ridiculous, of course, because this was a different room, and she had never lain beside him in this particular bed. That room, with that bed, was still locked and inaccessible. Idly, he wondered if the hotel manager, Mr Eastoe, would ever be able to make the room available once word got out that a horrible murder had taken place inside. But then he told himself that people sometimes enjoy the thrill of murder.

Hadn't he himself seen evidence of that, with people wanting to shake his hand and be close to the one who dispensed the crown's ultimate justice? Even that lunatic Pardew?

Strange. For some reason, the Goodfellow case came to mind. If things had gone more smoothly and the villain had dropped to his doom, why, the two brothers, Goodfellow's brothers-in-law, would have been the first to shake his hand as he stepped through the prison gates, thanking him for dispensing justice for their sister...

He gave a sad smile. No, he thought, Room Eight wouldn't be shunned. Mr Eastoe might even charge a premium to stay there.

He'd grunted his refusal when Batsford had knocked on his door for breakfast. He simply couldn't face food or making small talk with the journalist or his brother or anyone else who might find themselves in the breakfast room that morning. He wished to be left alone. Tonight, the inquest would be harrowing; a tremendous ordeal that he would have to get through, whatever he personally felt.

When he stood to wash himself in the basin, he did feel a certain guilt when he realised that Batsford would also be feeling quite devastated. After all, he'd lost his wife too, hadn't he? The cold water made him gasp as he realised that tonight's inquest was only the beginning. They all had another to get through, hadn't they?

*

Brennan walked down King Street in a good mood. He'd just managed to catch Father Clooney before he began the eight o'clock mass, and as usual, he felt almost a spiritual uplift once he'd left St Joseph's Church. The snow was now quite thick, although the bitter cold of the morning gave it a hard, crusted feel. He breathed in the air, its keen freshness sharpening his innards.

When he reached the station, the duty sergeant greeted him with a cheery wave.

'You look as if you've just found a sovereign, Mick!' he said, noting the smile on his colleague's face.

'Better than that!' Brennan replied.

'Well, I've got a couple of messages here, Mick. They might make you feel better or they might make you feel worse. I dunno.' He reached below the high desk and pulled out a sheet of paper. 'Two phone messages in two days. What will the wife think?'

Brennan grunted and took the message from him. For a moment, his good humour seemed to desert him.

'Not bad news?' said the duty sergeant.

'No,' said Brennan with a slow shake of the head. 'Not for me, anyway.'

With that cryptic remark, he made his way to his office and closed the door behind him. Then he reread the two messages. The first one, from the Bolton Police, merely confirmed that Thomas Evelyne did indeed live at the address he'd given. Not only his father, who lived with him, but also his neighbours had been spoken to.

It was the second one that caused him some anxiety. This one also concerned an address. But the information on the sheet of paper was quite different from the information he'd already been given.

*

In the hours before the inquest that evening, Brennan was busy. He paid another visit to the library and read the July 1st copy of The Graphic once more. The information in Maria Woodruff's article confirmed what he'd suspected, and he closed the magazine with a satisfied sigh.

Next, he spent some time going through his notes with the chief constable, who agreed it should be Detective Sergeant Brennan and not himself who should lead the police questions at the inquest. The coroner had the authority to consent to this.

Brennan knew there were two reasons why the chief constable had so readily agreed to him taking the lead at the inquest: one, his sergeant seemed fully in command of the facts and the motives – it would take him too long to acquaint himself with all that was required. The second reason was even more persuasive: Sergeant Brennan had promised that, by the end of the proceedings, the guilty one would be named in court and the necessary warrant would be immediately issued.

Neither Brennan nor Captain Bell could have foreseen the drama that was to come.

CHAPTER TWENTY-FIVE

Despite the densely falling snow and the bitter chill of the evening, quite a sizeable crowd had gathered outside the Wigan Borough Police Court. Rumours had spread around the town that the hangman's wife had met a macabre fate, and the most oft-repeated scenarios ranged from the poor woman hanging from the ceiling with her neck broken, to her lying mutilated on the bed while her head (which had been completely separated from its body) had rolled beneath the bed and was only discovered after a frantic search.

The court itself was rather on the small side, and although the public was admitted, space on the benches was severely limited owing to the number of reporters – some of them national – and, of course, the area allocated to the men of the jury.

Once the formalities of the court had been observed – the proclamation, the calling over of the names of the jurymen, the election of a foreman, their swearing-in – the coroner declared that the jury and himself had already viewed the body of Violet Crosby in the mortuary, each juror having observed the relevant markings on the neck that indicated how she met her end. In an attempt to put the twelve men of the jury at their ease, he told them how, in former times, the body would be on full view throughout the inquest, 'A stipulation that has mercifully been rescinded in these more enlightened times,' he added with a melancholy smile. Then he addressed the jury in sombre tones, describing the circumstances of the body's discovery. 'It is difficult to imagine a worse sight for a husband to be presented with,' he said before proceeding to read out the police report of their enquiries.

High above the heads of the jurymen, a large window showed the snow falling heavily against the row of chimneys of the buildings behind the court. To Sergeant Brennan, who was sitting patiently in the area reserved for witnesses and police, it seemed almost unreal, the cold filtering through and causing more than one person in the courtroom to shiver. He glanced to where the witnesses were seated and noted, with some satisfaction, that the one responsible for the recent murders appeared to be trembling, though not from the chill of the room. He saw Constable Jaggery standing near the door, and once the proceedings had begun, he gestured to him to move to where the witnesses were seated. It was always reassuring to have the big man make his formidable presence known.

The house surgeon at Wigan Infirmary, Dr Donald Monroe, reported the findings of the post-mortem he had carried out on the victim. The woman had been strangled, he said, with considerable force, and the presence of other wounds and bruises showed a degree of struggling as the victim had fought for her life.

'There were punctuated ecchymoses on the conjunctiva,' he announced, 'and also on the upper part of the chest. There were also apoplectic extravasations on the surface of the lungs.'

Brennan watched several of the jurymen nodding in apparent agreement, though he guessed they hadn't any idea what the man had just said.

There was a slight murmur that spread throughout the public seating when one juryman asked the witness if the cause of death were said to be similar to that produced by hanging.

'There are some superficial similarities,' said Dr Monroe. 'But you must remember that with hanging, the body is suspended, and the subsequent marks on the neck are quite different. With hanging, the marks are of a certain angle and higher up than strangulation, where the marks are more of a circular nature and lower down.' He demonstrated the difference with his hands, and the juryman nodded, satisfied, not only with the answer but also the fact that he'd drawn a link between the woman's death and her husband's former profession.

Before the first of the witnesses was called, Mr Milligan, the coroner, explained to the court in general and the witnesses in particular, that the law insisted on the evidence of each witness to be set down in writing by an officer of the court and later signed by himself and the relevant witness.

'This is because you shall give your evidence on oath, and these depositions shall be forwarded under Section Five to the proper officer of the court when and where a criminal trial is to take place.'

Again, Brennan cast his eyes to the row of witnesses, one of whom was swallowing hard and folding and unfolding his hands. One person, Oscar Pardew, was absent from the proceedings for two reasons, closely linked. Because he was a lunatic, he was deemed incompetent to give evidence. And it was owing to that deranged mental state that Brennan had come to the conclusion that the murders of Violet Crosby and Maria Woodruff were simply beyond the man's capabilities. Certainly, the Crosby murder required a degree of cunning and a cool head. Pardew might have some of the former, but of the latter, he was sorely deficient.

The courtroom fell silent when the first of the witnesses, Mr Simeon Crosby, was called. As he stood to give the oath, those on the public bench craned their necks to gain a good view of the man who had, for many years, been one of the country's foremost and respected executioners. Brennan wondered if any of those on the public bench or serving on the jury had been in attendance on the night of the talk given by Crosby, the night Violet was killed. He didn't doubt that the hangman would present himself in a far different way this evening. When he spoke the words of the oath, his voice faltered, and he had to stop for a few seconds to take a deep breath.

Brennan heard one woman on the public bench whisper to her companion, 'Poor bugger, eh? Look at how red his eyes are.'

The coroner, addressing the witness with due respect for the man's predicament, asked a series of questions that related to the night the body of his wife was discovered. Crosby stated, in subdued tones, how his wife was quite well when he left her, despite the headache she was suffering, but upon his return, he was horrified to find her lying face upwards, her eyes discoloured and the whole appearance telling him that she was dead.

'I have seen more than my fair share of dead bodies,' he added, to the accompaniment of murmurings, mostly sympathetic, from the public benches.

Sergeant Brennan, having been accorded by the coroner the authority to ask questions on behalf of the Crown, asked Crosby to explain in greater detail the circumstances of earlier that fateful evening, when he left his wife in their hotel room.

'I don't know what you mean,' said Crosby.

'Was your wife in her nightclothes?'

A flurry of whispers from the public bench this time.

'Of course she was. She was in bed.'

'I'm sorry if this is painful, Mr Crosby, but I wanted to clear something up. When you found your wife in bed later, she was fully clothed, was she not?'

Crosby blinked several times. 'Yes. She was.'

'Yet you say she was in her nightclothes and in bed suffering from a headache?'

'Yes.'

There was a cough from the coroner. 'Does it follow then, Mr Crosby, that at some point she must have dressed?'

'I think that's obvious.'

The coroner looked puzzled. 'Why would she do that?'

In spite of the situation, Crosby stifled a smile. 'I really have no idea. Perhaps she felt better and decided to go for a walk.'

'Or perhaps,' said Brennan, 'she was getting ready to receive a visitor.'

Now, the ripple that ran along the public bench was louder, suggestive of both shock and intrigue.

The coroner looked about to impose order in the room when Brennan went on. 'You see, as we shall hear, it appears she was getting ready to meet someone: a female reporter.'

The jury foreman raised his hand and, under the direction of the coroner, turned to Brennan. 'Is that the same female reporter who was found murdered the same night?'

Brennan gave an equivocal nod. 'It's the same woman who was found dead on Tuesday night, yes.'

The coroner gave him a grateful smile. It wouldn't be murder until he and his court said so.

'I had no idea,' said Crosby when the court regained silence. 'But it explains her headache.'

290

'And you were the last person to see her.'

'Apart from the blackguard who killed her.'

There being no further questions, Crosby was excused and Ralph Batsford called.

*

When he was asked by the coroner as to the last time he saw Mrs Crosby alive, Batsford replied, 'During our evening meal. The three of us ate together.'

'Did Mrs Crosby give any suggestion that she was planning to feign a headache or some such, in order to meet with the female reporter?'

Batsford hesitated before replying, 'She gave no suggestion. The fact is, I knew what she was going to do. I knew she had arranged a meeting with Miss Woodruff.'

Another reaction from the public.

'How did you know?'

'Because Mrs Crosby had told me. Out of respect.'

The coroner frowned. 'Respect for what?'

'She knew that Maria Woodruff was my wife. My estranged wife.'

Brennan heard one man behind him say, 'Bloody 'ell! They'll all be related in a bit!'

The coroner ignored the latest interruption. 'What was your view of that?'

Batsford shrugged. 'I didn't like it, to be honest.'

'Why not?'

'Because if she had published an interview with the wife of a hangman, it might bode ill for the project we were working on, Mr Crosby and I. His memoirs.'

'Steal your thunder, you mean?' asked the coroner with some asperity.

'I suppose so. At any rate, I tried to talk Mrs Crosby out of talking with Miss Woodruff. I even took her for a stroll to the park here in town, so that we could speak privately, without her husband over-hearing us.'

'And she refused to give up the interview?'

'Yes. Violet said that the article would be about her, not her husband. Anything that would be in Simeon's memoirs would be swamped – that was the way she put it – by other things. It was the thought that, for once, she would be almost like a heroine in a novel.'

'Sergeant Brennan?' the coroner said. 'Any questions?'

Brennan nodded and stood up. 'You say the last time you saw Mrs Crosby was the meal you ate together?'

'Yes.'

'When you were about to leave for the meeting at the Public Hall, escorted by one of our constables, you suddenly remembered something you'd left in your room.'

'Yes. My notebook.'

'You went upstairs to retrieve it. Did you knock on Mrs Crosby's door?'

'No,' Batsford said with emphasis. 'Why would I?'

'Another attempt to persuade her? Or to see how she was feeling?'

'I did no such thing. I merely got my notebook and went downstairs.'

'Earlier, when you went to call for Mr Crosby in their room, you saw him emerge from the room.'

'Yes.'

'You say he spoke to his wife.'

'Yes.'

'Did you hear her answer him?'

Batsford frowned and considered the question before saying, 'I heard nothing.'

Brennan turned to the public bench, saw their faces all rapt with interest. Then he turned once more to the witness.

'Later that night, after you and Mr Crosby found the body, you met with Miss Woodruff, did you not?'

For a moment, Batsford looked frightened.

'Might I remind you, you're on oath, Mr Batsford?' said the coroner.

Batsford's shoulders sagged. 'Yes, I did.'

'You argued,' said Brennan. He presented it as a statement, not a question.

The journalist looked at him, blinking. Brennan could see realisation dawn on his face. *If you know we were arguing, you must have a witness.*

'So, Mr Batsford, what did you argue about with your estranged wife in Wigan Market Place only an hour or so after Mrs Crosby was killed?'

Batsford straightened his shoulders, looked directly at Brennan and said, 'I told her she was responsible for the woman's death. In effect, Maria Woodruff killed Violet Crosby.'

They weren't murmurs or whispers anymore. Now, the sounds from the public bench became a steady throb of excited and speculative chatter. The coroner had to raise his voice to make himself heard, and it took several minutes for order to be restored.

Finally, when some semblance of normality had returned, the coroner issued a warning against further disturbance and then asked Mr Batsford to explain his latest remark.

'Are you saying that Miss Woodruff, who herself was found dead a short time later, had anything to do with Mrs Crosby's death?'

Batsford cleared his throat. 'I'm saying she was responsible for Violet Crosby's death. Not that she actually did it.'

'Then for the benefit of the record, you need to be very accurate in what you say next.'

'I'm saying that if Miss Woodruff hadn't arranged to meet with Violet Crosby in her hotel room, then Violet would have been safe at her husband's side. I should think that's a very precise assumption to make.'

The next witnesses to be called were members of the hotel staff, who repeated, more or less word for word, what they had told Brennan on the night of the murder. Mr Gray, the desk attendant, told the court about the disturbance at just after eight o'clock that night, when someone threw a brick through the bar window. Mr Eastoe related how a young boy had come to the hotel and confessed to the incident. George, the bellboy, further testified that he had met the woman reporter who came to see Mrs Crosby. He had gone up to her room but had received no response. He accidentally bumped into a man who was making his way down the stairs. He thought it was one of the other guests in the hotel because the man had addressed him by name.

'Do you remember anything about this man?' Brennan asked.

'Aye. I mean, yes, sir. He smelt of cigar smoke.'

'Thank you,' said Brennan, and the witness was excused.

When David Morgan gave his oath, he seemed to everyone in the room in a most agitated state. He made no eye contact when the coroner began his questions but simply looked down at the floor or examined his hands or even, at one stage, stared up at the thick snowflakes through the window high above the court.

The first question the coroner asked was for David Morgan to confirm his address in Chester. He stated it quietly.

'You were resident at the hotel on Tuesday night?' The coroner glanced down at the statement he had been given by Sergeant Brennan.

'I was. I was actually in my room from around eight o'clock.'

Brennan raised his hand. The coroner nodded.

'Was anyone with you in your room, Mr Morgan?'

Once more, those on the public benches reacted, this time with sniggers. This inquest was getting juicier by the minute.

Morgan swallowed hard. Then he said, almost inaudibly, 'No.'

'You had no visitor? No one at all? Perhaps you forgot. Being under oath can make people forgetful.'

Given the lifeline by Sergeant Brennan, Morgan raised his head and said, 'You're quite right. I did have a visitor. A fellow guest, Mr Dodds, came to see which train I would be catching the following day. I was due to go to Manchester, you see.'

'But in your statement, you have said you dined with Mr Dodds a short while earlier. Didn't you discuss train times then?'

Morgan lowered his head again. 'It mustn't have occurred to him then.'

Now the coroner spoke. Brennan could see from the stern expression on his face, that he considered the witness to be treading on dangerous ground.

'How long did Mr Dodds stay in your room, Mr Morgan?'

'A few minutes,' came the hasty reply. 'Not long enough even to finish his cigar.'

The coroner and Brennan exchanged glances.

'Did you hear anything from Room Eight?' asked the coroner. 'Or from the corridor? I believe your room lies around the corner from Mrs Crosby's room.'

'Nothing.'

The coroner now spoke sternly. 'Mr Dodds, your visitor, has absconded. I have already issued a warrant against him for contempt of the summons, so we have no corroboration for your testimony. The police have informed me that you do not know the man's address. Is that still the case?'

The witness seemed to consider the question for some time before saying, 'Yes. I have no idea of his address.'

'Do you know, in fact, if Dodds is his real name?'

'No, I don't.'

Again, the coroner gave Brennan a meaningful glance. Then, after once more consulting his notes, he said, 'The young chap, George Barker, the bellboy at the Royal, has stated that he bumped into a man on the stairs, a man who was on his way down and who smelled of cigars. You say Dodds left your room after a few minutes. Could that have been Mr Dodds the boy encountered?'

'It's possible.'

The coroner shook his head. 'Sergeant Brennan? Do you have any further questions?'

Brennan nodded reluctantly. 'In your room, Mr Morgan, you have a framed photograph of a young woman. A beautiful young woman.'

Morgan shifted his stance, clasped and unclasped his hands. 'Yes.'

'Who is she?'

'I told you.'

'Tell me again.'

Beads of perspiration began to trickle down from his forehead, despite the rather chilly conditions in the room.

'It's my wife.'

'And you live with your wife?'

'Yes, of course.'

Brennan sighed. 'Mr Morgan, after I enquired into the address you gave me – a genuine address, admittedly, the Chester police informed me that they paid your home a visit. The only young woman living there – a looker, by all accounts, is your sister. And while she was alarmed at the sight of the police on her doorstep, nevertheless, she told them the truth. That you are unmarried. There is no wife. You live with her and your mother. Your sister is a schoolteacher.'

A loud roar went up from the public bench, some of the men laughing and pointing accusatory fingers at the witness, while many of the women sat there shaking their heads and not knowing what on earth to make of it all.

Brennan knew well that it's no criminal offence to lie about your marital status, although if the coroner were feeling awkward, he could have the man arrested for contempt. He knew there was a reason for the man's lie, just as there was a reason why Edgar Dodds had left the town in such a hurry. There was a connection, and he knew very well what it was. Still, he would decide on his course of action as soon as the jury brought in its verdict.

Until then, there were two more witnesses to be presented in court: Gilbert Crosby and Thomas Evelyne.

*

'Mr Crosby,' said the coroner, 'what is your profession?'

'I have none,' came the reply.

'Then how do you live? Are you of independent means?'

Gilbert Crosby flashed a look across the room at his older brother, who was sitting with his head in his hands. 'I'm looking for a suitable position.'

'I see. The report I have here from the police informs me you went missing from the hotel from Monday night until Tuesday night. Where were you?'

'I was with some people I'd met. I spent all Monday night in their company.'

'Where would that be?'

'A rather foul-smelling place that goes by the ridiculously inappropriate name of the Gibraltar Inn.'

The murmurings from the public suggested they didn't take too kindly to the man's arrogant and condescending tones. One or two of them might be regulars, Brennan thought.

The coroner read through Gilbert's statement before him. 'You were gambling?'

'I was.'

'And you failed to return to the hotel the next morning?'

'I was invited by my new acquaintances to accompany them to the races at Liverpool. Aintree, to be exact.'

'You arrived back in Wigan at what time?'

'Nine o'clock.'

'And according to the information I have before me, no one can confirm that time?'

'I can confirm it. You have my word.'

The coroner raised an eyebrow and said, 'You have spent time in prison, I see?'

Another murmur from the public bench.

'An unfortunate misunderstanding.'

The coroner looked at Brennan, who once more stood up to speak.

'Mr Crosby, you are a gambler.'

'I have been known.'

'And your gambling caused friction between you and your brother and your sister-in-law.'

Gilbert smiled. 'Not really. They have always helped me when I've needed it.'

'Apart from the time when Violet Crosby persuaded her husband not to pay off your fine, which led to your being sent to prison. Is that right?'

'Poor Violet was right, of course. I needed teaching a lesson.'

Brennan pointed at Crosby's face. 'It was in prison, as a result of Violet Crosby's influence over her husband, that you were in a fight and received that scar on your face. Isn't that so?'

Automatically, Crosby lifted his right hand and ran a finger along the scar.

'I was attacked. It was nothing to do with Violet. I bore her no ill will.'

Brennan indicated to the coroner that he had no further questions, and the witness was dismissed.

*

Once Thomas Evelyne had taken the oath, several of those present looked forward to fireworks. Here in court, facing each other, were two men who held quite opposing views on hanging, and the recent violence in King Street was fresh in the memory of many in the room. Indeed, Evelyne stood rigidly to attention, his eyes shining with what appeared to be something more powerful than anger. As he glared fiercely at Simeon Crosby, the people could see hatred in his eyes.

The coroner, when presented with the list of witnesses suggested by the police, had queried the inclusion of Evelyne, who had been nowhere near the Royal Hotel on the night of the murder. But Sergeant Brennan had explained his reasons for the man's presence on the list, and the coroner had eventually agreed.

'Mr Evelyne,' began the coroner, 'can you describe to the court the events of Tuesday night?'

Taking a deep breath, apparently to calm himself, the witness proceeded to give a factual account of the meeting in the Market Square, the march down King Street and the sudden appearance of a madman who charged at the hangman. He also described how he suffered a blow to the head causing a painful swelling which rendered him unconscious, whereupon he was rescued by a Catholic priest who gave him sustenance.

Brennan took up the questioning.

'Mr Evelyne, what is your opinion of Simeon Crosby?'

A scowl darkened the man's features as he once more cast a glance in the hangman's direction. 'As low as it is possible to get.'

'Can you explain why that is?'

'The man is responsible for suffering and death.'

'Whose suffering and whose death, Mr Evelyne?'

The question seemed to throw the witness. 'I beg your pardon?'

But Brennan ignored him. 'Tell us about the moment you were saved by the priest. Father Clooney.'

Evelyne spoke sharply. 'As I've already testified, after I was assaulted by the Wigan police, resulting in a swelling on my head, I collapsed outside a Catholic church. The priest came and helped me.'

'You told me in your statement that he found you and helped you.'

'Yes.'

'But in his statement, which I have recently checked again, he told me you knocked on the door of the church.'

'Then that is what I must have done. I'd been unconscious, remember.'

The coroner spoke up. 'It seems quite reasonable, given the circumstances.'

Brennan went on. 'On the afternoon of the murder of Violet Crosby, you spoke with Maria Woodruff.'

'Yes. She came to see me. To interview me.'

'And she told you about her secret rendezvous with Mrs Crosby later that evening? When she was to feign a headache.'

Evelyne shook his head. 'She told me no such thing.' He affected the beginnings of a smile. His word against a dead woman's.

Brennan ignored it. 'You live in Bolton, Mr Evelyne.'

'Yes. Doubtless, you've checked my address.'

'I have. You live there with your father.'

'He's not in the best of health these days.'

Brennan paused before asking the next question. Then he said, 'You told me you were married.'

'I was.'

'What happened?'

For the first time, Evelyne's composure seemed to waver. He glanced over at Simeon Crosby, but the hangman was hunched forward, looking at the palms of his hands.

'My wife died,' said Evelyne in a voice now so low that many in the room couldn't hear him.

The coroner spoke up. 'I must ask you to speak louder, Mr Evelyne. Your responses are being written down.' He pointed across the court to a small, bewhiskered man, wearing pince-nez, who was scribbling furiously.

'I said my wife died.' Evelyne raised his voice, putting emphasis on the last word.

'And yet you told me,' Brennan went on, 'that you were anxious to return to your wife.'

'My wife's grave, Sergeant. Her shrine.'

Now it was Brennan's turn to speak low when he asked, 'How did she die, Mr Evelyne?'

Simeon Crosby turned to Ralph Batsford and said, loudly enough for those closest to him to hear, 'How in God's name is this relevant? It's *my* wife's death that's at issue, surely?'

The witness gave no sign of having heard. He held his head high, and those close to him could see that tears were beginning to form. There was a new inflection in his voice now, and later, people argued over which was the dominant emotion: anger, sadness or love.

'My wife was murdered, Sergeant.'

There was an audible gasp from the benches.

Brennan chose his next words with care. 'And who was responsible for her murder, Mr Evelyne?'

The witness stared at Brennan with understanding in his eyes.

'Simeon Crosby killed my wife, Sergeant. He was responsible for her death.'

CHAPTER TWENTY-SIX

There was uproar in the court, leaving the coroner with no alternative but to order an adjournment. Once the public and the reporters had left, only the witnesses were left in their seats on the instructions of Sergeant Brennan. The coroner and the other officials had also left the room, leaving only Brennan and Jaggery as representatives of the forces of law and order.

Thomas Evelyne was still standing facing the others in court, but now he had his head bowed low, with his right hand pressed firmly to his face.

When Evelyne had made his accusation, pointing a wavering finger at the man he'd accused, Simeon Crosby had stood up and told Evelyne, the coroner and everyone else in the court that this was *absolute nonsense!*

His brother had also stood, placed an arm on Simeon's shoulder and yelled at the witness in a similar, though more colourful, vein.

Now, with the exodus from the court complete, accompanied by strange looks and speculative murmurings, the room was eerily silent, with Constable Jaggery standing just behind Sergeant Brennan and surveying the row of witnesses with a fearsome scowl that precluded any further protest.

Outside, the snow fell ever more heavily, the tops of the chimneys still visible against the black night sky.

Brennan began to speak. 'Mr Evelyne has answered my question as I suspected he would. It's true that his wife was brutally murdered, just as yours was, Mr Crosby.' He looked at the hangman and held his gaze for a few seconds. 'It's also true that the two murders are connected by a thread more powerful than any hemp rope used on the gallows.'

There was confusion on the faces of most of the witnesses.

'When I asked Mr Evelyne who was *responsible* for his wife's murder, he gave what he believed to be the absolute truth. Two years ago, you, Mr Crosby, made rather a mess of an execution.'

Simeon Crosby rose in anger. 'I did *not*! I presume you are referring to the man named Goodfellow.'

'I am indeed.'

'The prison was to blame. I checked and rechecked the equipment as I always did on the night before a drop. The bolts and the trapdoors worked perfectly. But when the man stood on the trapdoors and I pulled back the lever, the doors moved only fractionally. After several attempts, I was instructed by the under-sheriff to stop the execution and the man was led back to his cell. It was the fault of the prison authorities, not mine.'

'Goodfellow escaped, though.' It was Evelyne who spoke, his eyes burning with hatred now.

'I cannot be held to account for that!'

Brennan held up his hand. 'I'm afraid you have already been held to account, Mr Crosby. Mr Evelyne, you have all but admitted to the murder of Violet Crosby. An eye for an eye. A wife for a wife. Was that not the case?'

Evelyne said nothing.

Brennan continued. 'Was that your original intention? To kill Mrs Crosby? Or did you plan to kill Mr Crosby instead?'

Evelyne glared at Brennan, defiance in his eyes now. 'I admit to nothing, Sergeant Brennan. The fact that Simeon Crosby failed to carry out justice on Goodfellow, the fact that as a result, Goodfellow escaped, the fact that he broke into my house and murdered my wife, the fact that she was halfway through our first pregnancy, even the fact that my ailing father doted on his daughter-in-law and was hoping against hope to see his first grandchild before he died... all those indisputable facts are as much evidence of proof as a straw in a whirlwind.'

Jaggery gave his usual cough whenever he was presented with a tricky problem. Brennan, on the other hand, remained calm.

'I believe that you had only intended to kill Mr Crosby, for how could you have known his wife would be travelling with him? Besides, I really don't think her death was part of your plan. Not until you discovered she was here in Wigan. Otherwise, why not simply travel to Lancaster, find out where they lived and do what Goodfellow did? Kill her in her own home. But no. I think her fate was settled when Maria Woodruff told you she was here in town and she had devised a simple trick to deceive Mr Crosby, which would leave her alone in her hotel room for a short time.'

'You bastard!' It was Gilbert Crosby who spoke, his hand pressed firmly on his brother's shoulder.

Brennan ignored him. 'The clever part of your plan was to present yourself as a denouncer of capital punishment in general and Simeon Crosby in particular. In that way, you could make life very uncomfortable for the hangman while no one would suspect that, far from despising the existence of the gallows, you were its greatest supporter.'

Evelyne cleared his throat. 'If Goodfellow had been hanged, my wife would still be alive. I would have a son or a daughter. We would be leading happy and fruitful lives.' He looked high up, towards the snow-filled blackness beyond the glass. 'It's what murderers leave behind. Empty, cold and beautiful dreams.'

'Something else conspired to help you that night. Oscar Pardew, an escaped lunatic who merely wished to shake the hand of the man who executed his father's killer, caused the disturbance in King Street. You took advantage of that, left the scene and went directly to the Royal Hotel, where you knew Mrs Crosby was in her room, awaiting the arrival of Maria Woodruff. You had to act fast. So you paid a young street rat to throw a brick through the bar window and cause a distraction. Then you entered the hotel, probably stole a glance at the hotel register and discovered Mrs Crosby's room. You probably knocked and presented yourself as the bellboy or the desk attendant, and Mrs Crosby opened her door, thinking all the while that her visitor had arrived. She would be dead within minutes.'

Suddenly, Simeon Crosby rushed forward before his brother could stop him and launched himself at Evelyne. The act took everyone by surprise. Jaggery moved quickly for a man his size, but even he wasn't fast enough to prevent the hangman from ramming Evelyne to the ground and locking an arm around his neck.

Evelyne began to gasp and kick out, but the hangman tightened his grip, one arm pressing hard against the back of his neck, the other forming a choke-hold at the front. Evelyne's eyes were wide open and bulging, his lips already turning blue.

'Stay back!' Simeon Crosby yelled as Jaggery got near. 'I know exactly how much pressure's needed to dislocate a murderer's neck. It'll only take a few seconds. No closer!'

'Constable!' Brennan snapped.

Jaggery began slowly to back away.

'You killed Violet!' the hangman hissed into Evelyne's ear.

Evelyne's face was turning a deep red. He was unable to speak.

'She had done nothing wrong!' Crosby went on. 'Nothing! Her books… she lived for those books!'

Now Gilbert Crosby, perhaps sensing the gravity of what they were witnessing, left his place and slowly drew near, his arms raised. 'Simeon,' he said urgently. 'You're killing the man! Let him go.'

Ralph Batsford, too, stood up. He addressed not the hangman but Brennan.

'Is this the same man who murdered Maria?'

Brennan, who was watching the hangman's eyes closely, gave a shrug. 'Until I can speak further with him, who knows?'

'But it's highly probable? There's no reasonable doubt, is there, Sergeant?'

Brennan understood the implications in the journalist's words. He kept silent.

Batsford raised his voice and spoke directly to the hangman. 'You must do what you have to do, Simeon. But he has killed two women who did nothing wrong. Innocent, innocent women. Do what you have to do, man! If I were in your place…'

Brennan slowly knelt down a few feet from where Crosby had Evelyne in his grip. 'You ready to die?' he asked.

'He can't speak!' rasped the hangman.

'I wasn't talking to him, Mr Crosby.'

There was a tense hiatus. It seemed that the room had grown much colder, darker.

With a sudden jerk, Crosby tightened his grip even more, and from Evelyne's throat there came a desperate, choking rattle. Brennan saw his eyes roll upwards, and now, only the whites of his eyes could be seen, tiny veins seeming to throb angrily in protest.

Then, as if the full import of Brennan's words had finally sunk in, the hangman relinquished his hold and lay back, leaving Evelyne gasping for breath and clutching at his throat with both hands.

CHAPTER TWENTY-SEVEN

It was another death that prompted Thomas Evelyne to make a full confession.

While he was being held in police custody that weekend, word came from Bolton that his father had passed away. The police sergeant from Bolton, a personal friend of Brennan's, had told him that a neighbour had found the old man slumped at the bottom of the stairs when she'd knocked on his door to check on him. She'd heard the strange bumping sounds, and when she'd flipped open the letterbox, she'd seen his body lying at an unnatural angle, his skull fractured by the fall.

Brennan refused the man permission to be escorted back to his home to pay his respects.

Thomas Evelyne blamed himself. He spent the morning cursing and railing against the whole world, finally calming himself down and whispering, in an almost sing-song voice, how only he was to blame, for if he hadn't come to Wigan, he would have been there in the house to prevent the accident. And his dear, dear father would still be alive. Ailing, but alive.

His sense of guilt proved too much of a torment, and he asked to see Sergeant Brennan.

Within minutes, the two men were facing each other across the table in the small interview room.

When he spoke now, there was a hoarseness to Evelyne's voice that was only partly due to his recent brush with a broken neck.

'Everything you said was true,' he began. 'And now my father is yet another victim.'

'You were in Violet Crosby's room when the bellboy knocked on the door, weren't you?'

Evelyne nodded. 'I knew I didn't have much time. Once the boy threw the brick through the window, I found the room she was in from the register and ran upstairs. When I knocked on the door, she just said, *Enter.* The door wasn't locked. But then she was expecting someone, wasn't she?' He glanced down at his hands. 'When the bellboy knocked, she was taking her last breath. A more merciful end than the one Goodfellow gave my beloved. And our unborn child.'

There was a long silence.

'Maria Woodruff, too, was an innocent victim, wasn't she?'

Evelyne nodded slowly. When he looked at Brennan, there were tears in his eyes. 'I didn't mean to kill her. That was a pure accident.'

'There's nothing pure about a crushed skull, Evelyne.' There was harshness in Brennan's voice. He had a fleeting vision of a young woman, beautiful, alive, eager to succeed in the career she had chosen.

'But it *was*!' Evelyne insisted. 'It was an accidental meeting, you see? I was looking for that lunatic who'd drowned me with beer when she saw me across the street from her hotel. She came across. But she was the last person I wished to see. Not after I'd done what I'd done back at the Royal. I just wanted to be left alone and savour the fitness of what I'd done. A wife for a wife.' His voice fell. He examined his hands once more, held together in prayer.

'She'd discovered your real name, Mr Ridge, hadn't she?'

Evelyne was too filled with grief and remorse to show any sort of surprise at Brennan's words.

'How did you know?'

'My colleague in Bolton has spoken to your neighbours. Apparently, you've only recently moved to that address. Under the name of Evelyne. When I looked further into the articles Maria Woodruff wrote, I remembered one person – *a frail elderly man* as Miss Woodruff described him, telling her of how his son came home to find his wife murdered. His *expectant* wife. Miss Woodruff also wrote in that same section that she saw a framed photograph of the son, a handsome fellow. She recognised you – or suspected she did – from that photograph, didn't she?'

Evelyne nodded. 'She wondered why I was here in Wigan railing against capital punishment when all the while my wife had been murdered by an animal who escaped the gallows because of that man's mistake.'

'Why didn't you deny it? Or even tell her the truth? There was no proof that you had done what you did. You could have brazened it out.'

Evelyne – or Ridge – shook his head. 'I could see the light in her eyes. She demanded an interview, urging me to explain my side of the story. How would that have looked? It would be the equivalent of putting my head in a noose of my own making.'

'So, what happened?'

'There's an alleyway opposite. We went in, to speak more privately. But she wouldn't let it go. Told me I had a great opportunity, to explain my feelings. Why I, the bereaved husband of a murder victim, was even now supporting abolition. She said it was a noble and selfless thing to do, and she would be sure that my motives would be clear and prove influential. She had no idea, even then, even when she knew of Violet Crosby's fate, that I was the one responsible. She thought I was filled with *a selfless nobility* as she put it. We argued. I made to go and she grabbed me. I turned and swung out at her, pinioned her against the wall. Then she slumped to the ground.' He raised his voice now. '*I didn't mean to kill her!*'

The room was silent for a while.

'And now my father… my poor father…' He looked Brennan directly in the eye. 'I, too, read that article, Sergeant, though I didn't say as much when I spoke with Miss Woodruff that first time. There was no mention of surnames. How did you know our real name?'

'I checked up on the case, despite the fact that Miss Woodruff printed no names. I discovered the woman's name was Ridge. I had all the clues I needed. The crime, the fact that it was committed by an escaped murderer. The murderer's name being Goodfellow. The fact that Goodfellow's survival from the gallows was attributed to a mistake on the executioner's part. And finally, the name of the executioner being Crosby. It was, as I said, a thread leading directly to you.'

Thomas Ridge sat back and exhaled heavily.

'Just one more thing, Mr Ridge.' Brennan reached down and produced from a small folder a sheet of paper.

'What's that?'

Brennan placed it on the table and slid it across. As Ridge began to read, Brennan spoke softly.

'It's an official report from the prison where Crosby tried to hang Goodfellow. As you can see from the conclusions at the bottom of the sheet, the authorities completely exonerated Mr Simeon Crosby from any culpability. It was discovered sometime later, after Goodfellow had escaped and killed your wife. One of the prison guards had become ill and was dying, and he subsequently confessed to being the cause of the equipment being faulty and failing to complete Goodfellow's execution.

He and a colleague, who had since left the job, had found themselves drinking in the execution shed on the night before the murder. They'd fooled around with the trapdoors. A silly game of Dare. With the most tragic of consequences. Until the following morning, they had no idea they'd damaged the equipment.' He paused. 'You see, Mr Ridge, *it wasn't the hangman's fault.*'

Ridge took his time. Then he said quietly, 'Then whose fault was it?'

EPILOGUE

There was confusion on Constable Jaggery's face as he reached for his pint in the Crofter's. The place was already filling up, for it was Saturday evening, the snow outside making the warmth of the public house, with its roaring fire spitting sparks onto the large hearthstone, an inviting refuge.

While that was a far from unusual expression on the big man's face, this evening, Detective Sergeant Brennan felt it his duty to help him become unconfused.

'With the confession of Thomas Ridge, the inquest into Violet Crosby's death will return a verdict of Wilful Murder when the court reconvenes. Whether the second inquest – into Maria Woodruff's death – brings in a similar finding, or judges her death to be manslaughter, is the only point at issue. Ridge will be brought to trial later for both deaths.'

But it was obvious that wasn't the issue as far as Jaggery was concerned. 'That Dodds bloke,' he said.

'What about him?'

'Well, why did the bugger run off like that? If he'd nowt to do wi' owt?'

'I never said that, Freddie.'

It always pleased Jaggery when the sergeant addressed him by his Christian name. He couldn't repay the compliment, of course, but it

313

established a deeper intimacy between them. He liked that sometimes, like warming your hands on a cold night.

'No,' Brennan went on to explain. 'Mr Edgar Dodds fled from the town for an entirely different reason. It had nothing to do with the Crosbys or Maria Woodruff and everything to do with David Morgan.'

Jaggery frowned. 'But he were his mate, weren't 'e?'

'Oh yes,' said Brennan, taking a long, slow drink from his glass. 'He was his mate all right. But in not the way you mean.'

Jaggery licked his lips. He looked across at the dancing flames in the grate. Suddenly, his face felt hot. 'You mean they were... *that way*?'

'I do.'

'So why didn't we drag that Morgan lad in then? They can get two years for that sort o' thing.'

'What proof did we have, eh, Freddie?' Brennan sat back, gave a smile and took another drink. 'Dodds left Morgan's room when he heard the commotion at the front of the hotel. The smashed window would mean police showing up, and it wouldn't look good if two men were found in a room together. That's when young George bumped into him. Crosby's room was round the corner of the corridor, remember? He thought he could slip out and not be noticed.'

Jaggery sat forward, shaking his head. 'We 'ad proof, Sergeant. They were in each other's rooms for a start. Morgan admitted as much. An' when we went to Morgan's room, that bugger were there again. I'm sure that's proof enough. What did his lordship say about it?'

'Captain Bell? Oh, I didn't tell him.'

Jaggery's eyes widened. 'Bloody 'ell, Sergeant! He'll go mad. You know what 'e's like for the letter of the law.'

'That's exactly why I didn't tell him.'

'I don't get it.'

It was Brennan's turn to gaze into the flames. 'What Dodds and Morgan did is against the law. Dodds fled and Morgan lied about having a wife. No law against that, of course, but lying to the police isn't recommended. At any rate, I know nothing about Dodds or whatever his name is, but I do know something about the lad Morgan. He has a sister. And she is a schoolteacher. Has she done anything wrong, Freddie?'

Jaggery shrugged. 'How do I know?'

'Well let's imagine she hasn't, shall we? What do you think the effect would be on her career if it became known that her brother was a homosexual and had been sent to prison for gross immorality?'

Jaggery thought about it for a few seconds then shook his head. 'But if we thought that road every time we felt some bugger's collar, we'd never arrest anyone. Every one of 'em 'as relatives of one sort or another. His lordship would have a blue fit! Besides, we're policemen, not vicars.'

Brennan closed his eyes for a second. Then he said, 'Let's just say I'm fed up with seeing victims at every turn. A victim's not just the poor bloke or woman or child on the receiving end of a good hiding or worse. It goes further than that. Maria Woodruff understood that, all right. Tried to write about it.'

He recalled the passage she'd written:

Imagine a still and quiet pool… a stone dropped in its centre. See the ripples flow outwards, disturbing even the calmest of places! Imagine now, that that self-same pool is filled not with water but with blood. Ripples of blood! That is the common theme with all of these acts.

He kept his thoughts unspoken, for neither Jaggery nor Captain Bell himself would understand exactly how he felt.

But if he had the chance to prevent anyone else from becoming a victim, he would take it.